DANCE ON BLOOD

Nell Bray would do almost anything to get the Vote—but she draws the line at planting a bomb in a house belonging to David Lloyd George. Her friends, however, have other ideas and, in trying to head them off, Nell becomes a leading suspect. She receives an urgent invitation to breakfast at 11 Downing Street with Lloyd George himself when he asks Nell to help him recover some embarrassing letters in return for which he will drop the charges against her. There's only one disadvantage—the last person sent by Lloyd George ended up dead in a bath with his wrists cut!

DANCE ON BLOOD

Herod Antipas: No. She is going to dance on blood. There is blood spilt on the ground. She must not dance on blood. It were an evil omen.

Salome
Oscar Wilde

DANCE ON
BLOOD

by

Gillian Linscott

Magna Large Print Books
Long Preston, North Yorkshire,
England.

British Library Cataloguing in Publication Data.

Linscott, Gillian
   Dance on blood.

A catalogue record for this book is
available from the British Library

ISBN 0-7505-1385-3

First published in Great Britain by Virago, 1998

Published in Large Print 1999 by arrangement with Little,
Brown and Company (UK)

Magna Large Print is an imprint of
Library Magna Books Ltd.
Printed and bound in Great Britain by
T.J. International Ltd., Cornwall, PL28 8RW.

Prologue

One night in November 1912 a young man was found dead in a bath in a flat in Mayfair. He was wearing trousers and a shirt unbuttoned at the neck, his tie on the floor beside the bath and his jacket hung tidily over a chair. His wrists were slit, probably by the cut-throat razor open on the bath mat, and he had bled to death.

There was a piece of paper on the chair beside the bath with three smudged words scrawled on it: 'I love you.' They had been written in blood, probably with the small brush that was found bloodstained on the bath mat beside the razor, the kind of brush that a dancer might use to put on her eye make-up.

A few hours after the body was discovered, still in the dark hours of a winter morning, a woman travelling on her own arrived at Victoria Station and bought a ticket for the boat train to Paris via Calais. Although I can't claim it for a fact, I'm sure from what I came to know of her later that she was warmly wrapped in furs and those furs had been paid for by somebody else.

The inquest took place nearly two months later, when what little press interest there had been in the apparent suicide of a romantic young man had faded to vanishing point. The verdict was that he'd committed suicide while the balance of his mind was disturbed.

I knew nothing of this at the time, being deep in other things. If I had happened to notice one of the very few press references to it I'd have turned the page without much interest, beyond a fleeting curiosity that with so many people in the world a man should end his life over just one who preferred to do without him. But I didn't notice and when, in the end, I had to take an interest in what had happened that night, it was part of a larger story that led through a golf course in Surrey to a room in Downing Street and began, of all places, in the offices of the Women's Social and Political Union or, as most people preferred to call us, the suffragettes.

Chapter One

The girl was a cold on two legs; you could see that from yards away. It was a bleak day in mid-February, with the sky outside only a few shades lighter than the dark grey pavements. It wasn't much warmer here in the hall of our new offices in Kingsway. She'd been standing beside a table with stacks of leaflets on it. There was a tea chest on the floor beside her, its top covered with canvas tied down with twine. More leaflets, I thought. Her nose was pink, the rest of her face as pale as paper under a brown felt hat without trimmings, lips cracked from the cold, scuffed brown leather boots that probably didn't keep out the wet. The coat of dark green cloth looked like a hand-me-down, too large for her thin figure. She couldn't have been older than eighteen. As she moved towards me a whiff of friar's balsam came with her, but inhaling it couldn't have done her much good because her voice was still choked with the cold.

'You're Nell Bray, aren't you? I heard you speaking in Southwark last year.' Her hand in its brown woollen glove grasped mine, a grip like a bird's on a frosty branch. 'It's because of you that I came into it ... into the Movement.'

She glanced to the packing case, then back at me, as if she wanted to explain something. Her eyes were bright and feverish. I suppose I'd started making the appropriate modest noises, but what I really wanted to tell her was: Never mind about the Movement for one day, it will still be here tomorrow and for as many tomorrows as anybody can see. Just go back home and burrow under the blankets.

I might even have said something on those lines, but at that moment a door opened off the corridor and Bobbie Fieldfare looked out. She managed, even on this grey indoor morning, to look as if she'd just got in from a fast day's hunting—hair in a mess, eyes bright, sparking energy in all directions. Then she noticed the girl with the cold.

'June, you're not supposed to be here. What are you doing?'

When annoyed, Bobbie tended to revert to the tone of her military ancestors.

June looked scared but stood her ground and muttered something in a low, cold-ridden voice. I caught: '... thought police might be watching the house' and '... have to take them somewhere'.

'Not here, of all places. Can't you find somewhere near you in Paddington?'

'Emily says we—'

'I don't care what Emily says. The whole point of having other places is not to involve this office. Then you go and bring them here.'

'Emily says it's quite safe. They won't—'

'I don't care. Just move them.'

'If we need them tonight—'

'You'll be told. You know the arrangement.'

Bobbie, having issued her orders, was about to shut the office door on June when she noticed me standing there. 'Nell, I want to talk to you.'

We hadn't spoken for several weeks and were annoyed with each other, not for the first time. Bobbie and I have been in enough tight places together to respect each other's motives, but not each other's methods. She thinks mine are too roundabout. I think hers, on her good days, stop just this side of lunacy. The difference this time was that most of the leaders of the suffragette movement, including two out of three Pankhursts, were on Bobbie's side. That was all on account of one little word. The word was arson. Pillar boxes first, then public buildings. Not the work of a few out-of-control hotheads but deliberate policy, sanctioned by the leaders of our Women's Social and Political Union. Now, I'm not a patient person. I've broken windows, stormed the Houses of Parliament and thrown things at cabinet ministers with the best of them. But I was passionately opposed to this arson policy on the grounds that it would do us harm in the public mind that was just being won round to our case. I was outvoted.

Bobbie was one of the enthusiasts for the fire policy. Since then, I'd kept my distance from what was going on and had concentrated on what I thought was the right way ahead, trying to recruit more working men and women, speaking at factory gates, union meetings, even public houses on occasions. It had mostly kept me away from our office and, in particular, from Emmeline Pankhurst. I'd only come in that day, Tuesday 18 February 1913, because I needed to pick up some leaflets. I still intended to collect them and get out as soon as possible. My journalist friend, Max Blume, had written a few days ago to say he wanted to see me, and I planned to go on to his office in Fleet Street. Anyway, I didn't like the tone she'd taken with the girl. I said I was in a hurry.

'It won't take long. Just let me finish with something in here, then we'll talk.'

The door shut, leaving me and the girl June standing there staring at each other. She looked ready to sink to the floor with tiredness and worry, as if this problem of the packing case were the last straw. It sat there looking immovably solid and heavy. Goodness knows how she'd managed to carry it inside in the first place. She walked slowly over to it and started pushing it towards the door. It moved a few reluctant inches.

'Oh for goodness' sake, let me help.'

She accepted without protest. We managed to slide it through the hall, then she held the door open while I pushed it on to the step.

'Right, that's far enough. I'll call a taxi.'

'No.' She seemed terrified at the idea.

I thought it was because of the expense. 'Don't worry, the Movement will pay for it.'

I went to the kerb and signalled. Two motor taxis went past without stopping. The third came to a halt and luckily the driver was young and solid. Together we got the tea chest into the cab.

'What you got in here then, ladies? The Elgin marbles?'

We didn't answer. I thought he might take fright at the idea of carrying a suffragette and subversive leaflets around

13

London and wanted to get June and her tea chest off my hands. I gave him five shillings, said his passenger would tell him where they were going, and watched them drive off, June's pinched white face looking back at me and mouthing thanks.

Bobbie was waiting for me inside the hall.

'Where have you been?'

'I was helping your friend with her leaflets.'

'Leaflets?' She looked puzzled. 'Oh, the packing case. What did she do with it?'

'I put them both in a taxi.'

She made a wry face.

'Was that wrong?'

'It's just funny in the circumstances, you helping her move them.'

The unease that had been nagging at the back of my mind for the last few minutes flared into a crisis warning. 'What exactly is going on?' Then, hastily, 'No, don't tell me. If it's what I think it is, I don't want to know.'

I turned away. She took my arm.

'Nell, I know how you feel about this, but we need your help. You don't have to be directly involved, but there's something important happening in the next few days, and the police—'

'I said, I don't want to know.'

14

'If you'd just come in here and let me explain ...'

I'd started pulling away from her when another door opened and a voice called for Bobbie. 'Bobbie, the Epsom trains don't go to Walton Heath, so we ...'

'Oh, bother it. Just wait a moment, Nell, while I see to it.'

While Bobbie was distracted, I snatched up the bundle of leaflets I'd come for and made smartly for the door.

Her voice came after me. 'Nell. Nell, I said wait.'

There was a motor bus coming, slowed down by the traffic. I jumped on it with a feeling of escape, but as it throbbed and crawled down Kingsway, the sense of crisis went with me. There was no doubt that Bobbie was planning something and the girl, June, was involved as one of her lieutenants. Well, not my business. The girl was young, pathetically young, and yet old enough to know what she was doing. She struck me as a person who'd be easily led by somebody with Bobbie's glamour and energy. But a natural leader has natural followers. It would have been intrusion on my part to tell her to get out of it while she still had the chance—but that was what I'd been aching to do. She'd said: 'It was because of you that I came into the Movement.' Had she really been won over by some speech that I couldn't even remember after so many? Even if so, did that make me responsible for everything that happened? Suppose she and Bobbie did go and set fire to something (and given Bobbie's record, it would be something more than usually spectacular), was that my fault? And if she got caught and went to prison, that was still her choice and I had no right to take it away from her. That should have closed the matter as far as I was concerned, only it didn't.

Two things worried me. The first was the reference to somebody called Emily. I knew it couldn't mean our leader: she was Emmeline, and anyway the girl June wouldn't have called her anything but Mrs Pankhurst. I knew an Emily. We all did. She was brave, determined, and to my mind very near the edge where conviction becomes madness. She'd made no secret of her belief that we wouldn't win the Vote until a woman died for it. If she was involved in this, then June was on the edge of a cyclone.

There was something else bothering me, but it didn't hit me until I was out of the bus and crossing Fleet Street. The tea chest. What would June want with such a weight of leaflets? And besides, it hadn't felt like leaflets. There'd been

16

something inside that rolled and shifted when we tilted the chest to get it into the cab. Bobbie couldn't wait to get it out of the office. Then she'd been amused that I should have helped transport it.

'Oh ye gods!'

A cyclist dodged round me, ringing his bell furiously. I leapt to the kerb and a conclusion, landing on both at the same time. This was going to be more than simple fire raising. All you needed for that was rags and matches, petrol or paraffin. Therefore whatever was going to happen that night or in the next few days at Walton Heath, wherever that might be, was something more elaborate than any of the attacks so far. Bobbie was engaged in it, which was bad enough, and an even wilder spirit in the shape of Emily, which was worse.

I thought about it as I walked along Fleet Street, and still hadn't made up my mind whether to do anything when I got to building where Max Blume worked. It was a tall and thin place, grimy with soot and the fumes of printer's ink. In the delivery road beside it, I had to shuffle sideways to get past the pair of heavy horses delivering print rolls to the presses. Their breath on my face was warm and smelt of hay.

Up some steep stone stairs, a knock on a frosted glass door, and I was in the little cubicle that served as Max's latest office. Max migrates from one magazine to another, in response to the splitting and re-aligning of small groups in radical politics. The more advanced the political views of the publication, the smaller his office. The size of the present one suggested that his latest was very advanced indeed. There was just room for one chair, a crate full of books and a desk with a corner sawn off so that it would fit diagonally into the available space. It felt colder in here than the air outside and Max, who'd been writing when I walked in, was still wearing scarf and overcoat. He gave me the chair and sat on the edge of the book crate. Before he could tell me why he wanted to see me, I asked him if he knew where Walton Heath was. His eyebrows rose.

'You're not thinking of taking up golf, are you, Nell?'

'Golf?'

'It's in Surrey, not far from the Tattenham Corner part of Epsom race course. There's a golf course out there where half the Cabinet spend their week-ends. Especially David Lloyd George. He likes the place so much he's even having a house built there.'

The Welsh Wizard—but not a name to conjure with for us. Lloyd George was Chancellor of the Exchequer, far and away the most able and powerful man in the Liberal Government. If he'd wholeheartedly supported the demand for the Vote, it would have been ours within months. And yet smooth words from him, even encouraging words, got washed away by other parliamentary business that was supposed to be more important.

Max must have seen the expression on my face. 'What's up, Nell? I thought you were refusing to get involved in that side of things.'

He knew almost as much about the inside workings of the suffragette movement as I did, and the same thought had hit both of us. Golf courses, with all they implied about smug male leisure, were tempting targets for our sabotage squads. A fortnight before, some of our people had etched 'Votes for Women' in acid on putting greens at Birmingham. A golf course used by Lloyd George, or even its club house, would be irresistible to Bobbie and Emily. That was where they'd be going, taking June and her cold along with them, that night or soon.

'Is something wrong, Nell?'

'Very wrong, I think.'

'I'm not asking you what you're involved

with, but be careful. The Government's sure to put the pressure on for arrests over this arson business. They've got a man in plain clothes watching your offices in Kingsway. Unmistakable.'

Bobbie must know that, but instead of lying low like any half sensible person she was rushing into something I guessed was more desperate than anything before.

'I'm not involved. Only ...'

Only I'd just helped a conspirator load a bomb into a taxicab, almost certainly under the eyes of a plain-clothes man from the Scotland Yard Special Branch. I stood up.

'Don't go dashing off already. I haven't even told you why I wanted to see you.'

'Will it wait?'

'The fact is, I heard something the other night that might be a case to interest you.'

'Max, I don't need cases. I'm not a private detective. Goodness knows, I've got enough problems without taking on other people's.'

'I know, only this poor girl did seem so distressed and she has no idea who to turn to. I thought if you'd agree to see her and let her tell you her troubles it might ease her mind at least.'

'What troubles?'

'She was engaged to a journalist. He

killed himself sometime last year in a piece of foolishness over a woman, but she's convinced he didn't.'

'Didn't kill himself?'

'She says he loved her.'

I moved towards the door. 'I'm very sorry, Max, but I've no time to sit through sad love stories. How did you meet her?'

'She's a barmaid at a pub down the back where I go to write when this place gets too cold. Nice girl.'

'She probably is, but I haven't got time to see her. Anyway, I'd only be raising false expectations.'

He sighed, but made no further protest when I left, only telling me to be careful.

I took the underground train home to Hampstead, trying to work out what to do and wishing I'd chosen any day but that one to look in at headquarters. It was a near certainty that Bobbie, June and Emily planned to blow up the club house at Walton Heath golf course. Even at best, if nobody was hurt, it would turn public opinion further against us and give the Home Secretary the excuse to lock up as many of us as he pleased. The worst case was that somebody would be hurt or killed. I knew two of the conspirators well enough to be convinced that they didn't intend to endanger anyone's life and would wait till the place was empty, but bombs are unpredictable objects (especially, it seemed to me, any bomb in which Bobbie had a hand). Even if they managed not to blow up themselves or anybody else they'd probably be caught. They were behaving with a recklessness that almost guaranteed it. They had to be stopped, and as far as I could see there was nobody but myself to stop them. The question was: how? Reasoning with Bobbie or Emily would be like howling into a whirlwind. Telling the police was unthinkable.

The only hope was to take some action that would make it impossible to go ahead with the plan. The trouble was I'd no idea where June had taken the bomb. I cursed my stupidity for not waiting to hear the address she gave the taxi driver. It was somewhere in Paddington, but I could hardly walk round thousands of houses asking if they'd seen a girl with a cold and a heavy tea chest. Anyway, there was no time. It might be happening that night. Since I didn't know the starting point, the only way was to be there waiting for them at the destination. If I got to the golf club before them, I could create some sort of fuss—I couldn't think what at the moment, but that would have to wait—that would ensure they had to go away without planting their bomb.

From Hampstead underground station, I almost ran up the hill to my house. It was still early on a grey winter afternoon, but as I went up the path to the front door I saw that the electric light was switched on in the living room. After years of living mostly alone, apart from the cats, it still came as a surprise to me to find another human being at home. When I pushed open the door, Bernard was sitting at the old dining table with its ink-stained red cover, my typewriter pushed to one side and a pile of music paper stacked beside him.

He stood up, beaming. 'You're early, Nell. Tea?'

'No time. I've got to change and go out.'

'I'll make it while you're changing.'

He bent to poke the fire and move the kettle on to the hob, while I searched through piles of books for Bradshaw and a map of Surrey. In spite of his broad build, he moved neatly, as he always did, like a man who was used to living in small spaces. That was just as well, because with his piano added to my files and bookcases there wasn't much room to move around. When I'd decided, six months ago, to take Bernard in as a lodger, the question of how on earth we'd fit in the piano had loomed much larger in my mind than the decency of the arrangement, much though this had bothered some other people who had nothing to do with it at all.

A lodger of some description had become a financial necessity. Up until then, I'd managed to scratch a living from translation work, but as the campaign for the Vote took over more and more of my time, that income faded dangerously. Besides, I was away a lot for one reason or another and it was useful to have somebody to feed the cats and keep the house warm. To be honest, I had intended to let the room to another woman, but when Bernard's need for a roof over his head coincided with mine for money it seemed illogical to worry too much about the proprieties.

I knew him by the time the question came up, though not well. He was in his mid-forties, hair and beard already flecked with grey, but what I'd liked about him from the first was his air of optimism and taking life as it came. To look at him, you wouldn't have put him down as a composer, but that was what he was. Twenty years before, he'd forfeited the chance of a comfortable living from the family firm, quarrelled with his father—who thought that music was a suitable hobby for a woman, not a proper career for a man—and worked as a labourer and a deck hand to finance his musical studies. Since then, there'd been two symphonies, eight quartets and several song cycles that gained some success with the critics but hardly enough money to keep him in beer and bread and cheese. He played the violin and viola well, and most of his fitful income came from occasional sessions with orchestras when they needed extra players in the string section, but the passion of his life was his opera, Wagnerian in scope, on Joan of Arc. He'd been working on it for three years and there was still a long way to go. That distinguished composer and human dynamo, Ethel Smyth, had taken an encouraging interest in his work and hauled him into the suffragette movement in return. Although his life was in music not politics he had a reputation as a loyal helper in things like putting up stalls for bazaars, addressing envelopes and writing the occasional march for special occasions. In the past six months I'd had reason to congratulate myself on my choice of lodger. He was even tempered, much tidier around the house than I was, good with the cats and paid his rent as often as could be expected from a man who never knew where his next pound was coming from. As for the busybodies who assumed lodger and lover were the same words, we both had better things to do than worry about them.

I found Walton Heath on the map, unearthed Bradshaw and started looking through it for Tadworth, the nearest station to the golf course.

'Will you be late back?'

'Yes. In fact, I might not even be back tonight. Would you mind feeding the cats? There's some boiled fish under the enamel dish in the meat safe.'

If the bomb party didn't arrive that night, I'd wait around Walton Heath until it did, sleep under a bush if necessary. I went upstairs and changed into my walking clothes: thornproof tweed skirt and jacket, green felt hat.

When I came downstairs carrying walking boots, Bernard raised his eyebrows. 'Hiking, this weather?'

'Not quite. Just a trip in the country.'

I didn't know his opinion on the arson campaign and had deliberately not discussed it with him. We tended to keep off politics at home. The teapot and two cups were already on the table, alongside a plate of hot dripping toast. I ate a slice and gulped some tea. There was a little pile of money on the table too.

'Last week's rent and this week's. Sorry you had to wait for it.'

'Sure Joan of Arc can afford it?'

She was expensive in manuscript paper and I knew he'd had no orchestral work for weeks in this sinking time of the year between Christmas and Easter oratorios.

'Sure. I got some work giving composition lessons. Nell ...'

He hesitated. I was bending down to put on my boots and glanced up to see him staring at me, worried.

'You will be careful, won't you? And if there's anything I can do ...'

'Nothing. But thanks all the same.'

The journey to Tadworth was by the South Eastern, second class return two shillings and ninepence. The train ran through the suburbs of Croydon, and by the time we were out in the Surrey countryside the light was already going. The remains of it glinted on broad wet leaves of ivy in the cuttings and was absorbed into fields where the faded grass looked as damp as a sponge beside a neglected wash bowl. As we got near the end of the line there were few passengers on the train, which wasn't good from my point of view. I wanted to be unnoticeable, not knowing how things might develop.

At Tadworth I was the only person who got out. It was after five o'clock by then, still just light but with night in the air and the temperature falling rapidly. There was a coal yard alongside the railway line, a bridge and a small cluster of shops and houses. A boy was putting up the shutters on the bakery. I was tempted to ask him the way to the golf course, but after the attack on the greens at Birmingham that would have made me an instant object of suspicion.

I'd tried to memorise the map and decided to make for the open heath, choosing a little flinty road through a copse. It took me past a round pond where a man was throwing sticks for a dog, then on uphill. By dusk, still following the path, I was out on the heathland with rough grass on both sides and the occasional copse of bare birches, tangled with brambles. I could see a few lights, probably the village of Walton-on-the-Hill, which meant I was still on track. Then, when it was still just light enough to make out figures, I saw the golfers. There were two of them plus two caddies on the other side of a clump of trees, walking briskly. I stood still and they passed without noticing me. At this time of a winter afternoon they'd be making for the club house. I waited for ten minutes then went in the same direction, but keeping to the rough grass of the heath.

After a while there was a drive running alongside and the sound of a motor car.

I saw its lights and stepped back to let it pass. There were two men in it and no sign that they'd noticed me—perhaps they were the golfers I'd seen, now on their way back to London after the game. I walked along the drive until I saw a building. Quite a substantial building too, brick and mock-tudor timbering, with electric lights blazing from windows and over doorways, and three more motor cars parked outside. There were several men standing among the motor cars in the tweed caps and plus fours of caddies. They looked as if they were waiting for their golfers to come out, but at dark on a winter evening, that would be ridiculous.

I'd envisaged the golf pavilion as a wooden shack, but this was a palace of its kind. My belief that it was Bobbie's target became a near certainty. At any rate, I had plenty of time. They'd have to wait until the building was empty so the attack would come late at night or in the early hours of the morning and it was a question of what to do with myself till then.

I went back along the drive, still unnoticed, then saw light coming from the other side of a low hedge. A man was sawing something on a trestle, out in the open by the light of an oil lamp. Behind him was the bulk of a large house, with the light of another oil lamp coming through its blank, uncurtained windows. The mud underfoot was churned up with cart tracks. A voice shouted from inside the house and the man stopped sawing. 'Right you are. Another five minutes.' Then started again. A building site. I found my way back to the heath and sat down on the damp grass with my back against a birch. Five men and a handcart came out of the building site and went away down the drive, taking their oil lamps with them, leaving the house in darkness. I stood up, walked around, sat down again. An hour passed. It struck me as odd that I'd seen nobody else leave the golf club. Then, odder still, people started arriving. First another motor car, a large one, went along the drive. Then a group of half a dozen or so men, judging by their voices, came walking up from the direction of Tadworth on one of the footpaths. They must have been local men because they knew their way without a lamp in the dark. They seemed in a cheerful mood and they too turned along the road to the golf pavilion. Even more odd.

I pulled my coat collar up, turned the brim of my hat down and walked along the drive, ready to melt away on to the heath if I met anybody. The lights were still on at the pavilion and what I saw made me catch my breath. Where there'd been a few caddies lounging outside the building, there were now thirty or forty men, standing purposefully as if waiting for something. Most of them looked like caddies but some of them were gamekeeper types in jackets and leggings. Nearly all of them carried sticks or golf clubs and there were several dogs in attendance. As I watched, pressing back against a hedge, a man came out of the clubhouse and stood under the light above the door. He looked like an ex-military officer, very stiff and upright, and spoke to them in a parade-ground voice that carried easily to where I was standing.

'I'm glad to see you all here. We've just had word on the telephone from the police at Leatherhead. They tell us that tonight is definitely the night.' A kind of murmuring growl at this. One of the crowd said something I couldn't catch. There was a laugh, quickly stilled. 'Now, you all of you know your stations. I want you to number off, green by green.'

'One, one. Two, two ...'

In voices varying from embarrassed to soldierly, they gave their numbers up to eighteen, two men to each green.

'You'll take up your positions now and stay there until relieved. Hot drinks will be brought round to you, but if any of you men have brought bottles or hip flasks, you'll hand them to the chief caddy now. We want you watchful, vigilant and sober.'

A pause, with no action. If there were hip flasks under the coats, nobody was admitting to it.

'Police Constable Luff will be here as soon as his other duties permit. He and I will be patrolling throughout the night. The clubhouse is the HQ and the secretary will remain on duty here at the telephone. If any one of you hears anything suspicious, he is to run to the clubhouse and report immediately, leaving his partner at his post. Otherwise, no man is to leave his post unless instructed by me or a police officer. Are there any questions?'

'What do we do if we catch one of them, sir?'

Laughter, and various suggestions. The officer-type was unamused.

'You are legally entitled to use sufficient force to restrain her. Remember, we are dealing with women ...'

Cries of 'Is that what they are?' and more laughter. It sounded as if a few had been at the hip flasks already.

'... so they may scratch or bite. However, you will not use any unnecessary force. Now, if that's all, I suggest we take up our positions.'

I had to leap for the heath as some of

them came past me, practically marching. From my hiding place in another clump of birches, I listened as voices fanned out across the golf course and grew faint in the distance. The clubhouse was still a blaze of light. It was all about as bad as it could be. Granted, from what I'd heard, the club was expecting a repetition of the Birmingham incident, with an attack on the greens themselves, and I was sure Bobbie's plan would be more ambitious. Still, her forces would arrive to find the clubhouse manned, a police officer in attendance with a telephone to hand and about forty hostile toughs within running distance. They'd done my job for me in preventing any attempt to bomb the building, but by the time Bobbie and the others knew what was happening it would be too late. Simply by setting foot near the place they'd be walking into the biggest trap ever constructed for us. What was worse, the police were expecting an attack that night. How they knew was a problem that would have to wait until later. The question was what was I going to do about it?

The obvious thing was to stop them before they got anywhere near the golf course, but that wasn't easy. They might be coming by train with the tea chest in the guard's van but there was at least one motor car at the disposal of the WSPU. I found my way back to the footpath and went as quickly as I could back down the heath in the dark, running on the easier stretches. When I got back to the station at Tadworth, the platform lights were still on, and I found from the timetable that there was only one more train due from London that night, in half an hour. It arrived on time. Just one passenger, an elderly man in a muffler, got off, said goodnight to the station master and tramped away uphill.

Either the arson party had arrived earlier and I'd missed them or they were coming by car.

For the next few hours, I walked up and down the heath in the dark, keeping roughly parallel to the track for motor cars that ran across it, stopping every now and then to listen in case I shouldn't hear the noise of an engine in the distance above the swishing of my boots in the dead grass. Over the hours, I worked out a kind of beat—as close to the drive as I dared, then down towards the clump of lights that were Walton-on-the-Hill, ears strained all the time for voices or the sound of an engine. It wasn't the kind of place that would attract many motor cars, especially after dark. Sometimes, nearer the golf club, I heard a coughing fit or a distant voice that showed the guards were still out there. Once a bicycle lamp wobbled along towards the club, possibly the local police constable. I'd brought some chocolate in my jacket pocket and tried to ration it, two squares to what I calculated to be every hour. There were twelve squares when I started. By the time I'd eaten the last of them the lights in Walton-on-the-Hill had gone out and the whole place was as dark as the times when the highwaymen rode across it. Well past midnight, certainly. The dead early hours when nothing seems like a good idea.

Then I heard the motor car. It was coming from the south, from the far side beyond the golf club. When I heard it, I was at the northerly extent of my beat, in the wrong place. Cursing, I sprinted as fast as I could uphill, which, given the dark and the conditions underfoot, wasn't fast enough. My heart was pounding so hard that I couldn't hear the noise of the engine any more. I stumbled, fell. In the seconds while I was getting my bearings, I heard it again, much closer this time, on the road over to my left. No lights that I could see, just the sound of it driving through the darkness, very fast, maybe as much as thirty miles an hour. It took me a while to realise the significance of its position.

It had passed the drive to the golf club without turning off, was heading straight downhill and away. I felt like shouting with relief. Somehow, with the luck that favours the reckless, Bobbie must have sensed at the very last moment that she was driving into a trap. Perhaps one of the party had spotted the lights still on at the clubhouse. At any rate they were getting out of it, hell for leather. I stood there willing them on, dreading to hear wheels skidding and the crush of wood and metal, but the car roared on and the noise died away in the distance. The idea that it might not have been Bobbie's party didn't occur to me. Who else would be driving like a maniac over Walton Heath at that hour?

The problem seemed to have solved itself without my help, leaving the lesser one of what I was to do with myself until morning when the trains to London started running again. As the heat from the uphill run died away, I was aware of the coldness of the night and the fact that there were still hours to go until daylight. Shelter of some kind was a necessity, but there was very little to be had on the heath. I tried to make a nest for myself in a copse out of a fallen birch trunk and some dried bracken, dozed a little but woke up shivering. At that point the idea of the newly built house came to me. I thought it would make a better shelter than a birch trunk. I'd be away long before the workmen arrived.

I worked my way back up the heath to where I judged the building site to be, moving carefully because it was very close to the golf club, hugging myself at the idea of the caddies getting uselessly cold out there. There was a scrubby hedge and, on the other side, the dark bulk of the house. I squeezed through the hedge, picked my way carefully across what seemed to be a wasteland of churned mud and broken bricks. Then, from only a yard or two away, a dog started barking. I waited for it to come snapping round my ankles but nothing happened, except that I heard something moving in a dark mass that might have been an outhouse on my left. With luck, it might be chained up. Another few steps and the barking began again, deep and gruff. So close to shelter, I wasn't going to be put off. I made in the direction of the front door, found my foot on the concrete step. Still no teeth in my calf.

'You there. Don't go in.'

A voice from somewhere off to the left. A woman's voice. A woman's familiar voice.

'Bobbie?'

A groan from the darkness. 'Nell. What in the name of damnation are you doing here?'

I stumbled in the dark towards her. The builders had made what seemed to be a kind of a lean-to for tools. She was in there, crouched against a pile of something or other.

'Was that you barking?'

'Yes.'

'So why can't I go inside?'

'Because it's Lloyd George's house. We've put two bombs in there.'

'Of all the stupid things you've ever done—'

'Don't stay here arguing. Just get out of it.'

'Why don't you?'

'Because I'm staying here to stop people going in, in case the builders come early. I thought you were one of them. How did you know what we were doing?'

'I thought it would be the golf club. When are these things supposed to go off?'

'When the candles burn down to the wood shavings. They should have gone off by now. I'm going in to see what's gone wrong.'

She stood up. I pushed her back down again. There was a strong whiff of paraffin coming from her.

'Do you know what time the workmen usually get here?'

'Early sometimes. About half past six when it's getting light.'

'And what's the time now?'

A match flared.

'Twenty to six. I'd better go in there and—'

'No. I'll head them off. You'd better keep out of the way, especially smelling like that. The golf club is crawling with men. The police were expecting something tonight. They'd telephoned the club. It looks as if you've got a spy in your camp.'

'Isn't it your camp too? That's what I wanted to talk to you about this morning but you wouldn't wait.'

'You suspected something and still went ahead with this? Where are June and Emily?'

'They went off across country. The car was supposed to pick them up near Tattenham Corner. With any luck they'll be on the way back to London by now.'

'Is the car coming back for you?'

'No. I was going to make my own way back, once the things had gone off.'

'Well, it looks as if they're not going to. But we'd better try to head off the workmen and then somehow manage to let the police know there are unexploded bombs in there. Whereabouts?'

'A cupboard under the stairs and a back bedroom.'

She stood up again.

'Where are you going?'

'To head off the workmen.'

'Stinking of paraffin like that? A blindworm would know what you'd been doing. Do you want to get arrested?'

Even Bobbie will occasionally listen to reason if you hit her with it hard enough. Also, she was tired, dispirited that the attempt hadn't gone as she'd planned. She hesitated just long enough for me to take over.

'What have you got on your feet? Shoes or boots?'

'Boots.'

'Then you'd better walk to Epsom. It's only six or seven miles. By the time you get there the smell might have worn off.'

I took her by the shoulders and urged her across the waste of brick and mud. She resisted a little at first but was secretly glad, I think, to have the decision taken from her. Once she'd disappeared I followed the ruts in the mud out to the drive, then on to the road. The sky was still dark, but there was that kind of tensing of the air that you feel just before the daylight comes.

Then, from down in the dark, I heard men's voices. I walked down the empty road towards them and saw the glow of an oil lamp and heard the creaking wheels of a handcart. They took shape against the darkness, two of them. Up to that point, I'd been walking softly. Now I let my heels strike hard against the road and adjusted my stride to what I hoped were nervous little steps. In the dark, the rhythm of the walk and the tone of voice would count for more than appearance.

I started calling, in a high little voice: 'Al-add-in, laddin, laddin, laddin, laddi-i-in.'

They came walking on with their handcart. I pretended to see them for the first time. 'Good morning, have you seen a little dog, a Pekingese?'

They were kind men. They stopped, let the cart rock back on its end. 'You lost one, miss?'

'I think he saw a rabbit. I couldn't hold him. He's over there somewhere.' I gestured towards the heath.

They unhooked the lamp from the cart and stood at the side of the road, letting the light play on the clumps of grass.

'Lad, lad, laddin. Here, boy. Heel, boy. Lad, lad, laddin.'

'He's probably gone off home, miss. Find him waiting for you on—'

Then it happened. First a dull thump like a fist connecting, then a split second's

41

silence when heart and mind stopped, after that a tinkle of falling glass that seemed to go on forever.

'It sounds like the golf club.'

'Or our house.'

They left the handcart where it was and went running up the hill, not waiting to see my reaction. At least now there was no point in caution. I ran down the road then took to the fields and, very much later in the day, caught a train back to London at a station further along the line.

That was on Wednesday. The following Sunday, Emmeline Pankhurst made a speech to a big meeting in Cardiff. In the course of it, she said proudly, 'We have blown up Lloyd George's house.' Of course nobody, not even the Home Secretary, thought she meant that she'd done it with her own hands, but she'd encouraged the policy and, say what you like about Emmeline, she never backed away from her responsibilities. On the Monday, she was arrested. On Tuesday, the crowd hissed and booed as she was driven to Epsom police court for the start of committal proceedings as an accessory before the fact and on Wednesday she was committed for trial. During that time, Bobbie and I were keeping well clear of each other.

Chapter Two

A week later, just after eight o'clock in the morning, I was at home in Hampstead cleaning my shoes when I heard a cab trundling up to the kerb and stopping outside. Bernard was still upstairs in his room. I hadn't slept well and was as fidgety as a horse on a frosty morning. The cab could have been for anybody in my small street, but I was sure at once that it meant trouble. Shoe still in hand, I went to look out of the window.

A man of medium height, in a black overcoat and bowler hat, was already out and had turned to say something to the cab driver on the box. It must have been that the cab was to wait, because the driver slumped his shoulders under his waterproof cape and rested his driving whip in its socket. The man turned. He was in early middle-age, with an official air and a worried expression. His face was greyish from the cold, deeply folded across the forehead and down the cheeks. I moved away from the window and let him knock on the door, put down the shoe, and opened it in no hurry.

'Good morning, Inspector Merit,' I said.

'Good morning, Miss Bray.'

He was polite and formal. Even on a past occasion, when he'd suspected me of protecting a murderer, his manners never slipped. On another occasion, when some of his colleagues thought I'd tried to dynamite Scotland Yard, he'd been on my side—as far as a conscientious inspector in the CID can be on the side of somebody with a record like mine. Not very far, that is. Still, if they had to send somebody to arrest me, I was glad it happened to be Merit. Then I told myself not to be a fool. Things didn't simply happen that way. If somebody at Scotland Yard had chosen to send a plain-clothes inspector all the way to Hampstead in a cab on an errand that could easily have been done by two local constables, it was because they expected advantages from it. Never trust a policeman, not even when he has a face like a sad grey frog.

'What do you want?'

He stared at me gravely. 'I've been asked to bring you with me.'

'Are you arresting me?'

'No.'

'I could refuse then.'

'I don't think it would be to your advantage to refuse.'

There was no threat in his voice, more

44

of an apology, but the threat was there in the words. Come in quietly for questioning or be dragged.

There were hurried steps on the stairs and Bernard appeared. His hair was tousled, shirt open at the neck, and the waistband of his pyjamas showing above his trousers.

'What's happening, Nell?' Bernard took a step towards Merit. The inspector stood his ground on the doorstep but his face became more creased and turned pink. 'Who are you and what do you want?'

'My business is with Miss Bray, sir.'

'Who is this, Nell? Is he bothering you?'

'He's a police officer. He wants me to go with him.'

'Oh.'

Bernard stepped back—not being accustomed yet to my lawless life—but still looked ready to defend me.

The last thing I wanted was to see him get into a scuffle with a policeman. 'Don't worry. He says he's not arresting me.'

So far.

'What does he want then?'

'I suppose I'll find out if I go with him. If I'm not back this evening, get in touch with the office in Kingsway and let them know.'

He hesitated. A current of cold damp air

was coming through the open door. Merit was making no attempt to come inside, just standing there stiff and embarrassed. I could see he'd made his assumption about Bernard's place in my life but I certainly didn't owe Scotland Yard an explanation about lodgers.

'You'll have to wait while I clean my shoes.'

I shut the door on him and assumed he'd wait outside on the step. I finished cleaning my shoes, slowly and carefully, and put them on. In preparation for a working morning, I was wearing an old blue skirt and grey jacket over a blue flannel blouse, so that was drab enough for the cells. I went upstairs for my hat and overcoat and when I came downstairs Bernard was standing in the kitchen looking unhappy.

'I wish there was something I could do.'

'You're doing it, looking after things here. Get on with Joan of Arc.'

I opened the door and found Inspector Merit waiting as patiently as a statue in a pond. He held the cab door open for me, waited until I was settled and got in beside me, balancing his bowler hat on his knees.

As the cabman pushed a way into the

46

stream of traffic down Heath Street, I waited for Inspector Merit to say something so that I could snub him. Not a word. At the junction with the High Street, where we were held up by people crossing the road to the underground railway station, he slid a watch out of his fob pocket and looked at it sadly.

'A busy time of day to travel, I'm afraid.'

I said nothing. He glanced at me, sighed, then turned his attention to the grey pavements and the crowds on their way to work, hunched in coats and scarves against the damp cold. Silence all the way down Haverstock Hill to Chalk Farm, where he looked at his watch again and observed that the roads seemed to get more crowded every week. This didn't seem to need an answer and I didn't give one. By then we were halfway to Scotland Yard.

If he was playing a waiting game, he was doing it thoroughly. I began to wonder if I'd been wrong in thinking there was a reason for sending this particular officer and if, after all, his job was simply to deliver me to whoever would ask the questions. But he was too tense for that. He sat on the edge of his seat as if he could urge the cab forwards through traffic that became heavier the nearer we got to the city centre. When a brewer's dray that had shed its barrels held us up in Camden Town he hung out of the window and asked the cab driver if there wasn't some quicker way. Yes, the driver told him. If he'd kindly arrange to have this old cab horse fitted with a nice pair of wings we could fly over the whole bloody lot of them, couldn't we, governor? He drew his head in again, face more creased than ever.

'Please don't worry for my sake,' I said. 'I'm not in the slightest hurry.'

I couldn't help it. He gave me another of his sad looks but didn't respond. Was that the trick—that I'd feel so sorry for the man that I'd tell him everything? I remembered that had always been a risk with Inspector Merit and resolved not to utter another syllable.

We rolled on in our enclosure of silence among the traffic noise down Tottenham Court Road and Charing Cross Road into Trafalgar Square. Only five minutes or so of the journey to go, down Whitehall and left for Scotland Yard. The question of what Inspector Merit was supposed to be doing was irrelevant now. I had to think about what was going to happen when we got to our destination. I had no doubt that all this was to do with the bombing of Lloyd George's house. The two workmen had probably told the police about the woman with the lost dog. It was more than likely that they were both at Scotland Yard waiting for me. An identity parade, that was it. And once the workmen had identified me, as they surely must, the police would be quite sure of what I was doing at Walton Heath at six o'clock in the morning. In their place, I'd have been sure as well. So what was my defence? Oh no, officer, I had nothing to do with it at all. I was only there to try to stop other people, friends of mine. Not possible. Even a fair-minded juryman would find my story thin, and when it came to suffragette activities, fair-minded Jurymen were as rare as apricots in winter.

When I thought about this, all the greyness of the day outside seemed to come rushing in on me. Grey pavements, grey overcoats, grey stone of the sentry posts at Horse Guards Parade. This wasn't something like smashing a window that would mean three or six months in a cell. Bombing meant years. I thought of the irony that one of the few things I had not been prepared to do for the cause would get me a longer sentence than the things I really had done. I even considered for a moment whether I should wrench open the cab door and run away, but Whitehall probably has more police constables on duty than anywhere else in

London. An undignified scamper followed by close contact with the pavement was all that would bring.

I looked across at Inspector Merit, ashamed of ever having felt any pity for him. He was as much a part of the monstrousness as the rest. And as I looked, the cab moved over to the centre of Whitehall and took a turn to the right.

It shouldn't have been turning right. Scotland Yard was further down and to the left. But the look on Inspector Merit's face was relief. We drove slowly past the police constable on duty at the corner, into a stub of a street with a familiar house on the right, a front door opening direct off the pavement with another police constable outside.

'But this is Downing Street.'

I must have been goggling at him. He nodded.

'Rather late, I'm afraid.'

The cab didn't stop at the Prime Minister's door, Number Ten, but took two horse steps past it. Number Eleven. Official residence of the Chancellor of the Exchequer.

'Lloyd George.'

I was off balance, still thinking in terms of identity parades and cells. But why here? I tried to concentrate on what

Inspector Merit was saying. Something about breakfast of all things.

'Mr Lloyd George hopes you will be kind enough to join him for breakfast. I was instructed not to tell you until we got here in case you refused.'

Before I could say anything he swung himself out of the cab, walked round to my side and opened the door. I got out slowly, still trying to make my mind move. The Chancellor, it was well known, had a fondness for breakfast meetings, particularly when he was trying to charm trade union delegations or other awkward beings of that kind. But surely that self-interested hospitality would not extend to women suspected of blowing up his house.

Inspector Merit, almost jaunty now, led the way across the pavement and knocked smartly on the door of Number Eleven. It opened instantly. I found myself inside, with Inspector Merit outside and the door shut. I heard cab wheels driving away. An elderly woman with a disapproving look on her face greeted me without ceremony in a strong Welsh accent.

'He's upstairs waiting for you. You can leave your hat and coat down here.'

I parted with my coat and hat. In my old blue skirt and grey jacket, so suitable for a prison cell but so inappropriate for taking breakfast with cabinet ministers, I followed her upstairs, trying to look as if this were exactly what I had expected.

When I walked into the room, it was as if my presence were all that the Chancellor had needed to make his day complete. A lover couldn't have been more welcoming in the way he bounded towards me, and enclosed my hand in both of his.

'Miss Bray, so nice of you to come, on such a day. I do hope I haven't inconvenienced you too thoroughly.'

I'd heard his voice many times at public meetings and in the Commons, but that hadn't prepared me for the warmth and confidingness of it at close quarters. There was a kind of a humorous quality about it, as if he and I, who had met only that second, were a select little club with an uncomprehending dull world outside. There were early daffodils on a table by a window and I could have sworn they were standing in sunshine, though I knew very well it was a dim winter day. He kept hold of my hand seconds longer than politeness required, looking into my eyes as if this meeting were really the most delightful and surprising thing. He wasn't a tall man, in fact I think I was an inch or two taller, but that didn't seem to worry him in the least. He let go of my hand.

'What am I thinking of? I'm sure we've

52

dragged you out without your breakfast, haven't we? Sit down and make yourself at home. Do you like your tea strong or weak?'

There were cups and a teapot on the sideboard, along with silver-covered dishes with candles under them to keep the food warm. He poured tea with his own hands, while the woman watched as if she didn't quite approve, and placed it on the little table beside me. It was good strong tea. I sipped it, settled into the chair that was upholstered in comfortable and well-worn chintz, and waited for the trap to close.

'I'm very glad to meet you, at last. You haven't been on any of the suffragette delegations to me, have you?'

'The ones you promised government backing for an enfranchisement bill? No, I preferred not to waste my time.'

His sunny humour was quite unruffled. He gave a smile as if I'd complimented him, under his moustache that looked as sleek and petted as a small domestic animal.

'What makes you think it would be a waste of time?'

'Experience. With your support, if you meant it, we'd have had the vote by now.'

He sighed.

'Ah, if only things were that simple. Now, what about your breakfast. Do you prefer sausages or kippers? Sarah here does a very good kipper.'

I opened my mouth to say that I hadn't gone there to talk about kippers, then remembered that I didn't know what I was there to talk about. Surely he hadn't sent for me simply for the next round in the game of half-promises and disappointments that the Government had been playing with us for years. I said I'd like a kipper please. Sarah served it with a thick slice of buttered brown bread.

Lloyd George watched benignly as if he wanted nothing better than to feed me and had all morning to do it. Even his clothes looked relaxed: grey suit and loosely knotted blue tie. His hair was dark with some strands of grey in it, rather longer than was fashionable, touching his collar at the back. The whole air, both of the man and the room, was homeliness and comfort. The housekeeper tidied the things on the sideboard then left us alone. While I picked at the kipper he stood on a hearthrug by the fire, a teacup in his hand, and went on talking.

'But things are not simple, are they? You with your knowledge of Parliament would understand that. It's a matter of taking the House with us.'

'The House tends to follow where the Cabinet leads.'

'Oh, quite so. Quite so.' He nodded quickly several times, as if I'd said something clever. 'And what is the situation in the Cabinet? I'll tell you, Miss Bray, I'll tell you quite freely. The Cabinet—or certain members of it—believe that there are more important things facing us at present than the question of enfranchising women, long overdue though that may be ...'

I'd have interrupted here that if it were so long overdue they should have done something about it by now, but I'd got a kipper bone caught in my teeth. Tactical mistake. Never try to eat a kipper during political discussion.

'... more important things like the number of battleships the Germans are building in such a hurry and how we can possibly keep pace with them. There are colleagues of mine who believe we are facing war with Germany and everything else we might wish to do must be subordinate to that.'

He was telling me nothing that couldn't be gathered from reading the papers and yet he managed to give it a confiding quality as if he knew I could be trusted with Cabinet secrets. I'd disposed of the kipper bone by then and decided to call his bluff.

'I'd have thought you were capable of

dealing with Mr Churchill.'

He laughed. 'Oh Winston, Winston, what shall we do with him?'

I was on the point of giving him a suggestion or two but he went running on, still in that low confiding voice. 'But if I may say so, Miss Bray, your organisation's present activities do tend to give some ammunition to your critics. You don't make it easy for your friends when you go round planting bombs.'

We'd got to it at last. I had to fight the temptation to turn and look at the door to see if there were police standing there. I took a sip of tea, working hard at keeping my hand steady.

'If a hundred years of asking Parliament politely have had no effect, you can't be surprised if people take other measures.'

'Quite so, quite so.'

He was nodding and smiling again, as if we were talking nothing but constitutional theory. There was a knock on the door and a very correct young man of the civil servant kind came in.

'You asked me to remind you about the meeting with the bankers, sir.'

'Indeed I did, Philip. Will you go back over to the Treasury and see if they've finished copying those letters? Then try to get Sir George on the telephone and regret I can't manage lunch today.'

The young man left, not pleased. As the door closed noiselessly behind him, Lloyd George sat down opposite me on a straight-backed wooden chair and dropped his voice.

'Philip got a first in classics at Balliol. I'm sure he never thought he'd be taking orders from a man who was educated at Llanystumdwy National School.'

There was a straightforward gleefulness about it, like a child with an unexpected and succulent slice of cake. To my horror, I was in danger of liking the man. I'd heard, and been sceptical, about the magic he worked but now I was seeing it in action. Only why was he trying it on me and why had he sent away a possible witness to our conversation? The smile faded and his voice became more serious.

'I gather Mrs Pankhurst's out on bail.'

'Yes.'

'I suppose the trial will be at the Old Bailey next month.'

'I suppose so.'

'It would cause a great deal of damage to your movement if she were to be locked up for a long time, and for a crime that most people have a horror of. It's a nasty business.'

'Nobody's life was endangered. It was only against property.'

'My property, as it happens. My little

house by the golf course. Are you a golfer, Miss Bray?'

As far as I'd seen, it was a moderate-sized villa, although his tone made it seem a pitiful little bothy. I shook my head. He moved his chair closer to mine, looking almost tenderly into my face. I had the idea that he was almost on the point of placing a hand on my knee, and drew away.

'Tell me, did you ever find your little dog?'

I gasped, couldn't help it. His voice was still confiding, his lips smiling under the plump moustache, but the bright eyes were as hard as moonlight on ice.

'What was his name? Something from the pantomime. Buttons, was it? Or Aladdin? Yes, Aladdin, that was it.'

Chapter Three

I couldn't take my eyes away from his. It was like being hypnotised. Even though I'd been expecting it, I felt as if the blood and brain had been sucked out of me. I looked away at the daffodils. Not even the illusion of sunshine now. His voice was going on, gentle as ever.

'Of course, it would take more than one person. Three or four at least, wouldn't you say? The police are quite confident of finding them all sooner or later.'

I looked back at him and said nothing, hoping my eyes were giving away as little as his.

'But we were talking about Mrs Pankhurst. I take it that you agree, Miss Bray, that it would be an excellent thing if we could find a way to prevent her going on trial for blowing up my house.'

He wanted something from me. For all his relaxed air, there was an intensity in him that was willing me to agree. The logic of where this was leading seemed to be that the charge against Mrs Pankhurst would be dropped if I admitted my guilt. But that made no sense at all. Hers was a much more important scalp than mine and if they knew about my presence at Walton Heath, as they obviously did, they could take both without bargaining. I took a deep breath and leaned back in the chair as if I really were considering some negotiating point. This had the advantage of taking me a little further away from his magnetic field. I tried to copy his relaxed tone.

'Yes, it would be a good thing if the charge against her were dropped.'

He smiled. 'And what would you say if I told you I was in a position to arrange that?' Then, before I could answer: 'Oh, I know what you're going to say—that judicial affairs are nothing to do with the Chancellor of the Exchequer, that it's a matter for the Home Secretary, the courts and so on. All of that.' He waved it all away. 'But it was, after all, my little house and what I want might have some influence in the matter, wouldn't you think?'

'What are you offering?'

My voice sounded harsh. Perhaps the kipper bone was still doing damage. There was a long pause and all the time his eyes were on me.

'Supposing I were to arrange not only that the charge against Mrs Pankhurst should be dropped but also that no action would be taken against any of the others responsible. Against *any* of the others, no matter how much evidence we had against them.'

'Of course, you might be bluffing about your evidence.'

A smile, less kindly than his earlier ones.

'Quite so. I might be bluffing. Only I'm not. I can tell you the names of at least four other people who were involved.'

And he named three names: Bobbie, Emily, June Price.

'Am I bluffing?'

There was a long silence. I could hear a motor horn sounding in Whitehall, feet coming upstairs, going into another room.

'And yourself, of course. There's a taxi driver who remembers you. You certainly tipped him generously for carrying that tea chest, but I don't think you'll find he feels very grateful to you now he knows what was in it.'

More silence. No point at all in telling him I was innocent. By that time, I didn't even feel innocent. The voice went on, still caressing, like a poacher tickling the belly of a trout before flipping it helpless on the bank.

'So what would that be worth to you, a promise of no charges?' Silence. 'I'll answer for you, then. I think it might be worth a great deal. If I were to say to you: Miss Bray, there is a piece of work which you can do for your country, and if you do this piece of work for us you would deserve well of both your country and your cause and we'll forget this little matter of blowing up my poor house—if I were to say that, would you be justified in refusing even to consider it?'

The door opened; the young man Philip looked in, slightly breathless from his run back upstairs. 'Private office telephoned. The bankers have arrived, sir.'

'Let them wait. Tell them to practise the

virtue of patience.' The door closed. 'He won't, of course. Well, Miss Bray?'

'What is this piece of work?'

The small breathing space had given me time to consider whether to go or stay. My first reaction had been to walk out, but the bait was swallowed and the hook in place. If I walked out, the charge against Mrs Pankhurst stood and Bobbie and myself, plus possibly two others, would join her in the dock. If I stayed, heard his proposal and decided to reject it, that could hardly make things worse. I guessed his idea would be that I should act as a spy within the movement. If so, I could tell him what I thought of him, slam the door and let the skies fall. It would be almost a grim satisfaction to know how low this government would sink.

'It's a matter of collecting information.'

I'd been right then. Well, let the man damn himself utterly. 'What kind of information?'

'Information that might help us recover something that has been stolen.'

'Something stolen?' That wasn't what I'd expected. The suffragettes had been accused of many things, but not larceny. Then it struck me that he might be laughing at me. 'I suppose a secret naval treaty abstracted from a locked compartment on the Orient Express.'

'Not quite that. No, not quite that, although as it happens you are remarkably close.' He wasn't laughing. In fact, his voice and expression had gone more serious than at any time in the interview. 'Miss Bray, do you consider yourself a patriotic woman?'

'The word's got dirty. Too many scoundrels have used it.'

'I entirely agree with you. Remember, you're talking to a man who was nearly killed by the mob for opposing the Boer War.'

'I do remember. In fact I admired you very much—at the time.'

He smiled. 'A verdict you've revised over the past thirteen years, I take it.'

'You did the revising.'

He refused to be offended. 'Well, let's come at the question from another direction. I take it that you are in favour of peace between nations.'

'Of course.'

'And you'll accept that the peace of the world is much more likely to be secured if all nations understand there will be penalties for breaking it?'

'Meaning the threat of war?'

'Miss Bray, don't assume that because I was pro-Boer I am anti-war in general and should faint at the mention of a cannon.

I am not against war with Germany if it becomes inevitable for national honour. But I love my country too much, and above all I love peace too much, to see war break out with all its horrors through the machinations of people who know nothing about love or honour or peace. Can you blame me for that?'

It was amazing. Sitting companionably opposite me, no more than a few feet away and without even raising his voice, he'd launched himself effortlessly into one of his speeches, like a boat taking to the tide. Even his enemies had to admit that there was no better speaker than Lloyd George. Part of the magic was that he made every member of the audience feel that he was appealing to him or her personally out of the hundreds present. Now, for some reason still unaccountable, I was genuinely getting the full force of it to myself. It was like having a whole symphony orchestra playing just to me, an opera chorus singing Verdi. It was all that I could do to hold on to my critical faculties and not sigh yes, he was right, oh, of course he was right. When he finished speaking he looked, I thought, just a shade disappointed that I wasn't doing exactly that.

'Of course any sane person would want to avoid a war with Germany. But you were talking about something that's been stolen. Is that something that makes war more likely?'

He stood up and walked over to the window, looking out on Downing Street. Still turned away from me, he said, 'Miss Bray, I've naturally made inquiries about you. If you were to give me your promise that nothing I tell you will be repeated outside this room, I should accept it.'

'Are you asking me for that promise?'

'I am.'

'Could you promise me in return that it would be nothing to the detriment of the suffrage movement?'

'Indeed. In fact, if things go as I hope, it might turn out to be considerably to its advantage.'

I never quite believed that. There'd been too many broken promises and half promises. And yet I could no more have walked out of the room at that point than you can look away from a trapeze artist the moment before he catches the bar. I could say it was curiosity, and of course I was curious, but if I'm honest that was only part of it. There was a magic about the man, and if it swayed my judgement on that morning when I was already unsettled, then I can only plead that I was one of a long list.

'Very well. I promise.'

He turned quickly, came back and sat

down, knee to knee.

'That promise holds from now. If you can't help us, forget this and never think about it again, let alone mention it to anybody else. What was stolen is a bundle of letters. They were written in all innocence by someone very close to the inner counsels of the Cabinet to a lady friend.' He raised a finger warningly. 'Now, I can guess what you might be thinking and I assure you that there's no question of moral impropriety of any kind. No question whatsoever of anything at all like that.'

I said, sarcastically, that I was relieved to hear it. If he noticed the sarcasm he let it pass.

'This lady is an old and trusted family friend of the man who wrote the letters, the daughter of a peer as it happens. He was in the habit of writing to her frequently—little bits of social chit-chat, who he had lunch with, what books he was reading—all quite harmless stuff.'

And yet, he wasn't trying too hard to keep a touch of satire out of the way he was telling it. Social chit-chat with the daughters of peers was not part of his own life. He wanted me to know that, keeping us in league on the same side of a social divide.

'So far, so innocent. But unfortunately

he was also in the habit of including little bits of political chit-chat too—such as what had been discussed at Cabinet meetings.'

His eyes, hard and angry now, were holding mine. I said that was surely a serious breach of Cabinet confidentiality.

'Of course it was, but he didn't think of it in that way. Don't you find, Miss Bray, that there's often a kind of blindness about people who pride themselves on their intellects?'

'So this person close to the Cabinet chatters about its discussions in letters to his highly respectable lady friend. How does this affect the peace of nations?'

He shook his head slowly. 'There are details I can't go into, even to you ...' (*Even!* He'd met me only half an hour ago and thought I'd bombed his house.) '... But you will understand that the situation in Europe concerns the Cabinet frequently. It's a matter, you see, of drawing lines. Stay behind this line, and there's peace. Cross that line and we are at war. You understand?'

'Yes.'

'And you'll also understand that there must be no wavering. If the other party feels for any reason that a line which should be firm is, so to speak, a dotted line, not so firm after all, then the temptation to see what happens if it's crossed is that much stronger and war is more likely. That is what we must at all costs avoid.'

'In other words, there have been discussions in the Cabinet that might suggest our opposition to any possible expansion by Germany isn't as firm as the Government pretend publicly?'

He let the silence grow, waiting.

'And this Cabinet wavering was included in letters that were stolen by somebody?'

A nod.

'Who stole them?'

A long sigh. He seemed relieved that we'd got there, but still took his time about answering.

'Have you ever heard of a woman called Oriana Paphos?'

It took me by surprise but rang a faint bell. I had to think for some time because it came from a world so far away from what we'd been discussing.

'Isn't she some kind of barefoot dancer? Free expression in ancient Greek draperies?'

'That's the one. What do you know about her?'

'Very little, but a couple of my friends went to see her dance when she was in London.'

(One of them, a man, had come back misty-eyed, saying she transcended physicality and it was like watching the

Platonic ideal of dance. The other, a woman, said it was the most pretentious performance she'd seen in all her life and a woman with thighs like that should have the sense to keep them covered at all times.)

'We don't know much about the woman either. She sometimes claims to be the illegitimate daughter of an English aristocrat and a Hungarian gypsy woman. As far as we know, nobody in Debrett's owns up to it. She's lived and performed all over Europe—London, Paris, Berlin. She calls herself a citizen of the world, doesn't seem to have a home of her own but rents, no expense spared, wherever she happens to be performing. Usually travels with a crowd of hangers-on, most of them people of somewhat mixed reputation to put it mildly. Last year, she rented a flat in Mayfair, gave a few performances in London then travelled around the country houses, putting on private shows.'

'And living as a house guest?'

'Yes. You or I might wonder, Miss Bray, how a country house weekend would be improved by having the illegitimate daughter of a gypsy doing barefoot dancing in her chemise, but then I don't consider myself a fashionable man. Are you a fashionable woman?'

'Hardly. Was it during one of those country house performances that these letters were stolen?'

'Yes.'

'From the woman they were written to?'

'Yes.'

'Are you saying that Oriana Paphos stole them?'

'Not directly. We think it was done by a Mr Leon Sylvan, her manager. He travels everywhere with her and his past is as mysterious as hers. We gather that he's technically a citizen of the United States, although he doesn't look or sound like one.'

I wondered about the 'we'. Was it Lloyd George and his Cabinet colleagues? Lloyd George and the Special Branch of Scotland Yard?

'How would Mr Sylvan know the letters existed?'

'A very good question, Miss Bray.'

A very obvious question and we both knew it. He was still trying to flatter me. If I had to draw my knee any further away from him, the armchair would tip over.

'To know those letters existed, let alone have any idea what was in them, Miss Paphos or Mr Sylvan would have had to be deeply knowledgable about the gossip of English politics and society. Much more knowledgable than you'd expect from a barefoot dancer and her keeper. So I'm sure I don't need to tell you what question we're asking ourselves.'

'Who might be employing them?'

He let out a long breath.

'Exactly. As far as we can see, there would be two types of people who might want those letters. The first would be some not entirely friendly foreign power—let's call it, for the sake of the argument, Germany. If so, the damage is already done, the letters were passed on months ago and we need to know the worst so that we can make our plans accordingly. The second possibility is that this pair of scoundrels, or whoever is pulling the strings, is simply interested in them for the money they'll fetch and will sell them to the highest bidder. Either way, you see, we need to know.'

'In that case, wouldn't the easiest thing be to offer them money and see what happens?'

'We thought of that. Unfortunately, there were complications.'

'What kind of complications?'

He sat back in his chair, at last taking the pressure off my knee.

'The letters were stolen in September. In November, a young man who'd been a member of Miss Paphos's entourage for some weeks was found dead in the bath at her flat in Mayfair with his wrists cut. The inquest verdict was suicide. Miss Paphos wasn't called to give evidence. She rushed off to Paris that same night and Sylvan followed a few days later. He had to come back to give evidence at the inquest, but she hasn't been back since.'

'This young man who died, was he a friend or a lover?'

'I gather that in the case of Miss Paphos the words were more or less synonymous.'

He drew out the word, lingering on the 'sin'. Somewhere beneath his implication that we were both people of the world there was a whiff of chapel and hymn books on a wet Welsh Sunday. He'd come a long way, but that was still clinging to him.

'This suicide verdict, was there any doubt about it?'

'Wouldn't you say there's usually room for doubt? Suicides don't often have witnesses.'

I remembered that he was a lawyer by training as well as everything else.

'But the inquest jury were convinced?'

'Let us say they had no reason not to be.'

'And what has this got to do with the stolen letters?'

'The young man who died was trying to recover them for us.'

'One of your men?'

He sighed. 'Miss Bray, you're a very

persuasive character. I'm trusting you with things that I shouldn't be telling you, putting my reputation in your hands, so to speak.'

I hadn't been persuasive at all, and I'm sure he never made an impulsive move since the day he threw his last rattle out of his pram. Every word of this had been thought out in advance.

'He was not, as you put it, one of our men. Not directly.' Another sigh, as if I were dragging this out of him. 'I have a certain generous and wealthy friend. Unlike many wealthy men, he has his country's interests at heart. It happens that he owns several magazines. Under a promise of strictest secrecy, I confided in him our little difficulty over the stolen letters. He suggested that one of his young men, one of his journalists, should attach himself to Miss Paphos's entourage under the pretext that he was planning to write a series of articles about her for one of my friend's magazines.'

'And steal the letters back if they still had them?'

'Recovery is not stealing. Fortunately, Miss Paphos is almost insane in her vanity and saw nothing surprising in the fact that a journalist should travel with her for weeks on end. He reported back to us, through my friend, that he was making progress.

He was deeply in her confidence and thought it only a matter of time before she told him what had happened to the letters.'

'Then he was found in her bath with his wrists cut?'

'Yes.'

'Did he leave a farewell message?'

'Not that anybody's discovered.'

'What did he use to cut his wrists?'

'There was a cut-throat razor on the bath mat.'

'Was it tested for his fingerprints?'

He looked ill at ease. 'Please understand, there's no question of calling you in as a private detective to investigate this young man's death.'

'That's just as well.'

'I'd like to have the luxury of worrying about one man's death. If things go as some of my colleagues fear, it could mean many thousands of deaths. No, poor Gilbey has gone for good and there's nothing to be done about that. What we need to know is what has happened to those letters.'

'How am I supposed to help with that?'

'You could try to insinuate yourself into Miss Paphos's circle.'

'In Paris?'

'No. She's coming back to London in a few days' time. Her manager, Sylvan, is here already.'

'How would I get into her circle? Or am

I another of those with a somewhat mixed reputation?'

'Let's say a person of advanced views.'

Again, though he was trying to conciliate me, he couldn't keep out that whiff of the chapel.

'How are my political and social opinions supposed to help here?'

'There are other kinds of advanced views. On music for instance.'

'Music?' He really had me at a loss.

'Yes. I believe you enjoy the work of Mr Richard Strauss.'

The shock of how much he'd taken the trouble to find out about me left me speechless.

'If you remember, you wrote a letter to a newspaper protesting about the refusal of the Lord Chamberlain to license the libretto of his opera *Salome* for public performance.'

I only just remembered it. That had been years ago, when there was time to think about plays and music as well as politics.

'What in the world have my views on Strauss's *Salome* got to do with what we're discussing?'

'Quite a lot. Sylvan is a hard character. We can't make any progress with him. But we've been getting reports that all is not well between him and Oriana

Paphos—rows in public and so on. At one party in Paris he even slapped her face.'

'Over her lovers?'

'No. He seems quite complaisant about those, probably even encourages them. After all, if the man is a spy, affairs in the right places might be very useful to him. The cause of war between them seems to be money. Oriana earns it and he keeps it.'

'Why doesn't she leave him?'

'Perhaps it will take another woman to answer that. But you see the direction of our thinking. If there is a rift between them, then it might be an advantage if it can be widened a little.'

'I see. You hope she'll leave him and bring the letters with her.'

'Ideally, yes.'

'So where do *Salome* and I come into it?'

'We need her back in England, and since we can't order her we have had to tempt her. Miss Paphos has let it be known that she feels an affinity with the character of Salome. She wants to do the dance of the seven veils—which, from what I hear, is approximately five more than she normally wears.'

'You mean the Government is going to finance a production of *Salome* to get her back here?'

I couldn't help laughing. The problem was that the libretto of the opera was by Oscar Wilde and even the mention of him was enough to send the censor into nervous spasms. He had allowed the opera to be performed in Britain only on condition that the action was shifted from the Holy Land to Greece and all references to John the Baptist or any other Biblical character deleted. Lloyd George was annoyed with me.

'As you very well know, there's no question of the Government's doing any such thing. Fortunately, this good friend of mine has agreed to finance a private performance. Miss Paphos has eagerly agreed to take part. She'll be arriving for rehearsals any day now.'

'And the idea is that I meet her. You must have other people you could use for this—people used to this kind of thing.'

Odd how reluctant I felt to use the little word 'spies', because that was what we were talking about.

'Yes, but you have certain advantages.'

'My advanced opinions?'

'Your sex.' His hand descended on my knee before I saw it coming. I twitched it off and he laughed. 'If we send another man he'll only go and fall in love with the confounded woman.'

'And my fee, if I manage to do this?'

I wanted him to say it so clearly that even he would have trouble wriggling out of it afterwards.

'I thought we'd discussed that.'

'Dropping prosecution of Mrs Pankhurst. No further proceedings against anyone else you think might be involved.'

He nodded.

'Yes or no?'

'Yes. If you succeed and as long as you keep quiet about it.'

'What if I try and can't do it?'

He hesitated. 'If you honestly try and can't succeed for reasons beyond your control, yes.'

I said nothing. My instincts were to have nothing to do with it, but I thought of the damage that would be done to us by the trial and inevitable imprisonment of Mrs Pankhurst, of Bobbie and others, and knew I didn't have the right to say no.

'Another thing, Miss Bray.' His voice had gone back to its most confiding, softest tone. 'If you were to succeed, I can promise you my strongest backing, for what it's worth, in the next bill that comes before Parliament to give the Vote to women.'

He'd made his word a devalued currency. And yet, when I knew so much, could he risk going back on it?

'Will you do it?'

'I'll try.'

I felt as if I'd jumped off a cliff.

'I don't think you'll regret it.'

I was almost sure I should, but the alternative was worse.

'I shall telephone and make an appointment for you with Mr Belter. May I suggest three o'clock at his office?'

'Jack Belter's the man you were talking about?'

'Yes. You've heard of him, of course.'

I had because I had made it my business to know about the press. Jack Belter: self-made millionaire, former Birmingham industrialist, now the owner of a sports newspaper and several magazines, including a popular weekly called *Home and World*. He was known to be a crony of Lloyd George and a contributor to Liberal Party funds, hungry for a knighthood or baronetcy. Apart from that, I knew of nothing to his disadvantage. *Home and World* had even given us some cautious support, mainly because a lot of women read it.

'In case anyone recognises you in his office, he'll let it be known that he's thinking of doing a series of articles on women and politics. Anything you find out, report to him and he'll pass it on to me.'

He wished me luck, stood up and walked

over to the fireplace. He must have pressed a button on the wall because a few seconds later the Balliol classics first put his worried face round the door.

'Have we still got our bankers, Philip? Excellent. Miss Bray and I have had a very interesting discussion. Will you see if she'd like some more tea and find her hat and coat for her.'

He dodged round the young man in the doorway and we heard his feet practically skipping down the stairs. I said no to more tea and let Philip open the front door for me. The police constable at the door of Number Ten wished me good morning as I walked past, still in a daze. By the time I got out of Downing Street and into Whitehall, I'd collected my wits and was signalling for a cab. Barefoot dancers and stolen letters would have to wait. There was something more urgent to be settled.

Chapter Four

It took me some time to find Bobbie Fieldfare. She wasn't at the Kingsway office and nobody knew where she'd gone. Even in calmer days she never stayed in one place for very long, and since the arson campaign she'd taken to moving from friend to friend like an outlaw. The Chelsea friend thought she might be at an address in Bloomsbury. Bloomsbury, suspicious, sent me back to Chelsea. Finally, with expenditure on taxis exceeding my entire budget for a week, I ran her to earth in Kensington, at a flat in a red brick mansion block behind the Albert Hall. Bobbie herself opened the door to me.

'Nell, what's happened?'

Her face was pale under her untidy mop of dark hair and there were rings round her eyes. She'd aged years in the past few months.

'We have to talk.'

'Not here. Wait while I get my hat and coat.'

She left me out on the landing, the door just ajar. Inside I could see pale green carpet, the gilded leg of a table, a curve of Japanese vase. As Bobbie came out, shrugging into her coat, jamming her hat on anyhow, she explained in a whisper, 'One of my aunts, not the sympathetic one.'

I didn't explain until we were across the road and pacing along the Flower Walk in Kensington Gardens, past borders of winter-pinched plants and patches of bare earth.

'The police know the names of several

people involved in that business at Walton Heath. I can't tell you how I found out, but a few hours ago four names were mentioned to me. You, me, Emily and June Price.'

'Where did you hear this?'

'I said, I can't tell you. But it was somebody in a position to know what the police know.'

'Who?'

'I can't tell you.'

She walked a few quick, angry strides. A uniformed nanny passed us pushing a pram with a toddler in tow, probably on their way to feed the ducks on the Round Pond. The toddler took a look at Bobbie's face and started howling.

'I knew the police were getting close to us. I wanted to talk to you about it but you wouldn't help when I asked you. You didn't even wait.'

She was angry with herself, with me, almost beyond thinking.

'I didn't know how deep this went,' I said. 'How many people knew about Walton Heath? Don't tell me names, just how many.'

She started to say something, then stopped herself and thought about it. The pace got slower and her voice, when she answered at last, more hesitant. 'About ten, I think. Perhaps twelve.'

'Oh for goodness' sake. You plan something like this and a dozen people know about it. I suppose you had a committee meeting and people taking minutes.' Knowing the strain she was under, I should have spared her the sarcasm, but I wasn't feeling any too relaxed myself. She turned on me, stopping in the middle of the path, eyes hard and furious.

'What does it matter? You know we're all going to be arrested anyway sooner or later. It's not a question of getting away with it, only doing as much as we can before they catch us. If you don't want to be part of it, at least stay out and let us get on with it.'

She started walking again. I kept pace with her, trying not to be as angry as she was, remembering things we'd got through together. Perhaps, after long minutes of silence, this began to communicate itself to her because she sighed and said she was sorry.

'Only I am worried, Nell. I knew something was wrong. There've been too many things recently, too many close calls when we've had to pull back at the last moment. I know you don't approve of what we're doing, but you can't want this to happen to us.'

We were beside the Long Water by then,

near the statue of Peter Pan. They'd put it there the previous spring and it was the first time I'd seen it. Not the occasion, though, for stubborn boys and bronze rabbits. We stood looking away from it across the water, a streak of cold pewter between expanses of green-brown grass. A pigeon hunched on the edge of the water, feathers fluffed against the cold.

'What are we going to do, Nell?'

'Now you know it's compromised, wouldn't the sensible thing be to call off the arson campaign? For a while at least.'

'How can we, with Emmeline taking the responsibility for what's happened so far and probably going to prison for years? It would look as if we were deserting her—as if it were all her idea. No, we can't stop now.'

'Well, in that case you'll be going on with a police spy in the organisation.'

'We can't do that either. We've got to find out who she is and throw her out.'

'Yes.'

'So help me.'

'I've got other things to do.'

'Exactly what have you got to do that's more important than this?' It was as sharp as the crack of a whip. Bobbie's natural and hereditary tendency to give orders had been sharpened by running her outlaw band.

'The thing that's going to win for us in the end—taking the message out to the women in the factories and the homes. We could bring this country to a standstill if they were all on our side.'

'Soap boxes and soup kitchens. You could go on like that from now to the end of the century and it wouldn't make any difference. This thing you've told me about is central. It's the rot at the core.'

'Your core, maybe. Not mine.' The pigeon shook itself and strutted away on feet as pink as chilblains. I started walking. Bobbie came after me and grabbed my arm.

'The core for all of us, Nell. Surely you see that. Our strength has been trusting each other, knowing we can all rely on each other more totally than anything else in the world. If that goes, it's all gone.'

I said nothing. She let go of my arm but kept pace with me.

'Nell, I'm appealing to you. Whatever else you're doing, this matters more. Please, help us with this before it does some awful damage to us.'

If she'd tried to go on giving orders I'd have walked away from her. What kept me was a flat desperation in her voice, like somebody who was almost at the end of her resources.

'You're better placed than I am, Bobbie. You know the people you're working with. Who's joined within the last few months, for instance? Who's always around, or seems especially eager to do things?'

'It isn't that simple. There are a lot of people that might apply to. The point is we've been mostly using the younger members for this. It's young women's work. They're risking more than any of us risked in the past. The thought of letting them down makes me so angry, I could ...'

She made a neck-wringing motion with her gloved hands and started walking again, back the way we'd come.

'Spies, Nell, can you understand it? If somebody's against you, that's one thing. But to think of a woman pretending to be on your side, making you trust her then crawling away and selling you—what sort of woman does that? It makes me feel dirty to be on the same planet as someone like that, let alone in the same room.'

I said, as calmly as I could, that being angry about it was beside the point.

'Start thinking clearly. You said a dozen people might have known about Walton Heath. The first thing is to narrow the list down. Now, did they just know something was going to happen there, or did they know exactly what it was?'

'Both.'

'It's an important distinction. The police knew that something was going to happen. Then, probably just a few hours before, they got word that it was going to be Tuesday night. I heard somebody at the golf club telling the caddies that the police had just rung them with a warning. But even up to that point, they still thought it was going to be an attack on the golf course. There was no guard on Lloyd George's house. What does that tell us?'

'I see what you mean. We can rule some people out.'

'Yes. I'd say you can rule out anybody who knew exactly what you were doing. You rule in anybody who might have known it was something in the area of the golf course. That might be more than you think. I found out about it just by being in the office. But you rule out again anybody who couldn't have known on Tuesday afternoon that it was going to be Tuesday night. Does that help?'

'It narrows it. Have you got pencil and paper? We could sit down on that bench and make out a list.'

'No. I don't want to know names. It's your problem. I'm only advising you.'

We walked in silence for a while, back

towards the Kensington side of the park. I could see she was thinking hard.

'It helps, what you heard at the golf club. They'd only just been told that it was going to be that night?'

'Definitely.'

'I think it's six. Five or six. Am I supposed to go up to six people and ask if they're police spies?'

'In your place, I think I'd set up a dummy operation.'

'You mean, pretend to attack something that we're not?'

'Yes, and it's got to be something important enough to make your spy put all her energies there, something the police would want very much to prevent.'

'Like blowing up the Houses of Parliament?'

'Let's not go that far. Once you've decided on your target, you tell the five or six people on your list, one at a time. Let them know it's even more important to keep quiet about it than usual. You can do that?'

'Yes. It's a terrible waste of time and energy, but I can see it's got to be done.'

'Then each of them is given a separate time and meeting place for the operation. If the police aren't there before you, then it's unlikely that particular person is your spy. You make some excuse for why the thing has been called off and go on to the next one.'

'It would take so long to go through all that five or six times.'

Patience had never been her strong point.

'Well then, try it in pairs or threes. At least then you'll have narrowed it down and you can go on from there.'

'Except by then the police will have arrested us.'

'Either you'll have to meet somewhere with a sure getaway, or be doing something so obviously innocent they'll look stupid.'

'So what's our target?' Bobbie's eyes went roving round the London skyline and lingered longingly on the immense brick drum of the Albert Hall. 'Too solid. Pity. I've never liked the place.'

There was an awful relish in her voice. For a moment I understood the giddiness of destruction, the feeling of holding the city in your hand and deciding whether to crunch your fingers into it. A hateful feeling. Her eyes shifted to something closer, a gilded spike rising up from the bare trees at the edge of the park. She laughed.

'There. That's our target. The memorial.'

Queen Victoria's memorial to Prince

Albert. A gothic wedding cake of marble, enamel and gilding, with figures of Faith, Prudence and Temperance keeping watch over the massively sedentary prince. Bobbie led us over to it as if drawn by magnets.

'Perfect. It's everything awful in one. Women ministering to the man. The worship of the patriarch. The solid smugness of the whole damned thing.'

'But it was a woman who put it there after all.' I knew it was ridiculous, but I really quite liked the memorial.

'Misguidedly. We couldn't think of a better target. Can't imagine why we haven't done it before. How much dynamite would you think, Nell?'

She was glowing, all her old vitality restored.

'For goodness' sake, remember you're not really doing it. And don't even think of dynamite.'

'It's a pity though. You don't think we might ...'

'No.'

I pulled her away. Passers-by were beginning to look at us, struck by Bobbie's apparent architectural enthusiasm. We crossed Kensington Gore and walked along Knightsbridge. We were going our separate ways at Hyde Park Corner and Bobbie said she'd let me know how things went. As she turned to go I asked the question that had been been in my mind all the time.

'Supposing the charge against Emmeline Pankhurst were to be dropped. Would you think of stopping the arson campaign then?'

'What's the point of asking that? You know very well that it won't be. They'll find her guilty and send her to prison. If she goes on hunger strike again it will probably kill her. And if she dies, Nell, I can promise you there'll be no holding us. What's happened so far will be nothing to what will happen then.'

She disappeared into the crowds. Without knowing it, she'd raised the stakes and destroyed the last possibility that I could walk away from where I'd landed myself. I had an egg on toast and a pot of tea in a café, then took a bus to Fleet Street.

Chapter Five

The first thing to do was locate the office of *Home and World* and the rest of Jack Belter's empire. It turned out to be a new five-storey building at the Ludgate Hill end of Fleet Street, gleaming with large windows and bands of green, black and white tiles, two uniformed commissionaires on duty inside the revolving doors that rotated constantly with people hurrying in and out. The pavement outside vibrated from the thump of printing machines in the basement. With an hour to spare before my appointment, I walked back to the other end of Fleet Street and found Max at work in his rabbit hutch of an office.

'That barmaid you were talking about, what was the name of her fiancé?'

Max can play chess games in his head and knows the average working man's wage for every country in Europe. Remembering names is no struggle.

'Gilbey. Laurence Gilbey.'

'Do you know who he worked for?'

'Yes. Belter's thing, *Home and World.*'

Disgust in Max's voice. As far as he was concerned, journalism was about crusading, not entertaining.

'Do you know anything about Jack Belter?'

'Why?'

I said nothing, Max being one of those people who don't deserve lies.

'I see. A case of don't ask, is it?'

'I'm afraid so.'

One of the many good things about him was that he'd accept that, although he sighed and stared at me for a while before answering my question.

'Jack Belter. I can't tell you much that the whole world doesn't know. Father was a Birmingham businessman in a modest way, making parts for printing machines. Son took to making whole machines, then got the bug for magazines and newspapers. You know the result.'

'I've just been looking at it. And a friend of Lloyd George too.'

'That's the horse he's backing at the moment. He's very big for trade and the empire—by which he means if something's good for the Birmingham businessman, then it must be good for the whole world. Angling for a baronetcy of course, but aren't they all?'

'Baronetcies come expensive.' As expensive, for instance, as a life of an employee and a private production of *Salome*.

'Oh, he can afford it. He's a millionaire several times over. It's probably just a matter of time.'

'Do you know anybody who's worked for him?'

'Fleet Street's half populated with men who've worked for Jack Belter. He hires impulsively and fires explosively.'

'Does that get him disliked?'

'Oddly enough, no. Funny people, most journalists. They'll stand anything but tedium. Go into any pub along the street and you'll find them telling Jack

Belter stories. They say the man has a flair for what the public wants to read. He gambles on where the next big stories are going to be and spends money to get them. He backs his men to the hilt—as long as they're successful. They never know from one day to the next whether they'll be sent to Paris or Cairo or kicked out into the gutter.'

'I think I'd like to meet Gilbey's fiancée after all. Will you arrange it?'

'Yes. I'd like to know why you've changed your mind overnight.'

'I'll tell you one day. Not now.'

'I'll see her tonight and let you know. Will you be at your usual address?'

A delicate way of asking me if I were on the run from the police. The last time I'd seen Max I'd asked him about Walton Heath and he couldn't be blamed for drawing the obvious conclusion.

'Yes, unless you hear otherwise. You know, I didn't plant those bombs.'

'That wouldn't stop them arresting you.'

I wanted to tell him that, for the while at least, I was safe from that, but couldn't do it without breaking my word. I thanked him and went to keep my appointment.

At five minutes to three I was back at the Belter building. I walked through the revolving doors into a dazzle of colour and light. The circular entrance hall was surrounded by pillars of coloured serpentine stone. It ran all the way up to the top of the building, with a glass dome supported by a web of cast iron for a roof. Underfoot, a mosaic floor gleamed with colour, reflecting clusters of electric light bulbs on the walls. When the dazzle wore off, I saw that the mosaic was a great map of the world, with the seas azure blue and the countries of the Empire vibrant red.

They were expecting me, and a uniformed messenger boy led me across Canada and Greenland to an electric lift in the far corner. We went up without stopping until the indicator reached the top floor, then there was more mosaic to cross to a desk and a solemn young man with round glasses and a bright blue tie, his brown hair so sleek that it looked as if it had been painted on his head without a drip falling from the brush. He said Mr Belter was free, in a tone which might have been just about appropriate to a group of pilgrims coming to see the Pope. As I followed him along a wide corridor I noticed two young women at typewriters in a side room and it struck me that they were the first females I'd seen since coming into the building. Then the corridor turned a corner and there was suddenly empty space on our right. From this top floor you could look over a low wall and a rail, all the way down to the entrance hall, and there was the world again, its imperial red patches showing up even more brightly from above. The commissionaire was standing on India; a man in a raincoat was hurrying across the Pacific.

The young man stopped alongside me. *'Home and World,* you see. Like our magazine.' He hurried me on until we stopped outside a wide mahogany door, tapped discreetly and opened it.

'Ah, Miss Bray. Come in, come in.'

After all the solemnity, the man himself came as something of a relief. No amount of marble or mosaic could take away the slightly comic impression of Jack Belter when you saw him for the first time. He was like a geometry diagram in a child's school book, with an almost perfectly round head, bald-domed, perched on top of a square body without visible intervention of neck. The grin of greeting, too, was as uncomplicated as a child's drawing: square teeth, very clean and white, eyebrows like strokes of black crayon. In spite of the bald pate, he was probably no older than late forties or early fifties. There was a feeling of life, of pent-up force, about him, even in those first few words—implying that it was a big, exciting world and any new acquaintance had better add to the excitement. I could see why he and Lloyd George appealed to each other. He shook my hand then kept hold of it and practically dragged me over to a table by the window.

'Now, Miss Bray, tell me—what are your views on the electrical kitchen?' The table was covered with plans and drawings, strange devices that looked as if they belonged in a hospital or ship's engine room. He let go of me and grabbed them in handfuls. 'See, an oven that will decide for itself when the meat is cooked, switch off and ring a bell to call the family to table. A machine that will iron shirts. The woman of the future freed from domestic drudgery, to make more use of her creative talents.' He was practically waltzing with them. 'We're running it in our next issue. The question is, one page or two? What do you think?'

I forget what I said. The solemn man, whose name was Henson, asked if there was anything else, sir, and was told to go. I'd assumed that once he was out of the room Jack Belter would come to the real subject, but he pushed a page proof in front of me.

'What about this? I think there are too many penguins. Do you think there are too many penguins?'

It was an *in memoriam* tribute to Captain

Scott and his party, the news of whose deaths had just broken. An engraved illustration showed a snowbound tent in the foreground, penguins in the middle distance.

'I don't think you'd get penguins that far on the ice shelf. Don't they stick to the coast?'

He stared as if I'd said something of great importance.

'No penguins at all, you think?'

'No penguins.'

He picked up the telephone from a desk as wide as a hay cart. 'Get Peters. Peters, I've just been speaking to an eminent ornithologist, who says you don't get penguins inland. Delete the penguins.'

Once that was settled he waved me to a chair and settled himself behind the desk. His round, slightly pop eyes had a shrewdness that showed there was more to the making of millions than simple enthusiasm.

'Our mutual friend tells me that you can be trusted. If that's good enough for him, it's good enough for me.'

I wondered how much Lloyd George had told him about that interview. I suspected quite a lot. I knew my fee and, from what Max had told me, thought I knew his. I was bothered if I'd be treated as one of his hirelings.

'Perhaps—but is it good enough for me?'

His eyebrows rose.

'There are a lot of things I don't know.'

'In the circumstances, you should expect that.'

'Some of them I need to know. There's been at least one other attempt to get those letters back and it ended fatally. You know about that.'

I'd put him off balance. He wasn't used to other people taking the initiative.

'Has our friend told you to investigate Laurence Gilbey's death?'

'Quite the reverse. He said he wished he could have the luxury of worrying about one man's death.'

He let out a long sigh and leaned back in his chair.

'Miss Bray, you and I have been entrusted with a matter of the highest importance to our country. Our friend, who is one of the country's and the world's great men, has a right to ask that our own personal concerns should be set aside ...'

(Oh, has he? I thought, though I didn't say it. I was waiting for the 'but'.)

'... But that may involve some hard sacrifices. I have had to do nothing when one of my own men is murdered, even though I am quite certain of the identity of the people who killed him. I've had to stand by while he was labelled as a suicide, in the most squalid of circumstances, by an inquest jury. I have had to speak to the widowed mother of a promising son who has been told that he slit his own wrists in the bath of a notorious harlot. As I say—all that has been asked of me by a man who has the right to ask it, but it's still hard, wouldn't you say?'

'You don't believe it was suicide?'

He waved it aside.

'Of course I don't and neither does our friend. He was murdered by the woman who calls herself Oriana Paphos and the man who calls himself Mr Sylvan.'

'Tell me about Laurence Gilbey.'

'His friends called him Laurie. He was twenty-seven years old, came from Croydon, lived with his mother before he moved to London. We engaged him as a journalist and he became one of our best. I paid him eight pounds a week and a free rein with expenses and he was worth it. You never had to tell Laurie anything twice and he got some stories our rivals would have sold their daughters for. He was totally trustworthy, so when our friend first approached me with this problem I had no hesitation in putting Laurie on to it.'

'Did he know exactly what the letters were?'

'How much did our friend tell you about them?'

'That they were written in all innocence by somebody very close to the Cabinet to a lady friend.'

From the way he looked at me I guessed he knew a lot more about them than that, but then he was one of Lloyd George's trusted friends and I was anything but that.

'Yes, that's very much what Laurie knew about them as well.'

'Did he have a chance to report back to you before he died? Was he making any progress.'

'Yes to both questions. He followed them around for five weeks—London, Paris, Budapest, back to London. As we'd hoped, he was soon in her confidence. He reported that he was quite sure they had the letters, had even shown him one of them, but there was no question of handing them over. He had the strong impression that she was in the control of this man Sylvan, even scared of him.'

'Anything else?'

'More than you'd want to know about the life that woman leads—drink, drugs, gambling parties. As for men, she's insatiable. The list of her lovers ran to nearly a page and that was just a few weeks.'

'Was Laurence Gilbey's own name on the list?'

'Would you have expected him to tell me?'

'Meaning you think it should have been?'

He shifted slightly in his chair. 'Yes.' A pause, then angrily, 'How do they do it, these women? There should be biologists working on it.'

'So she's irresistible?'

'She's the wrong side of thirty, she's not even what you'd call beautiful. You've seen pictures of her?'

'Not that I remember.'

He opened a drawer and skittered one across the desk at me. A studio study, postcard size, taken from the side with her head curved round to face the camera, heavy hair flopping down over gauzy draperies, sole of a bare foot, also facing camera. Somehow an air of challenge about that face and foot.

'Not beautiful, is she?'

There was urgency in the question. While I'd been looking at the picture he'd been watching me.

'Powerful.'

He snorted. 'What kind of power is it that only makes trouble?'

'Do you think Laurie was the sort of man who'd kill himself over a woman?'

'Not in a thousand years. Before I put him on to this, I made all the inquiries about him I could. If he was a drinker or a gambler or a womaniser I had to know about it before trusting him with anything so important.'

'So he didn't drink, gamble or womanise?'

I didn't try to hide my scepticism. He laughed.

'Of course he did. There aren't many saints in Fleet Street and as far as I know I haven't got any of them on my pay roll. But not to excess, there's the point. Of course there'd been women in his life. He was a good-looking young man, well-paid, free with his money. I'll admit, if somebody had told me that some deluded young girl had killed herself over Laurie Gilbey I might have been sorry, but I shouldn't have been entirely surprised. But to kill himself over a woman or anything else—not Laurie.'

'So why do you think he was killed?'

'Because of something he'd found out about them. They killed him before he could report back to me.'

'It can't have been simply that he was interested in the letters. From what you say he'd already discussed them with her.'

'Yes. He says she was quite open about them. That was what gave us hope that the pair were prepared to sell them back—at the right price.'

'You don't hope that any more?'

'No. Our friend disagrees with me. He thinks there's still a chance they'll deal. But if they were ready to do that, why kill Laurie when he'd made it pretty clear to them that he'd be prepared to act as middleman?'

'So what do you think he'd found out about them?'

'That they're spies. For Germany. If they ever do condescend to sell those letters back, it will be after they've been pored over by every clerk in the German foreign ministry.'

'Have you any reason for thinking this?'

'Common sense and the fact that they killed him. Drugged his drink, probably, then put him in the bath and slit his wrists.'

The phone on his desk rang. He picked it up, snapped that he was busy and all calls should be put through to Henson. This gave me a few seconds to think how little I liked the situation.

'You're sure he was killed, but you didn't challenge the suicide verdict.'

'I'd have liked to have every policeman and every private detective in London proving he was murdered. As far as I'm concerned, that young man died for his country every bit as much as if he'd been killed fighting under the flag for the Empire. But what would have been the result? There would have been an investigation, because I can punch a lot of weight when I choose. That investigation would have come up with enough information to arrest Oriana Paphos and Leon Sylvan. Then what would have happened when they were brought to court?'

He pointed a stubby finger at me, like a schoolmaster in an arithmetic test.

'The business about those letters would come out and the Government would be embarrassed,' I suggested.

'Far worse than embarrassed. The consequences for both the government and the whole Empire would be incalculable. Can you imagine what the enemies of our country would do with a story like this?' He paused, to give me time to contemplate the political wreckage, then sighed. 'So that, Miss Bray, is why I did nothing. But that doesn't mean I've forgotten it, and when the opportunity comes to punish the murderers of Laurence Gilbey without harming my country, I shall take it.'

'I understand that, but my objective is those letters. If you're right, they're probably already in the hands of a foreign government and it's too late.'

'I told you, our friend is more optimistic than I am. Perhaps he's right. At any rate, while there's a glimmer of hope, we have to follow the game through. And if you did happen to come by proof that those two had committed a murder, you couldn't ignore it, could you?'

He was staring at me, as if trying to hypnotise me. He didn't quite have Lloyd George's almost supernatural persuasive ability but you could tell he'd been studying it.

'Proof of murder is hardly something I'd stumble across.'

'You've been mixed up in this kind of thing before, haven't you?'

'Unwillingly.'

He changed tack abruptly, perhaps sensing that he'd gone as far as he could in that direction.

'Now, about this dratted opera, this *Salome*. The performance is a week on Saturday, in the ballroom of my house by the river at Maidenhead. Private performance, invitation only, supper afterwards. The singers and orchestra and what-have-you are rehearsing away there already and there's a dress rehearsal a week today. Leon Sylvan got here a few days ago, allegedly to check that everything is in order for Miss Paphos. He's staying at the Savoy at my expense. She's supposed to be here any day now. I'm going to invite the pair of them to stay as guests at my house. I'll feel as if I want to have the place fumigated afterwards, but there you are. You'd better stay there too. That should give you as much opportunity as you need.'

'Won't everybody wonder what I'm doing there?'

He grinned. 'You'll be my cultural attaché.'

'What?'

'I need one. Here am I, supposed to be so mad for modern opera that I'm putting on a special performance of this filth, and all I know about music is just about enough to stand up when they play "God Save the King". I've kept away from it so far, but I've got to pretend to take some sort of interest, otherwise Sylvan will smell a rat. She may be stupid but he's not—far from it. I gather from our friend you actually like this Strauss business.'

'Yes.'

'God help you. Well, you can represent me. We need somebody to keep order down there. Would you believe we've got fifty singers and players all yowling away and eating their heads off at my expense?'

'Who's conducting?'

'Youngish chap called—what was it?—

Haddock, Shamrock?'

'Madoc? Meredith Madoc?'

'That's the one. You know him?'

'By reputation. He's good.'

'At what I'm paying the lot of them, he'd better be. I've invited a hundred people to sit through it.'

'People may be surprised that you've suddenly acquired a cultural attaché.'

'None of their business.' His lips curved in a schoolboy grin. 'They'll probably assume you're my latest mistress.'

It had been hovering over us since he'd produced that picture of Oriana Paphos, a desire to shock or possibly to see whether I'd be shocked. He liked unsettling people. I gave him a long look, taking in the plump torso, the bald dome. 'Only by people who don't know my taste.'

He laughed, entirely good humoured, as if rudeness had been what he wanted.

If he could play games with me, I could reply in kind. 'In my new capacity as cultural attaché, I want to add another player to the orchestra.'

His eyebrows went up.

'There's a friend of mine who's a good violin and viola player. I'd like to know there's somebody there on my side.'

It had come to me out of the blue. Since that morning, I'd been feeling entirely at the mercy of events, out of my depth with no foothold. If Belter could have the whole world in his lobby, I was at least entitled to my souvenir from home.

'You're not to discuss this with anybody else.'

'I've no intention of discussing it with him. I don't suppose he'd be interested anyway. But, by your own account, the last person you employed on this business ended up dead in a bath. It's only fair to me to have somebody I can call on in the last resort.'

I'd no idea how useful Bernard would be in a crisis but there was another reason for wanting to include him. Meredith Madoc, both as a conductor and director, was an up and coming name in British opera, and Bernard would give a lot to work at close quarters with him. Also, a little orchestral work would help in his permanent financial crisis. Jack Belter gave in grudgingly. I could see that he assumed that Bernard was more than just a friend, but it suited me to get back at him for that mistress business.

'He can't stay at the house. The orchestra travel in by train every day.'

'All right.'

He picked up the telephone. 'Send Henson in.' Then, turning to me, 'Henry Henson, he's called. If you need me in a hurry, he'll know where to find me.'

'Does he know what's happening?'

'He knows enough to do what I tell him and not ask questions.'

The solemn young man appeared almost immediately. Not so very young, after all, perhaps early thirties. He was not bad looking in his way, but beside the grotesque vitality of his employer he seemed no more than a shadow.

'Henson, I've just appointed Miss Bray my cultural attaché.' Henson didn't blink. 'She'll take up her duties at once. You'll find my house easily enough, Miss Bray. It's just up-river from Skindles. Good luck to you.'

In an outer office, Henry Henson provided a railway timetable for Maidenhead, his office telephone number which I had no intention of using with my mistrust of the instrument and ten pounds for immediate expenses, all without showing the slightest flicker of curiosity. I asked him if he were involved with the *Salome* production.

'I'm inevitably involved to some extent in all of Mr Belter's enterprises.' He made the line sound as if it had been drafted by a solicitor.

Still feeling dazed by all that had happened since the morning, I caught the underground railway back to Hampstead. When

I got home, Bernard had lit the fire and was at the table in the living room working on *Joan of Arc*. He jumped up, surprise and relief on his face.

'Nell, they've let you out. Did they charge you with anything?'

I'd forgotten that the last he saw of me I was being carried off by Inspector Merit.

'They had nothing to charge me with. Look, there's been quite a lot happening. You are free for the next ten days, aren't you?'

It was difficult to explain to him, with so much that I had to leave out. I reduced it to the bare and more or less true essentials, that an acquaintance had introduced me to Jack Belter as somebody who might help with his opera project and I'd accepted. The news that it involved ten days' paid work for him and an opportunity to buttonhole Meredith Madoc delighted him so much that he didn't ask awkward questions.

'Nell, you're a fairy godmother. There's bound to be a chance to get him to look at the first act. And it will be good to play some Strauss. I don't care if it's viola or second violin. I'd practically pay them to have a chance to hear it. Who's singing Salome?'

'I don't know. Oriana Paphos is dancing it.'

'Who's she? Oh yes, Grecian attitudes and so on. I'd better not take my opera in on the first day. If I wait and get to know him ...' And so on, while he dodged around the furniture making tea. I was glad that this small good was coming out of the tangle. It was the only good that I could see. The chances of getting what Lloyd George and Jack Belter wanted seemed even dimmer now I was away from the influence of their magnetic personalities.

As we sat by the fire drinking tea, Bernard went quiet for a while, then he said, 'You know what pleases me most about this, Nell?'

'The chance to lobby Madoc?'

'Not even that. That it's good for you.'

'Good?'

'Yes. I mean ... we all know what the cause means to you. But it's taken over so much of your life. It's a relief to know you're getting back to other things ... like music. What's up? Have I said something wrong?'

My face must have changed. I'd been thinking that the secrets that had been forced on me were already cutting me off from my friends, and of what Bobbie had said about spies.

'Nothing wrong, no.'

I was still glad he'd be with me, but guilty about all I couldn't tell him.

Chapter Six

On Thursday morning, I took the train from Paddington. Just before you reach the station at Maidenhead, the railway crosses the Thames and for a few seconds you look down over a wide stretch of river to the grey stone road bridge. In summer that stretch of river is alive with punts and steam launches, the lawns beside it flowering with silk dresses and striped blazers. Now, in early March, the river was brown and empty apart from a few wind-blown swans, the lawns deserted.

Jack Belter had said his house was just past Skindles Hotel on the far side of the grey stone bridge. I couldn't see it from the train, but I knew that living there confirmed two things about him: considerable wealth and a determination to take his place in society. With Cliveden no more than a mile up-river and Windsor a few miles down, the Birmingham businessman was making it clear that he knew his place. Good luck to him on that score. I preferred his energy and vulgarity to the languor of people who'd been privileged for so long that they were too bored to enjoy it.

There were cabs waiting by the clock tower in the station yard and I took one of them. The driver nodded when I said I wanted Mr Belter's house and didn't need anything else in the way of directions. I'd normally have walked the mile from the station to the river, but today I was travelling on Belter's money. Bernard would be following me down in the afternoon as I'd decided it was only fair to warn Meredith Madoc in advance of the extra member of his orchestra.

Those Thames-side mansions run to ostentation, but even by their standards Belter's was something remarkable. The centre part of it was Victorian mock-gothic, perhaps forty or fifty years old, built with every shape and colour of brick the architect could lay his hands on. Patterns of black, white and yellow fidgeted all over it, small and arbitrary towers mushroomed from the corners, dormer windows erupted from the roof line. On either side of this a more restrained architect had recently added two wings in ordinary red brick that almost doubled the size of the house and confined the spikey gothic like a hedgehog in a hutch. My first sight of it from the cab was the land frontage as we turned in from the small road that ran parallel to the Thames. There were a few shrubs but most of the grounds on that side were taken up with a wide sweep of yellow gravel for carriages or motor cars. A new brick rectangle that looked like a garage stood to one side.

I paid the cabman, walked up the broad brick steps and knocked on the front door. It was opened by a small, strongly built woman in a dark green dress. She was in her forties or early fifties, with dark curly hair and a slight squint that, oddly, made her more attractive, giving her an air of glancing back over her shoulder at something that amused her. I introduced myself and she said they were expecting me and invited me in. Her voice was soft southern Irish.

'I'm Bridget, Mr Belter's housekeeper. Will you be wanting a cup of coffee and something to eat or will you go straight through to where they're practising?'

'Straight through please,' I said, and followed her along a corridor that cut through the middle of the house, deep carpet yielding underfoot. After the bleak greyness outside, the house was warm as summer, heating pipes running along the walls and electric lights on. The walls were covered with paintings—reproduction Stubbs and Constables. I liked the fact that Jack Belter had chosen paintings so well known that nobody could take them for the originals.

At the end of the corridor, Bridget paused, her hand on the door.

'We have to go out in the cold to get to the ballroom. He's going to have a colonnade made, but it won't be done till the summer.'

We went on to a wide stone terrace at the back of the house. There was a lawn sloping down from the terrace to the river, a landing stage and diving board standing out against the brown water, fast and swollen from the rain, and a boathouse. The terrace was bisected by a structure that looked like a chapel with big windows, sticking out at right angles from the rest of the house. It was obviously part of the original building with the same bands of coloured brick. The sound of a piano was coming from it, and a voice. It came curving along the cold terrace, as warm and sinuous as a vine in summer. *'Thy mouth is redder than the feet of those who tread the wine.'* A few bars, a silence, then the piano again and the voice continuing. *'Thy mouth is redder than the feet of the doves who haunt the temples.'* The voice of Salome herself. As far as I'd been thinking of the opera, it was Salome dancing. But the dance was only a small part of it. Somebody had to be found to sing that wonderful, impossible part—a sixteen-year-old princess with the voice of Isolde. It stopped me in my tracks but Bridget went on and knocked at a door in the side of the chapel-like building. The piano and Salome's singing stopped at once and a woman spoke in a strong Yorkshire accent.

'My pies at last.'

There were four people looking at us as we went in. One of them, dark and intense, I recognised as the conductor, Meredith Madoc. Also a man sitting at the piano, a large young man standing and a woman. It was a huge room with an echoing wooden floor and a platform with the piano at one end of it. Rows of chairs and empty music stands were set out on the floor in front of the platform. After hearing that voice, I couldn't help looking round for Salome, but there was only one source of it and she looked as unlike a wanton desert princess as it was possible to imagine. She was large, in her forties, with a thatch of light brown hair caught up in a bun, like the knob on a cottage loaf, and a square face with determined eyebrows. She wore a blouse of bright kingfisher blue over a serviceable black skirt with a Paisley-patterned shawl round her shoulders.

Bridget said to her, undisturbed, 'Your pies are just out of the oven, Miss Wetherby. Cook will be sending them over in a minute or two.'

I crossed the echoing floor towards Meredith Madoc, feeling an intrusion into their world. Cultural attaché might do as a joke for Belter but it wouldn't do for Madoc, so I explained that I was representing Jack Belter and he should let me know if he needed anything and assured him of my perfectly genuine admiration for his work. He seemed quite happy.

'Mr Belter has given us an amazingly free hand so far. It's wonderful to find a man in his position with such an enthusiasm for modern opera. I begin to have hopes for English music after all.'

I didn't tell him that as far as Jack Belter was concerned they might as well have been doing *The Song of Hiawatha,* as long as Oriana Paphos would consent to dance in it. Why disillusion him? He was quite unconcerned too about the arrival of Bernard once I'd given him a few names of other people with whom he'd worked, taking it for granted that any musician worth the name would want to be in his production. He was taking the piano rehearsal with Salome and John the Baptist this morning and the orchestra would be back in the afternoon. While we were talking there was a knock on the door and the maid arrived with a covered dish. The woman fell on them.

'You'll have to excuse me. We left London before breakfast and this slave driver hasn't given me a minute to gnaw a crust.'

'You need a slave driver, Elsie. We've only got a week to the dress rehearsal. Miss Bray, Elsie Wetherby.'

'I could learn the whole Ring cycle in a week, let alone this little floozy.' She smiled, shook hands and turned back to the pies. 'You'd better have one of these, John. Keep your strength up.'

The large young man had been keeping in the background trying to look inconspicuous, which was difficult with his build. He must have been all of six foot six, broad and muscular in proportion, with shoulders straining at the seams of his decent dark jacket. He had a friendly but hesitant air and would be handsome when his face matured to catch up with his body. He looked just out of the egg, but a very large egg. Elsie, between slices of pie, introduced him.

'John Bartholomew, the best young baritone in Yorkshire, which means in the whole country. He's engaged to my niece Vera.'

She sounded like a miner staking a claim. John blushed and shuffled. Madoc seemed to have accepted that the rehearsal was going nowhere until Elsie was satisfied, and seemed quite happy to talk to me.

'You're doing it in an English translation?'

'Yes, as far as we can we're going back to Wilde's words. Of course, we're having to adapt them because the music was written for the German translation.'

'Of words originally written in French by an Irishman. Why not? At least this time there shouldn't be any trouble with the Lord Chamberlain.'

'That's the beauty of it. It's a private performance to invited guests so he can't do anything about it.'

'I gather Oriana Paphos is due to arrive in the next day or two.'

His face fell.

'She's a side show as far as I'm concerned. Salome's dance isn't the most interesting music in the opera and I need all the time I can get for the singers.' I promised I'd do what I could to keep Oriana off his hands until the dress rehearsal. By then Elsie had finished eating and they started rehearsing Salome's spine-tingling declaration of lust for the prophet's body and his denunciation of her. Even at this stage, it was clear that the performance was going to be remarkable. John Batholomew's voice was wonderfully mature for such a young man and his horror at what he was hearing entirely convincing. It became clear that this wasn't a matter of acting. Elsie, for all her homely appearance, was really throwing herself into Salome's music. *'There is nothing in the world so red as thy mouth. Let me kiss thy mouth.'* Although he must have read it in the score, John probably hadn't heard it sung before, and his solid body quivered with the shock of it. His face turned red; he took a step back from his prospective aunt-in-law as if he really expected her to sink her teeth into his lips, and he kept glancing towards the door, either in fear of spectators or hope of rescue. In a lull, when Elsie and Madoc were discussing something, he came over to me, looking like a man who'd collided with a wall.

'Are we really going to be singing this in public?'

'That's the general idea.'

'Those words, just as they are?'

'You don't approve?'

He rubbed his head, uneasy at the thought of having to approve or disapprove of anything. 'When Elsie sent the telegram and said I was going to sing John the Baptist, I thought it was oratorio. I've done mostly oratorio.'

'I suppose you could think of it as a kind of oratorio in its way. After all, she does come to a bad end.'

They called him back to the piano and

he went, not comforted.

'Never, daughter of Babylon! Daughter of Sodom.'

Perfect casting.

At lunchtime, cabs full of musicians and their instruments arrived from the London train, including Bernard. He'd met several friends among them on the train and after a few words with Madoc settled down among the violas with as little fuss as if he'd been there all along. It was an orchestra happy in its work, made up of more than usually competent players. I sat and listened for a while then, nodding from the heat of the room, decided to walk around outside to wake myself up.

I wandered for a while on the damp lawn beside the river, looking at the little steam launch moored at the landing stage and the newly built diving platform and springboard. A small wooded island opposite cut Belter's lawns off from the main channel of the Thames, but there was still plenty of room on his side for boating and swimming in summer. I imagined the more lissom of his house guests somersaulting off the springboard or jumping with noses clasped between thumb and forefinger. A little creek cut across the lawn and where it joined the river a rustic wooden bridge led across it to a boathouse with Indian canoes and a punt. Everything about the house and grounds shouted cheerfully of money spent for comfort and enjoyment, the sort of thing an ambitious boy might promise himself once he'd made his fortune.

I wandered away from the river on a path alongside the house to the sweep of gravel at the front. A lad was raking away at it, smoothing the tracks of the cabs that had brought the musicians. I was watching him as a motor car turned into the drive, its engine running so smoothly that the crunch of its tyres on the gravel was the first thing either of us heard, and the lad with his rake had to jump aside in a hurry. Even to my eyes, unskilled at distinguishing varieties of motor car, this one was something out of the ordinary. Two huge brass headlamps flanked a radiator with 'Mercedes' written on it in gold letters. The coachwork and wheel spokes gleamed glossy red, accented with lines of black, and the upholstery was buttoned red leather. It was driven by a chauffeur in cap and jacket of dark grey with red facings. At first I thought it must be bringing Jack Belter back from town but the way the lad was goggling at it showed he hadn't seen it before either. It swept round in a half circle and came to a halt with its running board on the left hand side practically touching the bottom step to the front door. The chauffeur leapt down to open the passenger door and, taking his time about it, a man got out of the back seat. He was wearing a shiny black top hat and a black cloak fastened with a silver chain and two lion-head clasps that swung back to show a mauve carnation the size of a small cabbage in his jacket lapel. I remembered somebody—my aunt probably—saying that only bridegrooms, bounders or foreigners wore carnations in the daytime. Whether bounder or not, he certainly looked foreign, if only from the confident way he turned round on the step and stared at the lad with the rake and me as if waiting for applause. It was hard to guess how old he was. He walked and stood like a man in the prime of life, but his stiff pointed beard was streaked with silver, the streaks so regular that it looked as much a deliberate design as a sign of age.

'Is this the residence of Mr Belter?'

The accent was a puzzle. Every country in Europe might have claimed a part in it. His eyes were strange—the pupils very large, the irises almost as dark. I took a guess.

'Are you by any chance Mr Sylvan?'

'Of course I am. Where is he?'

I knew from Bridget the housekeeper that Jack Belter was twenty-five miles away at his office in London and his return was unpredictable. I passed this on.

'Then I shall return to London too. You may tell him I was here.'

Having no intention of letting him slip away so easily, I introduced myself as Mr Belter's assistant and asked if I could do anything to help.

'I want to see if the arrangements are suitable for Miss Paphos to dance.'

I'd promised to keep Oriana Paphos away from Madoc as far as possible, but nothing had been said about her manager. In spite of Sylvan's arrogance, it seemed a reasonable request, so I suggested he should go with me to see the room where she'd be performing. He nodded, told the chauffeur to wait and followed me round the side of the house. When we got to the ballroom, the orchestra were rehearsing the interlude before the appearance of the Baptist. Sylvan showed an inclination to stride straight up to Madoc in mid-flow and I had to jostle him to get him to sit down on a chair by the wall. As our bodies collided I was aware of a field of nervous energy round him, the air almost humming with it. He sat with his legs stretched out, long fingers in grey kid gloves moving restlessly on his thighs.

'Is this the music she will dance to?'

'No. That comes much later.'

'Tell him to play it.'

His voice was loud and Madoc glanced round with an annoyed look. As far as I'd seen, he wasn't a temperamental man as conductors go, but to do what Sylvan asked would be like trying to give orders to a captain on the bridge of his ship. I was starting to explain this in a whisper when there was an interruption from another source. The door from outside was flung open, letting in a blast of cold air, and Jack Belter stumped in, hat in hand, overcoat flapping.

'Whose car is that outside?'

He looked furious, his crayon-stroke eyebrows merged into one black bar. His sleek assistant, Henry Henson, tiptoed in behind him, closing the door as he came like a man battening down hatches for a storm. Madoc, after another annoyed glance over his shoulder, signalled to the orchestra and the music stopped.

Sylvan stood up. 'Mine, as it happens.'

Until that moment I don't think Jack Belter had realised that Oriana's manager was under his roof. He was furious because he thought the car was an extravagance on the part of Madoc or one of the soloists. When he saw Sylvan, he came to a halt and seemed to swell out his chest, like a cock robin finding a rival on its territory.

'Oh, you're here, are you? What do

you mean, it's your Mercedes? Have you bought it?'

His tone stopped just short of rudeness. Even so, it was hardly a warm welcome but Sylvan was unperturbed. He was a head taller than Belter and the more striking of the two, with his showy clothes and jutting Olympian beard, like Zeus on a Greek vase. A stranger might have taken him for the millionaire and Belter for a tradesman.

'I told the hotel porter to hire it.'

'On my money, I suppose. A Mercedes and a chauffeur on my money. There's a perfectly good train service.'

'You don't use the train service.'

A giggle from somebody in the orchestra, hastily suppressed. There were about forty pairs of ears and eyes witnessing a struggle for power. Even somebody who knew nothing about their recent history would sense the tension between the two men, and perhaps the musicians were waiting or hoping for an explosion. In spite of Sylvan's coolness, he was throwing out a challenge like one playground urchin to another. Unspoken: I've got something you want so what are you going to do about it? It must have cost Belter an effort not to rise to the challenge, especially before an audience, but the cock robin let his feathers subside and stepped aside from confrontation.

'Is Miss Paphos with you?'

'No, but I have a message for you from her.'

'She should be here. Where is she?'

Slowly, with everybody looking at him, Sylvan shifted his cloak back over his shoulder, slid a hand into the pocket of his jacket and brought out a folded telegram form.

'She sent this message from Paris last night.'

'Paris? She's not meant to be in Paris. I'm paying her twenty pounds a day to be here at rehearsals.'

A gasp from Elsie Wetherby, over by the orchestra. I guessed she wasn't being paid a quarter as much.

Belter signed to Henson to take the telegram, as if he didn't want to risk contamination. Henson opened it and held it for his boss to see. I glanced over his shoulder. Five words.

CAN'T COME. NO CLOTHES.
PAPHOS.

Belter gulped. 'What does she mean, no clothes? All she needs is seven veils.'

'She has no clothes suitable for winter in England.'

Since she was presumably surviving Paris in March this seemed excessive. It was clear already that these two were playing with Jack Belter and he knew it.

'And exactly what kind of clothes does Miss Paphos need?'

'Furs, naturally.'

'I should have thought Miss Paphos would have all the furs she needed by now.'

'She has a generous heart. She gave her fine sable coat away to a little beggar girl by the Seine.'

'Henson.' Jack Belter forced the words through gritted teeth. 'You will get Miss Paphos's address from Mr Sylvan. You will go to Paris on the night train, buy her a fur coat at my expense and bring her back here by the day after tomorrow at the latest. Is that understood?'

Gasps and rustles from the direction of the orchestra, but Sylvan looked impassive, though something about the way he stood implied that he knew he'd won the round. Henry Henson looked a little surprised but no more than that, and I supposed a press millionaire's assistant was used to dashing around like Ariel. In any case, he had no time to argue even if he'd wanted to because Belter turned and stalked out with another rush of cold air. Henson followed him, more slowly, and Sylvan slower still at a languid walk and with a supercilious look over his shoulder at the orchestra. As Madoc rapped on his music stand to bring the orchestra to attention, I went outside too and got to the front of the house in time to see Sylvan climbing back into his hired motor car. The empty green two-seater parked askew beside it, probably Belter's own, looked speedy but decidedly less grand. As soon as Sylvan was settled his car went gliding away. Obviously he didn't intend to spend that night under Belter's roof, so there was no reason for me to stay either. When the rehearsal finished and the orchestra piled back into cabs for the station, I went with them. By then the green two-seater had gone as well.

Bernard sat next to me on the short train journey back to London, happy and half drunk from the music. He fell asleep after Slough, viola case across his knees, his head on my shoulder, and didn't wake up until we slowed down outside Paddington.

'Odd chap, that manager of the dancing woman.'

'Yes. Where do you think he comes from?'

'Could be anywhere. There was a man in the second violins thought he might have seen him before, but couldn't remember where.'

I'd been feeling sleepy as well, but this woke me up. 'Where? This country or abroad?'

'I didn't ask him. It was just a remark while we were waiting.'

'Could you ask him, get him to try to remember?'

'Nell, you're not involved in anything, are you?'

When I didn't answer, he sighed and looked aside at the iron girders slipping past us.

We bought fish and chips at a shop near the station and got the man to wrap them up well so that we could take them home on the underground train. Bernard insisted on paying, to celebrate the money he was earning, he said. As usual, there was a pile of letters on the mat inside the door, most of them dull-looking. I dumped them in a heap on the table and went up to change while Bernard lit the fire. I didn't get round to sorting through them until we'd had our meal and I was looking forward to spending what was left of the evening beside the fire with the cats and a book. Most of them were as dull as they looked, but in the middle of the heap was an envelope marked URGENT and addressed to me in Bobbie's sprawling writing. It had no stamp, so she'd delivered it by hand probably sometime between first

131

and second post which was why I hadn't seen it when I picked up the pile.

MEET ME OUTSIDE ALBERT HALL AT 11PM TONIGHT. MOST URGENT AND IMPORTANT. PLEASE, PLEASE BE THERE.

I looked up from it at Bernard's worried face across the table.

'Bad news, Nell?'

'Not really, only I've got to go out again.'

He didn't ask any more. I supposed he was getting used to that.

Chapter Seven

It was half past nine by the time I read Bobbie's message. The trams didn't come up as far as Hampstead and, with no cabs cruising for hire so far from the centre of things at that time of night, I had to travel by underground railway and bus. By the time I was in Kensington, hurrying towards the enormous drum shape of the Albert Hall, it was past eleven. At this time of night the place was quite deserted, with only a few dim lights on over the doors.

I started walking round its circumference, my footsteps echoing up the great curving cliffs of brickwork. Then I heard more footsteps coming to meet me and Bobbie appeared from the dark. She was wearing a black coat and a knitted cap pulled down low on her forehead. Her face in the faint light looked drained.

'I thought you weren't coming.'

'Why do you need me? I told you you'd have to handle this on your own.'

'I've got an instinct about tonight.'

'Why tonight?'

She took my arm and pulled me against the wall, away from the light. 'I did what you suggested. The first lot, last night, nothing happened. I told three of them to meet me here at the flat when my aunt was out for the evening. Nothing. Not a whiff of a policeman. So that was three ruled out.'

'Not necessarily. You might not have given the informer enough time.'

Typical of Bobbie to rush at things. Even now, she wasn't taking any notice of what I'd said.

'Today I started on the other three on the list. I went to them all individually, swore them to secrecy and told them to meet me at midnight on the east side of the Round Pond in Kensington Gardens.'

'And they all think you're going to plant

a bomb at the memorial?' I stepped back into the light to look at my watch. Half past eleven. 'You'd better start walking then.'

'Come with me. Help the two innocent ones get away. I know the police will be there.'

'Not necessarily.'

'They will. If it wasn't last night, then it has to be tonight. For goodness' sake, it's your plan I'm working to.'

With anybody but Bobbie I'd have thought it was fear making her voice tremble. With her it was urgent to get the business over. The knowledge of treason had got into her like a fever, overheating a judgement that was never cool at the best of times. She started walking back towards Kensington Gore and the park. I went with her, knowing very well that I should do what I'd said and leave her to it, but couldn't quite bring myself to desert her. Two lots of hurried steps echoing now. More than—

I stopped, grabbing her arm. For a full two beats the steps went on. I could feel Bobbie starting to say something, and squeezed her arm tighter. She said nothing, but the arm went as rigid as cast iron. We walked on. Listening for it now, you could hear the third set of footsteps, just out of rhythm with ours and heavier. The curve of the building helped the person following us, keeping him out of sight. We came on to the pavement and walked towards the main entrance. Kensington Gore was in front of us with horse carts and motor vehicles going along it, even at this hour. Beyond them, street lamps and railings, then the dark space that was Kensington Gardens, with the Round Pond in the middle and three women converging on it, nerved for sabotage. A policeman paced towards us on our side of the road.

'Goodnight, ma'am.'

An ordinary policeman on his ordinary beat.

'Goodnight, officer.'

With his measured footsteps and the traffic noise we couldn't hear now whether those other steps were still following us. Certainly there was nobody in sight as we went up to the kerb and waited to cross.

Bobbie said, 'We've got to get there. We can't just leave them by the pond to get arrested.'

There was a bull-at-a-gate quality about Bobbie that made her rush on into disaster. I remembered that one of her ancestors had charged with the Light Brigade. The best I could do for the present was try to supply some tactics.

'When we get to the other side, just turn

135

right and walk alongside the railings as if we're out for a stroll. If he's following us he'll have to cross the road too and we'll see him.'

We crossed, turned right. Bobbie was pounding along like a hiker and I told her to slow down. I counted twenty paces and looked back. Nobody was crossing the road from the Albert Hall. The same at forty paces. Bobbie took a long breath.

'Perhaps it was nothing to do with us.'

'Perhaps.'

The next thing was to get into the park. At this time of night, the gates were locked. We chose a stretch where the street lighting was dim, checked that the policeman on his beat on the far side of the road was out of sight and there were no vehicles coming, then scrambled over the railings. Once we were inside the park, we kept to the grass to muffle the sound of our feet. Bobbie knew the place well enough to navigate confidently in the dark, and started by striding out fast until she fell headlong over a low fence and learned some temporary caution. As we went, we heard a clock striking the quarter hour to midnight. Every now and then I made her stop so that we could listen. Nothing but the sound of our breathing and the occasional vehicle along the road. I began to hope that the person by the Albert Hall had been no more than a tramp looking for cigarette butts but didn't believe it.

We skirted round clumps of shrubbery that could have hidden whole platoons of watchers, then the bandstand loomed out of the dark. We took our bearing from it and walked on to the eastern edge of the Round Pond. It's a cheerful place by day, with children feeding ducks and sailing boats, but on that winter night it looked bleak enough for some slow monster to come crawling at us from shallow water. Instead two ducks that must have been sleeping on the edge took off as we came near, with a quacking loud enough to wake up half London. It was about as exposed a place as could be found in the city, open as a moorland tarn with no trees or bushes near the edge and a broad path running all the way round. That was an advantage on the one hand because we'd see the police coming, a disadvantage because we were as exposed as apples on a plate. Bobbie's choice of meeting place had been chosen more from her incurable sense of drama than from tactical thinking.

'I suppose they'll come singly.'

'Yes.'

'You'd better sit on this bench here and wait for them. I'll go for a walk round the pond and see if there's anything.'

As I paced I did some thinking. When

I got back to Bobbie I sat down beside her, struck by how depressed she looked hunched up in her coat.

'As soon as each of them gets here, tell her it's called off and there may be police watching. They'll all have to make their own way out. I suggest they go towards Bayswater, on the opposite side away from the memorial. If the police are watching they shouldn't be so thick on the ground there.'

'Suppose they want to know—'

'Shh.'

Something had taken shape quite close to us, a solider darkness against the dark.

'Bobbie?'

A whisper. A young woman's voice.

'Who is it?'

The shape gave its name.

'It's off. The police are there. Get away. I'll explain tomorrow.'

The girl hesitated and I took her arm. She was shaking, her breath coming short and harshly. The name was not one I recognised. In the dark I could see no more than an outline of a face. I practically pushed her away from the pond and got her facing towards Bayswater.

'Off you go. Walk, don't run, unless you think they've seen you. Keep to the grass.'

She resisted. 'What about Bobbie?'

'Bobbie's all right. Now go.'

By the time I got her on her way, clocks from buildings all round the park were striking midnight and still no sign or sound from the police. I began to walk round the pond and must have been a hundred yards or so from Bobbie on her bench when I was aware of a somebody moving in the dark, not far away.

'Who's there?' If this was the police at last, there was no point in hoping they hadn't seen me. I tried to make my voice loud enough to carry to Bobbie and to put into it the annoyed respectability of an insomniac walking in the park. A gasp, then a low voice.

'Bobbie? Bobbie, is that you?'

'No. Who is it?'

I thought I recognised the voice and, when she came closer and spoke again, I was sure. It was somebody I knew and liked, who'd been in the Movement for years. She recognised my voice too.

'Nell, I thought you didn't—'

'The police know about it. Bobbie says to get out.'

She took in the situation in an instant and was off almost before I'd finished speaking. I went back to Bobbie, cars strained for the shrilling of police whistles that would tell us somebody was being hunted, but none came.

'Who was that?'

I told her, and she drew a long breath. 'I'm glad. I never thought it was her. I was right then, wasn't I? It's well past midnight now and one of them hasn't come.'

'Neither have the police.'

'Number three's not coming. You know, I'd have trusted my life to her. I mean it. She's been in most things we've done and so keen to do more.'

'I told you that might be a danger sign.'

Soon, I knew, Bobbie was going to say a name. I wanted to keep the moment off as long as possible, hoping that it would be nobody I knew. Even if I didn't know her, linking a name to the treachery would make it real in a way it hadn't been before, even in Lloyd George's breakfast room.

'The question is what we're going to do now,' Bobbie said.

'Split up and get home as soon as we can. Or you can come back with me if you like.'

'No, I mean about her. You'll have to go and see her.'

'Why me?'

'Because I couldn't trust myself. Tell her what we know and how we know it. Tell her never to set her dirty foot in the same room as one of us again. Tell her to go and hang herself like Judas. Tell her—'

Feeling rather than hearing, I was conscious of somebody behind us. I caught Bobbie's arm. She stopped talking and we heard the sound of a step on the grass, heavy breathing, then coughing. Harsh, female coughing that would be audible a hundred yards away.

Bobbie's head came up. 'Who's there?'

From further away, a whistle shrilled, cutting through the silence. Then there were voices and pinpoints of light coming at us from the direction of the bandstand. Close beside us in the dark the coughing stopped and somebody drew a long, painful breath.

'I'm sorry ... I'm late. I think there are police ... or somebody ...'

I knew I should recognise the voice but still didn't. She was visible now, but only as a dark shape. The lights were still coming, the pinpoints growing larger, all on a level, moving fast towards where we were. Then, away in the darkness on our right, a dog barking, several men shouting.

'Stop. Stop her.'

Bobbie snapped, 'Did you tell them?'

'T ... tell them? Tell them what?'

The voice, still breathless, sounded confused.

'Tell them we were here? Tell them what we were doing?'

Bobbie's voice was harsh, no attempt now to whisper and still the shouting was going on and the voices and lights coming nearer, lurching up and down as if the men behind them were running. But Bobbie seemed determined not to budge until her question was answered. Then there was a commotion away on our left, the torch lights converging, the thump of somebody hitting the ground, shouting and swearing.

'Have you got one of them?'

The question, in an authoritative man's voice, came out of the darkness alarmingly close at hand, but the question wasn't to us. A reply was shouted from further away, where the lights were.

'No, it's just an old tramp and his dog.'

'Bring them over here.'

Although neither group of police seemed to have realised we were there, in spite of the coughing, we'd be caught in a pincer as they moved towards each other. Our best hope was to sprint away northwards and leave the question of number three's guilt or otherwise to be sorted out later. I took a step towards the sound of her rasping breath and grabbed for her hand.

'Come on, run.'

Bobbie started to say something, probably a protest, but she'd have to look after herself. After a moment of resistance, the other woman came with me, gasping and stumbling.

'Where are we going?'

By the sound of her, she was too exhausted to run far or fast. Then she started coughing again, a racking, tearing sound.

'What's that?'

'Is that him?'

The cries collided in the darkness, from one group of policemen to the other. Followed by two simultaneous shouts of 'No'.

'It's one of them. Just in front of you.'

'In front of you.'

I ran, dragging her, stumbling and coughing, along with me. There was a shout from behind: 'There she is', and I thought they were on us. Then a furious splashing, quacking of ducks and more swearing.

'She's gone in the pond. Get after her.'

The girl tried to pull back. I dragged her on. 'Bobbie will look after herself.'

Sick at heart, I doubted it, but to go back for Bobbie would have run us both into the arms of the police. Once the girl knew we weren't going back she did her best to run with me, but long before we'd got to Lancaster Gate on the northern side of the park we'd slowed to a walk. We helped each other climb over the railings on to the Bayswater Road and there was no sign of the police. Every man on duty had probably been assigned to the park. There was lamplight there and she looked half dead, hair fallen down and plastered round her sweating face, eyes hot and feverish. I recognised her, groped for the name.

'It's June, isn't it? We met at the office.'

The girl with the cold, worse now by the sound of it. Not the time and place to start asking questions. Besides, she wasn't fit for it.

'Can you get home from here? Have you got money for a cab?'

'I ... I live near here. What will you do?'

'I'm going to try and find out what's happened to Bobbie.'

'I'll come with you.'

'No. We don't need you. Go home.'

I watched her walk across the road and up a side street then started looking for a dark point between two street lamps to climb back into the park. I had my foot on the low wall at the base of the railings when, only a few yards away, I saw a figure climbing out. It was an agile figure that hesitated for a moment before jumping down on to the pavement. As it walked towards me, it left a wet trail.

'Hello, Nell.'

'How did you manage it?'

'That blessed old tramp saved me. I had to go into the water to get away from the police. I think two of them must have been holding on to him and when he heard me splashing about he decided to break away from them and try it too. What with him and the dog and the ducks and me, they didn't know who they were chasing. In future every tramp I ever meet gets a shilling from me as a thanksgiving.'

She was as wet as a cartload of spaniels, but her eyes were bright and she looked more like her old self. We'd have made a strange pair if anybody had bothered to notice, but two untidily dressed women walking the streets of Bayswater around midnight would only attract the attention of the drunk or desperate. Over in the park the distant shrill of a police whistle reminded us that the hunt was still on.

'What are we going to do now?'

'My aunt will have a fit if she sees me like this. I'd better come home with you and try to get back in the morning before she wakes up.'

We walked towards Paddington station and managed to get a cab with a driver who was too tired to be curious and glad to get a fare out towards Hampstead, where the horse was stabled. As we made our slow way up the hill, Bobbie lost some of the animation that had come from the chase and the old drained look came back.

'Is it her?'

'June?'

'The police came just after her, almost with her. And that coughing fit was as good as a signal.'

'I think the cough was real. And she didn't want to leave you. I had a job to drag her away.'

'Or was it her friends in the police she didn't want to leave?'

I could see the force of that. If she were a police informer, to be dragged off into the dark by me wouldn't be reassuring. 'What do you know about her?'

'She joined us quite recently. She's nineteen. One of Emmeline Pankhurst's soldiers.'

The youngest and most militant, the centre of the arson campaign.

'Does she live with her family? What's her job?'

'With a friend. She works at a milk depot or somewhere odd like that.'

The world where single women had to earn their living was unfamiliar to Bobbie. Not her fault, just the way she was brought up. Once I knew she was safe, a thought that had been knocking at the outside of my mind since we heard the police whistle found its way in.

'You know, there's one odd thing about tonight. You say you'd told all three of them to be at the Round Pond at midnight.'

'Yes, I had.'

'An informer would have passed that on. And yet the police weren't waiting for you near the Round Pond. They got there so late that they missed two of you completely.'

'That points to June. She was the last one I told. I couldn't find her till she came home in the evening.'

'But that would still have given her time to let Scotland Yard know well before midnight. And yet there was somebody following us round the Albert Hall. It's as if they didn't know where things were going to happen and had to follow you.'

'But how did they know to follow me tonight? And how were there so many of them in the park all of a sudden? They must have known something was going to happen there.'

'I admit it's odd.' I couldn't help getting interested in it as a problem. 'In fact, it's very much the same pattern as Walton Heath. The police knew what night it was happening, and approximately where, but not as much as you'd expect them to know if they had an informer right at the centre of things.'

'But those three were the only ones I told.' She thought about it for a while, then, 'Suppose she wanted to stop the bombing but didn't actually want us caught. Wouldn't that fit?'

'Except that she then leads the police straight to us—if it was June.'

Bobbie shifted in her seat. 'You'll have to go and see her. We've got to know.'

I didn't answer and we sat in silence for the rest of the journey. The light was on in the window of my living room and the door was on the latch. Bernard was still up, sitting at the table with a stack of music paper beside the last glowing embers of the fire.

'Nell, where have you been? I was worried about you.'

Then he saw Bobbie standing in the doorway. She'd pulled off her knitted cap and her dark hair had come over her shoulders, the ends of it still draggled with wet from the pond. She looked like a woman who'd arrived out of the sea in some dark Celtic drama. Bernard's eyes widened. He stood up.

'This is Bobbie. She's staying the night.'

I introduced them. Bobbie was surprised too, then recovered and was determinedly unembarrassed. We hadn't seen much of each other in the past few months and I'd forgotten that she didn't know about the lodger.

'You're wet,' he said.

'I've been in a pond, along with an old tramp and half the metropolitan police force.'

He seemed enchanted by her, almost mesmerised and I thought I could see why. For years, while he'd been writing his opera, Joan of Arc must have been at the centre of his waking thoughts and probably in his dreams too. Now the nearest thing to her he was ever likely to see had walked into his lodgings in the early hours of a winter morning. He tipped the last of the coal from the scuttle on to the fire in a grand gesture.

'Tea. You'll want tea, both of you.' He put the kettle on to the hob. 'Are the police likely to arrive here?'

I wondered if he intended to defend us like Horatius in the doorway, with the empty coal scuttle and a poker. 'Not very likely,' I said, hoping I was right, and Bobbie and I both collapsed into chairs by the fire. Bobbie began to steam gently. Bernard could hardly keep his eyes off her. I went up to my room to collect an armful of dry clothes and a towel, then we banished him upstairs while she dried herself and changed in front of the fire.

'Haven't I seen your Bernard at some of our demonstrations?'

'Very probably, except he's not my Bernard. He's my lodger.'

'Nell, you can be honest with me. I'm hardly a stickler for the social conventions. I'm glad to see you're exerting your right to—'

'I'm exerting my right to make forty pounds a year by letting my spare bedroom. Which means, by the way, that one of us will have to sleep on the couch down here.'

'No need to be annoyed with me. I told you, I'm not criticising.'

She wasn't convinced but I was too tired to argue. The kettle boiled and we called Bernard down to share tea and buttered toast. Bobbie, still being too polite for my liking, asked him about his opera and he told her about it at some length, kneeling there on the rag rug in front of the fire with a toasting fork and half a loaf of bread. Bobbie was wearing a skirt and blouse of mine with a dressing gown over them. Her feet were bare, stretched out to the fire, and his eyes kept straying to them. They were elegant feet, so why shouldn't he admire them? Even when she yawned in the middle of what he was saying about the difficulty of orchestrating battle scenes, he didn't resent it.

'You're exhausted. We shouldn't be keeping you up like this. Bobbie will have my bed, Nell. I'll sleep down here.'

By this time I was too tired myself to care where anyone slept, provided they didn't expect me to bustle around changing sheets. We left Bernard arranging himself on the couch with an armful of blankets and went upstairs.

'I'll have to be away early, Nell. I'll try not to wake Bernard on the way out.'

'I don't think he'll mind.'

'I've written down June's address for you here. You'll go and see her tomorrow, won't you?'

'I'm not sure I'll have time.'

'Please. As soon as you can, and let me know what you think.'

'Go to bed.'

I was dimly aware of her leaving, long before it got light. When I got up some time later, Bernard was already bustling around downstairs. He'd insisted on making coffee for her, he said, pleased as a child with a new pet, and got her to eat some bread. The last of the bread, as it turned out. Also the last of the milk for the coffee. He left early for rehearsal, humming to himself. I hadn't seen him so happy in weeks.

Chapter Eight

I knew they wouldn't need me at Maidenhead for the rehearsals. There was nothing for me to do until Oriana herself arrived and that could hardly be before Saturday evening, however rapidly Henson managed to buy furs for her. It should have been a day for getting on with my work but I couldn't settle to anything. The scrap of paper Bobbie had pressed on me the night before had an address off Praed Street, Paddington. Bobbie had dropped the problem on my doorstep like a terrier presenting a rat. Even though I knew I'd have to do something about it, sheer reluctance drove me away from it and towards the other problem. Oriana was still out of reach but her manager was in town and at the Savoy. If, as I thought, it was simply a matter of money, why not start negotiations with him directly? I could hardly do this without Jack Belter's agreement so I dressed in my best suit—far too severe to be taken for anyone's mistress—and made my way back to the offices in Fleet Street. It took time to convince the young man behind the desk that Mr Belter would want to see me and I had to do quite a lot of pacing over the countries of the Empire before I was escorted to the lift. It was down rather than up this time because he was in the basement overseeing the printing of his sporting paper. He saw me in an inky little cubicle to one side of the printing floor that vibrated to the thunder of the great machines gulping down their rolls of pink paper just a few yards away from us. It was like being on the enclosed bridge of a ship in a storm, especially as we had to stand close to each other to be heard.

I said, 'I wonder if we're being too elaborate about this.'

His eyebrows came together. 'How so?'

'It's obviously money they're out for. Isn't it simply a case of offering them enough of it?'

'If it were that simple they could have had it two months ago and Laurie Gilbey would still be alive.'

'If they're spies, they're carrying on in a very ostentatious manner.'

'You're an expert on spies, are you?'

'It's just common sense. If they've passed those letters on to a foreign power the last place they should be is back in London making themselves conspicuous.'

'Can't help it. Like a drug to them. Her especially.'

A hooter blared. The presses stopped with sudden brutality, like a horse rearing up against a fence. Men came running out from the sides of the machines. Belter reached across me, grabbed a stopwatch from a table and fixed his eyes on the printing floor and the running men.

'Paper tear. Third time this morning.'

The presses roared into life again, presumably in a satisfactory time, because when he turned back to me he seemed less annoyed.

'Was that what you came to talk about?'

'I wondered whether I should go round and see Sylvan at his hotel. It's one thing I might do while we're waiting for Oriana Paphos.'

'What good would that do?'

'It might help to find out more about him. That accent for a start. I'm fairly good at languages and I can't place it. It seems a mixture of several things.'

'You think it's fake?'

'He wouldn't be the first person in the theatre business to make himself sound more exotic than he is. Another thing, somebody in the orchestra thought he'd seen him before.'

'Where?'

'I don't know. I'm trying to find out.'

He looked away from me at the machines. 'Stay away from him. I don't want to be responsible for any more deaths.'

'He can't be that dangerous in a hotel lounge.'

'I'm not risking it.' He took a deep breath, turned to face me. 'Miss Bray, you might as well know it was our friend's idea to bring you into this, not mine. He's a great man, our friend, the greatest man our country's produced this century. But even greatness has its drawbacks and in his case it's a tendency to have too many ideas.'

He dropped his voice as low as the machine noise would allow when he said this, as if speaking treason. It wasn't just a matter of honours, his admiration for Lloyd George clearly amounted to hero worship.

'And my presence is one idea too many?'

'Bluntly, yes. Nothing against you. It's just that he's had this idea that our best chance of success is playing the Paphos woman against Sylvan. He thinks she's scared of him and would like to get away from him, and a bit of womanly sympathy might do the trick.'

A man outside our little cubicle was attending to one of the machines with a large oil can. Womanly sympathy. A little oil on the harsh wheels.

'My view is that it would take more than

a few kind words and a shoulder to cry on to get her away from that man,' he said. 'She's in it up to her fat white neck and even if she wanted to get away from him he wouldn't let her.'

'So you think I'm wasting my time anyway?'

'That's up to you. I don't suppose you're doing this for nothing.'

'Any more than you are.'

He glared. 'I'm doing this for my country and my friend, in that order.'

'If it comes to that, I might say much the same thing. But, whether you like it or not, it seems you're landed with me.'

'Yes. Our friend has said you're to have a shot at driving a wedge between the two of them and I'm giving you your chance to the best of my ability. But it's her you're dealing with, not Sylvan. Keep clear of him as far as possible and don't be alone with him.'

That seemed to settle any idea of tackling Sylvan, so I asked him if there was any news of Oriana.

'I had a telegram from young Henson this morning to say he'd arrived at Calais so he's probably in Paris by now. If he looks lively they could be on the overnight train back here tonight.'

'They've got to get the fur coat for her.'

'How long does it take to buy a fur coat in Paris?' His implication was that it should be as quick and easy as getting a cabbage from a market stall. 'Anyway, he should be on his way back with her by Saturday afternoon at the latest. I suppose she'll want to spend the night at the hotel, so they can come on to my place on Sunday.'

He beckoned through the glass at one of the men minding the machines and, when he came, told him to show me to the lift. I found myself out on the pavement of Fleet Street with my brain still numb from the noise of the machines.

Once my head had cleared, I decided it was still too early in the day to go and see June Price, who would presumably be out at work. I had a meeting to go to in the afternoon. Meanwhile, I filled in the time at two of the newspaper offices, looking for reports in the files of the inquest on Laurie Gilbey, and found very little that I didn't know already.

One report gave a brief summary of Leon Sylvan's evidence. He was described as the artistic manager of a dancer, Miss O. Paphos, and told the inquest that he had discovered Gilbey's body in the flat rented by Miss Paphos when he returned with her from a performance. He did not know how the deceased came to be in the flat, but it was possible that he had obtained a key. The coroner asked him if the deceased had been an admirer of Miss Paphos. He replied that Mr Gilbey had introduced himself as a journalist, anxious to write a series of articles about Miss Paphos. Had he ever threatened to kill himself over her? Not to his knowledge. No mention of Jack Belter. No mention of stolen letters. The verdict of suicide had probably been arrived at because of the manner of Gilbey's death, and the qualification 'while the balance of his mind was disturbed' added as the traditional rag of consolation for his family. I was surprised that the case hadn't attracted more sensational coverage, given Oriana's fame or notoriety, until I remembered that Lloyd George had many good friends among the press owners. The death had been as concealed as a half-democratic government could manage. I copied down the few useful details then went to my meeting near Euston Road.

When I came out, the street lamps were lit, starlings were jostling and bickering for space on windowsills, and office workers were beginning the trudge to bus and tram stops and underground stations. June Price would probably be on her way home as well, from the milk depot or wherever. Reluctantly, cursing myself for getting dragged into it, I joined a bus queue for Paddington.

June lived in a small street of blank-faced houses, mostly divided up into single rooms to judge from the many varieties of thin curtain illuminated by yellow gaslight and the unkempt state of the small rectangles of garden in front of them. There were only two lamp posts in the whole street, so it took me some time to find her house number. There were four bell buttons, one of them marked 'Hoddy and Price' on a piece of card in neat italic. I rang and after a few seconds a sash window slid open above my head.

'Hold on, I'm coming down.' A young woman's voice, more cheerful than I'd expected from the circumstances. Some time went by, then the front door opened.

'Hello. I suppose you're wanting June. She should be home any minute. Would you like to come up and wait?'

She had a round, pale face and the sort of red hair that looks as if it's had an electric shock. Her smile was warm, although as far as I knew she'd never seen me in her life before. It wasn't until she moved back from the door that I noticed one of her legs was in an iron brace and the shin, even under its wool stocking, as thin as a stick of kindling. She limped in front of me up two flights of stairs, quick and unembarrassed, and stopped in front of a door off the landing.

'We fly the flag, you see.'

The door was mostly purple, with a white border and a green frame—the colours of the Women's Social and Political Union.

'The landlord hates it, but we pay our rent so he has to put up with it.'

The room inside was quite a large one, with a high ceiling of moulded plasterwork, rather yellowed. The floor of worn brown linoleum, partly covered with rag rugs in a flare of greens and reds and yellows, might have been as slippery as ice for the young woman with the limp, but she negotiated it without fuss. There were two divans against two walls, one covered with a bright green bedspread, the other with orange. A big battered table under a gaslight bracket was littered with scraps of material, scissors, a pot of glue.

'I'm sorry, I was just going to clear that lot up before June gets home. Sit down. The armchair's safer than it looks, provided you don't put too much weight on the left back leg.'

I sat down cautiously while she began to clear the scraps into a big square basket, talking all the time.

'It's what I do for a living. You might have seen them at our fairs and so on.' She flipped a bookmark into my lap, beautifully embroidered, *Votes for Women.* The *V* of *Votes* was done in medieval style, like an initial letter in a Book of Hours. There was a woman riding a white horse on the reverse side.

'I do pen-wipers, handkerchiefs, scarves. Twenty per cent of the profit goes back to the Movement. I'd like it to be more, but you have to have something to live on, don't you?'

I mentioned that the design of the letters seemed influenced by William Morris, which pleased her.

'It was his daughter who taught me. I worked with her for a while.'

'Does June help you with it?'

She laughed. 'June couldn't darn a stocking. She works as a book-keeper for a big dairy firm. Apart from her real work, that is.'

Her voice went serious for the last few words and her head went down, intent on tidying up a skein of embroidery silk. Then, 'That sounds like her coming in. I should have had the kettle on by now.'

Running steps upstairs, then the door opened.

'Gwen, that awful dog from next door's been—'

She stopped dead when she saw me,

startled to find somebody else there. Then she smiled. 'Nell Bray.'

The other girl looked up. 'This is Nell Bray?'

'Of course it is. Didn't you recognise her?'

'I wish I had. June's told me the story of how you and Miss Fieldfare saved her last night.'

'I was never more relieved in my life when I looked in at Kingsway at lunchtime and found Bobbie Fieldfare there. I was sure she'd been arrested. I had to go into work as usual and sit there at those ledgers not knowing.' She still had the cold. An austere hat in navy blue emphasised the pallor of her face, the pink of her nose. But in spite of the shock of finding me there, nothing in the way she looked or spoke suggested my visit was an unpleasant surprise.

'I suppose Miss Bray's come to see you're all right,' Gwen said. She picked up a kettle from a table in the corner. We heard her going down one flight of stairs, the rush of a water tap on the lower landing.

June said, 'Are we going out?'

I suppose she thought I was there to take her off to some desperate action. 'No. I just wanted to talk to you about what happened last night.'

'I never thanked you.'

'That's not what it's about.'

She took her hat and coat off and hung them in a cupboard in the corner. I'd kept my coat on. The bright colours in the room gave it a look of warmth, but there was no fire in the grate and the air felt only a few degrees warmer than outside. Goodness knows how Gwen kept her fingers warm enough for embroidery. June sat down on the divan bed with the green cover, not tense exactly but keyed up for something to happen.

'The police knew you were going to be in the park that night,' I said. 'Can you think why?'

'I suppose they're always patrolling.'

The door opened and Gwen came in with the kettle. She sensed something because she stood there in the doorway.

'Should I go?'

'No. We're not saying anything you can't hear.' Gwen bent to put the kettle on a gas ring on the floor. June explained to me, 'Gwen knows everything I do. She'd be doing it as well if it wasn't for her leg.'

'You'd told her about the Albert Memorial?'

Her eyes didn't shift from mine. 'Yes. Bobbie Fieldfare would have expected me to. She likes Gwen. Anyway, we couldn't have secrets from each other, not living like we do.'

'Did either of you tell anybody else?'

Gwen shook her head and went over to sit on the divan beside June, not quite protective yet, but ready. June gave me a long stare. She'd looked bone tired when she came in from work and I guessed she'd been sleeping badly.

'No, we didn't. I suppose you're having to ask all of them.'

She was no fool. I'd expected her to be angry at the implication, whether guilty or otherwise, but she was a step ahead of that.

'You see, June, it wasn't the first time it had happened. That night at Walton Heath, the police knew something was going on. They didn't know it was Lloyd George's house, but they knew whatever it was would happen that night. Do you remember when we met at the office that morning? You said something to Bobbie about when the bombs would be needed.'

'Yes. They hadn't decided then. My orders were to be ready any night from Tuesday onwards.'

'What did you do with them?'

'Brought them back here.'

I glanced round the bright room, wondering where they'd put a tea chest of bombs.

Gwen caught my look. 'It was quite safe. They wouldn't go off until they were meant to.'

'Did you know what they were going to be used for?'

'Bobbie didn't say so directly, but June and I guessed it was something to do with a golf course not very far from London.'

I said to June, 'What else were you told?'

'To wear warm dark clothes and boots or goloshes. I lost one of the goloshes in the mud by the hedge.'

'When did you know it was happening on that Tuesday night?'

'When Bobbie Fieldfare and the others came to collect me.'

'In the motor car?'

'Yes.'

'When did Bobbie tell you where you were going?'

'In the car. She said we were going to blow up Lloyd George's house.'

'What time was this?'

June looked at Gwen.

'It was half past seven when you left here.'

'And neither of you knew till then?'

They both shook their heads. By that time the news that there was to be an attack on Walton Heath that night had already reached the golf club.

Gwen said, 'I didn't know until she got back at about four in the morning. She was a sight too, only one golosh and all over mud and paraffin. Still, it was a relief to see her. When she didn't come back earlier I thought it was the Black Day, didn't I, June?'

'Black Day?'

Another glance at each other.

'When the police catch her and she goes to prison.'

'So then it will be all over.'

There was something like relief in June's tired, cold-muffled voice.

'Even prison doesn't mean it's all over.' She shook her head. 'Not for the cause, but it will be for me. I won't eat and I won't let them feed me. I'll die in there. That's what they want. They won't give us the Vote until one of us dies for it.'

Gwen said, subdued now, 'Only it might be Mrs Pankhurst if they send her to prison.'

'Well, she won't be on her own then. If Mrs Pankhurst dies in prison, we'll blow up the homes of every politician in the country with them inside. Then they can do what they like with us.'

There were bright red patches on June's pale cheeks. She started coughing and Gwen moved closer and put an arm round her.

June said, 'So if you find the police spy, you can tell her that. It won't make any difference.'

'Have you any idea at all who it might be?'

They both shook their heads.

'Somebody knew the precise evening of an attack on Walton Heath. Somebody knew something was supposed to happen near Kensington Gardens.'

'I can't believe it's anyone Gwen or I know.'

The kettle boiled. They urged me to stay for tea, but I wanted to get away. Somehow the room looked less bright than when I'd come into it. As I picked up my hat from the table, I almost dislodged a little vase of flowers and recognised the source of the scent that had been at the edge of my consciousness while we'd been talking.

'Violets.'

There was a shade of annoyance on June's face, as if detected in a weakness or a frivolity. 'Gwen's young man brought them.'

'He is *not* my young man. He's just a customer.'

Gwen was mock-indignant, seizing the chance to lighten the atmosphere. I guessed she'd be the one who chose the bright colours, made rugs to warm the linoleum.

June wouldn't have cared. As she showed me down the stairs she asked me just one question.

'This spy business, does it mean we can't do anything until you find out who it is?'

That was a question for Bobbie and the others, I said. She sounded disappointed at the thought of it.

Chapter Nine

When I got home there was a savoury smell in the air and Bernard was prodding at something in a frying pan on the stove, cats in attendance. 'It's a kind of beef and potato hash. I've made enough for two if you like.' He'd served a few weeks as a ship's cook on a coaster, collecting impressions for a maritime song cycle. The songs were more impressive than his cooking skills, but I was too hungry to be fussy.

'Bobbie Fieldfare called here an hour ago. She said to tell you she'll be back later.'

I felt slightly less hungry.

'Did she say anything else, or was she in a rush as usual?'

'Not really. In fact, she stayed for quite

a while. I showed her Joan's aria from Act One and she even sang part of it. She's quite musical.'

The first I'd heard of it. I felt a pang of something regrettably like jealousy. I'd never sung any part of his opera. Perhaps I'd been too busy, but Bobbie was usually worse, hardly staying in one place long enough to whistle two notes, let alone sight-read arias.

'Do you like the burnt bits? There's a bottle of sherry opened on the table, but I couldn't find glasses.'

'Sherry? What are we celebrating?'

'I'll tell you when we're sitting down.'

He flipped the hash on to two plates with a fish slice. I took a quick look at it, poured large sherries and got the pickles out of the larder.

'Meredith Madoc has promised to look at Act One. He knows some of my other work and he's definitely interested.'

'Marvellous.'

'It could be the chance I've been hoping for. If he likes it enough, he might do a concert performance of just the one act. What do you think?'

I made encouraging noises while covertly feeding a piece of beef to one of the cats under the table, wishing I had his capacity for optimism.

'There's only one problem, though. Even

a concert performance costs a lot. I was wondering ...'

He hesitated.

'Wondering what?'

'Wondering whether we might think of approaching Jack Belter. After all, if he's trying to build up a reputation as an opera patron ...'

I hated to disappoint him and couldn't explain how reluctantly Belter was playing patron to even one opera. 'I shouldn't build up your hopes too much. He's a mercurial kind of man. Next time, it might be something quite different.'

'You think so?' He looked disappointed and forked moodily at the hash. 'I say, this stuff is pretty awful, isn't it?'

'Try a pickled onion with it.'

After a while we gave up and poured another sherry. While we were drinking it, Bobbie paid her second visit of the day. She stayed at the open door, hat and coat on.

'Are you coming out, Nell, or am I coming in? You and I need to talk.'

Bernard, taking the hint, said he had work to do up in his room. He went slowly, with wistful looks at the warm fire and Bobbie. She was glowing from the walk uphill from the underground station in the cold, and from impatience.

'Did you see June Price?'

I cleared the plates off the table, sat her down and told her about it, every detail that I could remember. She listened, elbows on the table and chin on her hands.

'Well, was it her?'

'I honestly don't know. If she is a police spy then she's an exceptionally intelligent one. She put up a convincing performance of being totally committed to us.'

'You believe her?'

'Yes, I think I do. Is it right that she didn't know you'd be going to Walton Heath that evening until you picked her up?'

'Yes. She was to be ready any night that week.'

'You didn't tell her that morning in the office?'

'No, because we still hadn't made a final decision.'

'And by the time you picked her up, the people at Walton Heath already knew something was afoot for that night. That points away from June. Of course, there's her friend Gwen ...'

'Oh, I know Gwen. She's totally trustworthy.'

'Yes, but that's what we think about all of them. Did you know that Gwen had a male friend—somebody in the Movement or close to it who buys her bookmarks and so on?'

'No. That could be any one of dozens. I'll make inquiries if you like.' She seemed even more fidgety than usual, twisting around in the chair, tugging at a curl of hair that had escaped. 'But it's all taking so much time.'

'What did you expect? Anyway, for what my guess is worth, it's not June after all. Which points to one of the other two.' One of them a friend of mine, somebody I trusted as much or more than I did myself. No point in saying that, though.

'Unless the police heard about both things some other way.'

'You know who you told. Anyway, Bobbie, I'm afraid I'm handing the problem back to you. I've got other things to do from now on.' Oriana and Henry Henson might be crossing the Channel at that moment.

'Working for Jack Belter?'

'Temporarily, yes.'

She made an exasperated noise. 'I don't understand you, Neil. Getting involved in an opera of all things, for a man like that and now of all times.'

I couldn't have explained to her, but in any case I was annoyed at the implication that I had to give reasons to her for what I did. A spirit of contradiction came over me.

'Aren't I entitled to have other interests then?'

'No you're not. None of us is entitled to other interests now, any more than a soldier in the middle of a battle is entitled to other interests.'

'It's been a very long battle.'

'Is that a reason for giving up? When we've won you can spend as much time organising operas and things as you like and work for a money-grubbing vulgarian like Jack Belter for all I care. But to walk away from it now, with everyone's hand against us and Emmeline probably going to prison for years—I just don't understand it, Nell.'

She'd started off being simply angry, but that last sentence was a wall of puzzlement, quite untypical of Bobbie. Although I couldn't tell her what I was doing, I tried at least to preserve a plank of a bridge between us.

'You can't always go at things as straightforwardly as you'd like.'

'Do you think I don't know that? Do you think I like all this secrecy and wondering who you can trust? If I had my way I'd like to march a regiment of women with pick-axes up to the House of Commons and take it apart stone by stone in broad daylight.'

I couldn't help smiling at the picture.

She grabbed my hand. 'Nell, don't desert us now.'

'I'm not deserting you.'

'Then will you go on helping me find this spy?'

'No.'

She let go of my hand and sighed, staring into the fire. 'I suppose it happens to most of us, sooner or later.'

'What are you talking about?'

I was aware of something going on unprecedented in my experience—Bobbie trying hard to see another person's point of view. Naturally she got it wrong, having had so little practice.

'Most people can only keep campaigning for so long, then they start thinking about all the things they're missing. How long have you been in the WSPU, Nell?'

'Nine years. I joined soon after it was formed.'

'Did you ever think it would go on for this long?'

'No. Back then, it seemed so obvious that we were right I thought any half reasonable government would give us the Vote within months.'

'Except we've never had a half reasonable government. We've changed too, haven't we? There used to be more ... I don't know, you can't exactly call it light-heartedness, but it was more of a lark in its way. Now

174

there's all this criticising and back-biting amongst ourselves. The police spy business is only part of it.'

'Yes.'

From Bobbie, emotional analysis was as unlikely as embroidery. She was in a strange mood, but then perhaps we both were. We'd been drinking Bernard's sherry without much noticing it and our glasses were empty. She refilled them to the brim.

'Have you ever thought, Nell, what we'll do when we finally get the Vote?'

'Race around shouting in our bath chairs, probably.'

'Don't.'

'You know all the things we've discussed, getting women elected to Parliament, all the laws that want changing.'

'Oh, I know all of that.' She dismissed a decade of planning, writing, debating with a wave of her hand and another gulp of sherry. 'Nell, how old are you?'

'Thirty-five.'

'I'm twenty-six next month. Do you know, these girls of June's age are already making me feel old? They're so sure the sacrifices—any sacrifices—are worthwhile.'

She sat back in her chair and looked at me over the glass. I had the feeling that Bobbie was embarrassed—Bobbie of all people, who had the cheek of a whole mantelpiece full of brass monkeys and a skin like rhino hide.

'So I suppose, Nell, if you do feel like cutting some of the ties, making a life for yourself, I shouldn't criticise you. Only if you could do this for us first ...'

'What on earth is this?' I stared at her, wondering why she was making such a drama out of a few days away at Maidenhead, then her eyes shifted briefly away from me and upstairs and I understood. 'Oh, for heaven's sake, not again. He's the lodger, L-O-D-G-E-R, tenant, person who pays rent. That's all. We are friends. We are not lovers, or prospective lovers or would-be lovers. We simply live under the same roof.'

'Shh. He'll hear you.'

'I don't mind in the least if he does.'

Then I understood something else, with the lightning understanding that comes to you when you know somebody very well and you're drinking a little too much together. She was relieved at what she'd just heard. Unmistakably, what I'd just said in my annoyance was exactly what she wanted to hear. Which was another shock. For one thing, Bobbie and I had known each other for five or six years and I'd never heard her express the slightest romantic interest in any man. For another, if I'd ever speculated on the kind of man who might attract her—and I never had—it would have been some character as tough and desperate as herself. An explorer, say, like her uncle, or possibly a revolutionary anarchist. A composer would never have made it on to the list of also-rans. Which just showed, I thought, how wrong you could be in these matters, even about your friends. I guessed too why she'd raised, out of the blue, the question of finding a life apart from campaigning. She hadn't been talking about June, or even about me. Bobbie herself was the one thinking of branching out.

'What are you grinning about, Nell?'

'Nothing. Have we finished our talk? If so, I'll let Bernard down from his room.'

'If you like. Anyway, I'm just going. What time does the last train back to town leave?'

Definitely embarrassed now, she grabbed her hat and coat and left, practically at a run. Bernard came down when he heard the front door bang and seemed disappointed that she'd gone.

'That wasn't a very long discussion to come all this way for.'

'Long enough. I'm afraid we've drunk quite a lot of your sherry.'

I told him that I'd be staying at Jack Belter's house at Maidenhead from Sunday night onwards to look after Oriana Paphos.

Like the rest of the orchestra, he'd be travelling up and down from London each day, so he'd have to look after the cats and the house. I mentally included in that the washing up of the frying pan which looked like some unidentified archaeological object. He nodded, but his mind seemed to be elsewhere.

'Bobbie's a very good friend of yours, isn't she?'

'Yes, I'm fond of Bobbie. Shall I lock the front door, or will you?'

His question sounded like the prelude to what might well turn into a sentimental fireside discussion about Bobbie's admirable qualities. I was tired and there were limits. I picked up a book and went to bed.

Chapter Ten

On Sunday morning Bernard was out and I was up in my room, packing a small suitcase for the move to Jack Belter's. I was just wondering if his guests would be expected to change for dinner, and if so into what, when there was a knocking on the front door loud enough to set the whole house quivering. I leapt for the window, half expecting to see Inspector Merit again and instead found myself looking down on the navy blue top of a chauffeur's cap. Beyond it, a red motor car took up most of the width of the street, blazing like a geranium in the grey day. Another of Jack Belter's cars. When I went down and opened the door the chauffeur, without a word, handed me a note addressed to 'Miss Nell Bray. Cultural Attaché'. It consisted of a few words in an impatient scrawl: *Henson missing. Come to office prepared to travel.* Quite how a man could be described as missing when he'd left for Paris less than three days ago I couldn't understand. Also, I was annoyed at Jack Belter for ordering me about as if I were one of his reporters.

I offered the chauffeur a seat in the kitchen but he wouldn't leave his motor car unattended. By the time I came down ten minutes later with my suitcase, a crowd of children had gathered, admiring it from a respectful distance. With only Sunday morning traffic on the streets, we managed the journey to central London in about half the time the inspector's cab had taken. Fleet Street was almost eerily deserted in contrast with its usual day and night bustle and I'm convinced we must have hit forty miles an hour as we scorched along it, with the bells from St Bride's and St Paul's ringing a calmer accompaniment.

Inside the building there was just the one commissionaire on duty, standing solidly in mid-Pacific, and within seconds I was whisked up to the top floor and shown into Jack Belter's office. He started talking as soon as I put a foot over the threshold.

'Where have you been? You don't have a telephone.'

'Of course not.'

'All of my people have telephones. I'll put one in.'

'Not while I live and breathe. Awful things.'

'Anyway, you're here now. I want you to go over to Paris and find Henson.'

'Isn't he on his way back?'

'He should have been back last night. No sign of him. What's more, he hasn't been heard of since that telegram I told you about from Calais on Friday morning. I've drilled into all my men that they have to be in touch with the office every twelve hours, no matter what.'

'Have you tried the hotel where Oriana Paphos is staying?'

'They haven't got a telephone either. We've sent three telegrams, no answer. My car will take you down to Dover then you can catch the next ferry.'

Normally I'd have jumped at a trip to Paris, but not on this tame goose chase.

'I'd probably just cross with them mid-Channel on their way back here. After all, he's not even a day late yet.'

I supposed I had to allow for the fact that the last young man Belter sent to Oriana Paphos had ended up dead, but this anxiety seemed almost superstitious. He looked annoyed at my opposition and we'd probably have had an argument, but at that point there was a bang on the door and a young man came in with a telegram.

'It's from Mr Henson,' the young man said, looking at his employer like a stable lad at a horse that bites.

'At long last.'

Belter grabbed it from him, read it at a glance, made an explosive sound with his lips and handed it to me.

DEEPLY REGRET DELAY DUE TO NECESSARY ALTERATIONS TO FUR COATS. HOPE ARRIVE LONDON MONDAY.

'Has he gone stark raving mad?' Belter, eyes popping, glared at the two of us as if the question really needed an answer. 'Has Henson gone mad? Alterations? Haven't we got any needleworkers in London? Does he say coats? With an s?'

The young man nervously confirmed the s.

181

'One coat, that was what I said, though why she needs that goodness knows. Is he buying up Paris? Are they trying to make a corner in furs?'

'At least you know where he is.' He ignored me and snapped at the young man. 'Send a telegram to Henson at their hotel: "Damn alterations. Return next train with Paphos." '

'I don't think the telegraph office accept "damn", sir.'

'Well, whatever they will accept. Only make it strong.'

The young man left at a brisk trot but Belter went on fuming for some time. Still, he accepted that there was no point in my going to Paris now that we'd heard from Henson, however unsatisfactory the message, and no need to take up residence at his house until Oriana got there on Monday.

I went down in the lift, picked up my suitcase from the commissionaire's desk and left it with the chauffeur to take to Maidenhead when he drove Mr Belter home. Strolling back towards Charing Cross, I'd got almost as far as the Law Courts when I was conscious of running feet behind me, echoing along the almost empty street. I turned and there was Max Blume, hat in hand and overcoat flapping.

It was typical of Max to be in Fleet Street when everybody else was away for the weekend, probably writing an editorial predicting the collapse of Western capitalism for a magazine in far more imminent danger of collapse. I waited for him to catch up with me.

'I was going to write to you, Nell. She'll talk to you very willingly.'

Luckily, he didn't ask what I was doing there. With my mind still on Oriana Paphos, it took me a few moments to understand what he was talking about.

'You mean the barmaid, Laurence Gilbey's fiancée?'

Lloyd George and Belter had warned me off investigating Laurie Gilbey's murder but if the Fates were pushing this woman into my path it would be black ingratitude to step aside.

'Can we go and see her now?'

'Now? I don't suppose the pub will be open on a Sunday with no journalists or printers around.'

'Does she live on the premises?'

'I think so.'

'What's her name?'

'Everybody calls her Lizzie.'

We turned left into a side alley that broadened out at the bottom to provide a few feet of pavement outside a flat-fronted public house. It had no sign out, only advertisements for beer and spirits painted on the walls, and I couldn't see a name on it. As Max had predicted, the shutters were up and the doors barred.

'Perhaps we should come back on a weekday.'

I knocked on the door before he had a chance to retreat. A sash window went up above the door and a bald, middle-aged man looked out. He was unshaven and in his shirtsleeves.

'Is your barmaid at home? I wondered if—'

Without waiting to hear any more he turned and bellowed into the room behind him, 'Lizzie, lady and gentleman here to see you.' Pause, then, 'That's right, I said lady *and* gentleman. Well, I don't know, do I? No, I don't think they're from the Sally Army, they haven't got no tambourine or collecting box.' Pause, then down to us, 'Lizzie says she's changing to go out but you can come and wait for her down in the snug.'

We heard heavy footsteps coming downstairs, wheezing breath and bolts being drawn back. Shuffling in worn-out slippers, the landlord showed us into a dark square of a room just inside the door, brown-painted benches, brown curtains drawn against the winter light, brown smell of stale beer in the air.

'Her ladyship says she's just coming but so's next Christmas. Anything I can get you?'

We said no thank you and he went back upstairs, wheezing at every step. It was ten minutes or so and I felt half-pickled in beer fumes before there were lighter steps on the stairs, the door opened and a young woman came in. She was wearing a bright green coat with darker velvet lapels decorated with an unseasonable posy of silk cornflowers, a jay's wing in her green hat. The hair under it looked naturally fair, the face round with blue eyes and a turned-up nose. Probably eighteen or so, about the same age as June Price. Whatever she'd been expecting, it wasn't us, because she stopped in the doorway, looking alarmed. Then she recognised Max, gave him a smile and me a wary glance.

'I'm sorry to come as you're going out,' I said. 'I wondered whether we could have a few words with you.'

'What about?'

The accent was south of the river rather than Cockney, a little harsh but that could be nervousness.

'I gather you were a friend of Mr Gilbey.'

The blue eyes went instantly cloudy.

'He was my fiancé.' Then, more sharply,

to Max, 'What about him? Is she from the lawyers?'

'I'm not. Were you expecting something from the lawyers?'

'I don't know. Not the money I don't suppose. I suppose his mum got that. But I thought he might have left me some ... some kind of keepsake. He never got round to buying the ring, you see. He said we'd go up the West End and buy one as soon as he got the day off from his work, only he never seemed to.'

As she was talking she sat down on the brown bench on the other side of the table. Her eyes were on me, like a neglected child's, still hopeful against experience that the promise of a treat would be kept. Max moved uneasily on the bench beside me.

'Were you surprised when you heard he'd killed himself?'

'He didn't.' She said it immediately, quite flatly. 'Laurie wouldn't kill himself. We were going to be married.'

'When was the last time you saw him before he died?'

'The Thursday. It happened on a Saturday night. He came in the Thursday before and took me out.'

'As usual?'

'There wasn't any usual with him because of the way he had to work. I hadn't seen him for ten days before that.'

186

'Did you know what he was working on?'

'Yes, he told me he was doing this big thing about this dancer. Like Pavlova? I said, and he said not quite like Pavlova, heavier for one thing, but he had to spend a lot of time with her for his piece, which was why he wasn't seeing me as much as he usually did.'

'Did you have the idea at any point that he was at all attracted to her?'

'Attracted!' It came out of her round mouth as a little screech of protest. 'Of course he wasn't. She was old for one thing, over thirty. He used to do impressions of her dancing with her behind stuck out and her hands waggling all over the place till everybody in the bar nearly died laughing.'

'You weren't called to give evidence at the inquest?' I couldn't remember any of that from the newspaper reports.

'No, I didn't even know it was happening that day until one of his friends come in the bar and told me. "The jury says it was suicide, Lizzie." I went mad. I just screeched out behind the bar that they were all lying, then I couldn't stop. In the end they had to take me upstairs to bed.'

'That last Thursday, did he seem cheerful?'

'Cheerful? He was like a man who'd had a hundred quid on the Derby winner. I've never seen him so cheerful. He came in here about seven o'clock, new hat, new coat, grinning all over his face and said, "Lizzie, I'm going to take you out for the evening of a lifetime." He paid old misery upstairs a quid to let me off for the evening, told me to go up and change into my best things, then we went to the second house at the Oxford and met some of his friends in the bar. After that we all went off to this restaurant and had oysters and stout and champagne, a whole crowd of us with him doing all the paying. On the way back in the taxi-cab I asked him when we were going up to the West End to get the ring and he said on Saturday I could have a diamond as big as the Koh-I-Nor. Only he didn't come.

There'd been a sparkle about her as she described the evening out. With the last four words her voice went flat and she stared down at her gloves—green silk gloves too thin for winter, a tear in one thumb clumsily mended.

'And didn't send a message?'

She shook her head, still looking down.

'Did he tell you why he was so cheerful that night?'

'He said he was going to be rich. "More money than you can think of, Lizzie. Buy that rotten old pub ten times over if I wanted." '

'From his work as a reporter?'

'I shouldn't think so. I thought maybe ...'

'What?'

'Maybe he'd had a good tip on the stock exchange or saved the life of some old millionaire and got remembered in his will. Something like that.'

'Weren't you curious?'

She raised her head and her blue eyes met mine. 'Not really. We were too busy having a good time.' She was silent for a while then, 'Are you related to him?'

'No, I never met him. I just know someone who knows him.'

It seemed to be all the explanation she wanted.

'Well, you can tell them Laurie didn't kill himself and if I'd known about that inquest I'd never have let them say he did.'

'Then what do you think happened?'

'I think she killed him, the dancer. I suppose she wanted him and when she found he was faithful to me she just took a knife to him.'

'Did you tell anybody that's what you think?'

'What good would that do? She's famous and I'm nobody. You can get these things covered up if you've got friends in the right places. Only it makes me sick to

189

my stomach to hear people say he killed himself over her.'

A rapping on the street door, very sharp and peremptory, probably with the head of a walking cane. She jumped up, a miserable look on her face.

'It's my gentleman, come to take me out.'

I glanced at Max and we followed her into the passage. When she half-opened the door we caught a glimpse of a fat, middle-aged face, glossed with sweat even on this cold day, between an astrakhan collar and a bowler hat with a curly brim.

'Come on, Lizzie, don't keep me waiting.'

His thin jocularity couldn't conceal the greed under it. He gave Max and me a glance of suspicion.

' 'Course I wouldn't keep you waiting.'

Her cheerfulness would have been almost convincing if it hadn't been for that glimpse of misery back in the snug. She let him take her arm without protest, put her hand on his coat sleeve and they walked away together up the street. The landlord wheezed down the stairs behind us.

'Gone out with her young man then, has she? Get what you wanted?'

We heard him bolting the door behind us.

Max looked angry with the man, with me, with the world. 'What chance has she got? Sunday outings with old lechers.'

'Precious little. But then what chance did she have as Laurie Gilbey's fiancée?'

'Fiancée! There are probably half a dozen barmaids in public houses like that one who considered themselves Laurie Gilbey's fiancée.'

'So you got that impression too?'

'Of course I did. The absences, the boasting, the expensive dinners in a noisy crowd. If he'd felt anything for the girl, it would have been a walk in the park and dinner tete à tete, not second house at the music hall and oysters with a mob of paid friends.'

It was the first time I'd heard Max say anything even hinting at an emotional life. Strange this view I was getting of my friends.

'So what did you think of her, Nell? Is there anything to investigate?'

'I'm not sure.'

'I'm afraid I've brought you into this on false pretences. When it comes to it, there's nothing firm enough in what we've heard to challenge a suicide verdict. Poor Lizzie naturally can't accept it.'

'It's interesting though, his belief that he was going to get his hands on a lot of money.'

'Meaningless. Just swagger to impress her.'

'She was impressed in any case before that. By the sound of it he really was excited about something.'

'Probably a gambler then. They tend to lose all touch with reality.'

This with the austerity of a man who believed international currency reform would abolish war and make all men brothers. I left Max at the corner by his office, already turning his mind to the more congenial subject of international politics, and walked on thinking that it was just as well that I probably shouldn't have liked Laurie Gilbey. That made it easier to follow my instructions and not care if the coroner's court had been wrong. Unlike poor Lizzie—indignant and sorrowing, but clutching that plump overcoated arm in her thin silk glove because a girl has to survive somehow. Not my responsibility.

Chapter Eleven

On Monday I travelled down to Maidenhead with Bernard and the rest of the orchestra. This time there was a whole fleet of vehicles, motor and horse powered, waiting to transport us and the instruments. We attracted a lot of attention from shoppers and errand boys as we went in an impromptu procession through the town and across the river bridge, and the musicians were in good spirits with the prospect of another week of well-paid work. Bernard said little, his viola case across his knees and the manuscript of Act One of *Joan of Arc* in a brown paper parcel under his arm.

When we got to Jack Belter's mansion, his motor car was outside, the chauffeur already in the driving seat and the engine running. As soon as I'd set foot on the gravel, Belter himself came running down the steps from the front door. He was wearing a long waterproof driving coat and carrying a cap with earflaps. He gave the orchestra, unloading itself from the vehicles, a look of collective dislike and turned on me.

'We've lost them again. Henson's not answering telegrams.'

'They can hardly telegram if they're on a train or ferry.'

'He should have telephoned me from Dover. I've got to spend the day in town. I want you to wait here till they arrive, and as soon as they do, telephone my office and let me know. Bridget knows the number. And for goodness' sake get those bloody carts out of the way. I'm late already.'

He got in; the car threaded its way through the clutter of vehicles and musicians and sped off Londonwards.

With the reluctant patron out of the way, the rehearsal went well. Elsie, even singing at half voice, was impressive and young John Bartholomew was superb. Either nobody had told him to save his voice at rehearsal or he had so much voice that he could be spendthrift with it. His denunciations of Herod's court and Salome rang out with all the contempt of the north for the soft south, but even constant repetition of Salome's gloating praise of his black hair and white body couldn't take the shock out of his eyes. I thought he wouldn't be entirely surprised if we were all swallowed up in fire and brimstone. Towards the end of the afternoon, they were rehearsing the scene where Herod is trying to persuade Salome to dance for him. It was dusk outside and the long velvet curtains had been drawn across the windows overlooking the lawn and terrace. Madoc had stopped the orchestra to correct something the strings were doing so there was silence apart from his voice and the faint gurgling of the water in the heating pipes. There was a knock on the outside door, a glimpse of the housekeeper

Bridget's face as it opened, then the entry of Salome.

The newcomer walked into the silence as if it were a fanfare playing for her: quite slowly, with a lazy but concentrated step, like a cat sizing up the bird table. A coat of thick black sables, so glossy that they reflected the electric light, swung from her shoulders; under it a dress of fine violet-coloured wool, draped at the front so that it swung as she walked to show ankles in the sheerest of grey silk, and shoes of violet leather that looked as supple as ballet pumps, with a little heel. Her hat was a kind of turban, also black sable, that set off her pale powdered face and lips stained violet-red as if she'd been munching mulberries. Her eyes were dark and enormous, with an upswept oriental look to them. One surprise was that she was small, almost dumpy. Her face, apart from those eyes, wasn't remarkable—the cheeks on the plump side, her black hair growing low down on her forehead over plucked black brows. But none of that mattered alongside her air that said, as clearly as if she'd shouted it, 'I am beautiful. Look at me.' We all looked. There was a rustling in the orchestra and Madoc stopped talking. She walked slowly up to him and spoke in a voice like a note on an oboe, husky but penetrating.

'Play.'

At that point Leon Sylvan came in, wearing his cloak and top hat. It was as if he'd deliberately held back to let Oriana Paphos make her entrance, but now he stalked behind her, eyes ranging over the orchestra and singers like a priest watching for heretics.

After these two, few people there would even have noticed the third figure that sidled in a few steps behind Sylvan, carrying a hat box, a fur muff, a bouquet of mimosa and a make-up case. Henry Henson.

Madoc, usually so totally in charge at rehearsal, seemed taken aback for once and gave me a do-something look. I got up from my chair by the wall and walked over to the woman, holding out my hand.

'I take it you're Miss Paphos. I hope you had a good journey.'

She turned, but ignored my hand. 'Tell them to play my music.'

Madoc might justifiably have been annoyed at somebody treating his orchestra like a dance band, but luckily he was a showman too and rose to the situation.

'Very well, gentlemen—Salome's dance.'

A moment's surprise, then rustling of scores. Elsie gave Oriana Paphos a cold glance then pointedly left the platform and went over to sit by the wall, followed after some hesitation by the other singers. The music started.

I think we'd half expected that Oriana would dance there and then in her fur coat and turban, but she stood, eyes closed, chest rising and falling as if drawing it in. She was almost motionless, and yet her head and upper body moved a little as if searching for something by smell. At first the movement was towards Madoc, then away to the wall where the singers were sitting. Elsie was watching with an expression of amusement and disgust but the blind questing didn't linger on her. It slipped just a few degrees to the right and the person standing next to her. John Bartholomew, jaw dropped, eyes staring. It was if, by some magic, she'd fastened on the best-looking and most bashful man in the room. The music stopped.

'Yes. That will do. That will do very well.'

Her eyes were open, back on Madoc. Henry Henson coughed, not an attention-seeking cough but a necessary throat-clearing. All the time the music was going on, he'd been standing there with his burdens, marooned in the middle of the gleaming ballroom floor and nobody was taking any notice of him.

'Introduce me to people.'

She said it as: 'intradoos me to pipple.'

197

If there was some mystery about Sylvan's accent there was none about hers. It was as unconvincing an attempt at a French accent as I'd ever heard and I was prepared to swear that the voice underneath it was English Midlands.

Madoc, a little impatient now because rehearsal time was short and the dance was a small matter for him, introduced the leader of the orchestra then led her over to the singers. He walked briskly but she went slowly behind, as if the rhythms of the dance music were still in her head.

'Elsie, Oriana Paphos. Miss Paphos, this is Elsie Wetherby who's singing Salome.'

'Ah, you are my voice.'

Elsie, making no attempt to get up or put out her hand, gave a glance at the grey silk ankles.

'Oh? I rather thought you were my legs.'

Madoc hurried on through the rest of the cast. Herod, Herodias and the others got only the briefest of acknowledgements. Then he came to John Bartholomew.

'And this is our John the Baptist.'

She put out a hand to him, high up as if for kissing. He grabbed it, blushing like a furnace, dropped it as if burned.

'The holy man who loves me.'

'As a matter of fact,' said Elsie, 'he's the only one who sees you for what you are.'

Oriana shook her head, not resentful. 'Everybody loves Salome. Only some resist it more.'

There was a crash and a rustle behind us. It was Henry Henson, dropping the mimosa and the hat box.

'Oh, mind my poor flowers, lambkin.'

Oriana swooped to rescue the mimosa, almost treading on Henson who was on his knees trying to cram a hat like a purple butterfly back into its box.

While this was happening Jack Belter came in. He was still wearing his driving coat and clearly in a worse temper than the morning, crunching bits of gravel from his soles into the polished floor, leaving Bridget to close the door behind him. He stepped round Henson, disregarding him.

'When did they get here? Why wasn't I told?'

Everybody looked at me.

'They only got here half an hour ago.'

Oriana, clutching the sheaf of mimosa to her sable breast, went gliding up to him and put a violet silk hand on his arm.

'Mr Belturr, I promise you we shall make something beautiful.'

Behind her, Sylvan stared at Belter, his expression unreadable. Belter stared back over Oriana's shoulder, not reacting to her at all.

'You're already in breach of contract.

She should have been here four days ago.'

'My art is not about contracts,' Oriana said, still in that cardboard French accent.

'Well, my money is.'

He couldn't stop himself giving a look of disgust and pulled away, leaving her hand in the air. Gracefully she let it drift back to her side, unaffected by his rudeness. Belter turned his attention to Henson, still on the floor.

'What are you doing down there and where have you been?'

Henson straightened up slowly, clutching the hat box. He hadn't quite managed to confine the hat, and a wing of it flopped over the side. His face was pale, his eyes sunken and blank with tiredness, his trousers creased.

'I ... I sent a telegram from Paris, sir.'

'*One* telegram. Didn't you get all of mine? You were supposed to be back two days ago. What in the world did you think you were doing?'

'It ... took Miss Paphos some days to make her arrangements and pack, sir.'

'Pack! Does it take three days to pack? I suppose it does if you've bought her half the Paris fur trade on my money.'

'You told me to get her a fur coat.'

'Any old fur would have done. I don't

suppose the Queen herself has got sables like those. You'll be hearing more about this, young man.'

Sylvan's voice cut in. 'Miss Paphos is tired from her journey. If you wish us to stay here, she will go to her room.'

By this time Oriana had gravitated back to the singers. She looked anything but tired and was talking animatedly to John Bartholomew. He'd stood up politely and had bent his head to listen to her. His face was as red as a sunset, with Elsie Wetherby's providing the storm clouds.

Sylvan said, like a parent giving orders to a child, 'Oriana, go and rest.' She touched John's arm lightly, smiled at him then went obediently towards the door where Bridget was waiting. On the way she stopped beside Jack Belter.

'Is my John the Baptist staying here as well?'

Jack Belter looked at me and I started to explain that the singers travelled in from London every day.

'No.' She cut me off, not rudely but as an irrelevance. 'He must be here. If we are to perform together, there must be a rapport.'

She sounded the 't' of 'rapport'. I mentioned that since John the Baptist and the dancing Salome were never actually on the stage at the same time it didn't much matter. I might as well have saved my breath.

'He must be here. If the vibrations are not sympathetic, I cannot make my dance.'

Belter said to me, 'Which one is she talking about?' I pointed out John Bartholomew and he strode over to him. 'Miss Paphos wants you to stay here in my house. I'll send the chauffeur to your hotel for your bags.'

'No.' This time it came from the singing Salome, Elsie Wetherby. John himself just gaped, not saying a word. 'If John's staying here, I'm staying too. He's never been out of Yorkshire before and he's engaged to my niece.'

'Sort it out, sort it out, sort it out. Have the whole pack of them to stay here if you like. I'll see you later.'

Having dumped the problem in my lap, Jack Belter strode out, banging the door behind him. Henson stood rooted to the spot but head turned round in the direction of the slamming door, torn between his employer and Oriana, who had hardly glanced at him since she walked in. The first task was to smooth down Elsie.

'Would it suit you to stay here? It really is a very comfortable house and quite warm.'

Singers, careful of their voices, are

usually as greedy for warmth as kittens, but she wouldn't be placated. 'I'd sleep on sacks in a coal hole rather than leave this young man on his own.'

In the end it was settled that both Elsie and John would be added to the guest list. Bridget and I took Oriana over to the main house and saw her settled into her bedroom. She hardly said a word to either of us, as if a current had been switched off once she was away from her audience. On the way back I met Jack Belter in the hall.

'Is it settled?'

'Yes. John Bartholomew and Elsie Wetherby are staying. Miss Paphos is resting.'

'What's she done to young Henson? He looks like an opened oyster. Three nights in Paris and those furs on my money.'

It was in my mind to say that this was proving so expensive he'd better hold out for an earldom instead of a mere baronetcy but I bit my tongue. Something else was bothering him.

'Did she call him lambkin? Did I hear aright?'

'I'm afraid so.'

'God help us. Anyway, I'm stopping the sables from his wages.'

He might mean it too. I thought, from the look of the furs, it could leave Henson a pauper for a very long time.

'And now she wants this other one as well, the singer. I've never met a woman like it.'

I mentioned that her life seemed so crowded, with Sylvan, Henson and now John the Baptist that my chances of getting into her confidence seemed slim.

'Well, that's what you're here for. You'd better find a way. I'm sure there are some things women talk about with each other that they don't with men. And get on with it. I don't know how much more of these people I can stand.' He strode out.

For the next hour or so I was so occupied with consulting the housekeeper and arranging the collection of luggage that I didn't even see the musicians go. I'd have liked a word with Bernard as some kind of hold on sanity, but that would have to keep. By seven o'clock, with everybody allocated a room and the luggage organised, I was sitting in the lounge feeling as if a cyclone had passed overhead when the next instalment of it arrived in the shape of Elsie Wetherby.

At first I was glad to see her because I'd liked her down-to-earth manner. But her first words were not encouraging.

'Oh, there you are. I want a word with you.'

'Problems with your room?'

She plumped herself down opposite me in a leather armchair. The furniture in Jack Belter's mansion was substantial and comfortable, custom-built for a man who knew what he wanted, but she was in no mood to be appreciative.

'What are we going to do about that female python?'

'Python?'

'Don't try looking innocent at me. Something's going on and I think you know what it is.'

'What kind of something?'

'Feeding time at the zoo, and she's not getting poor John. If Jack Belter wants to keep her in his menagerie and feed her a new young man every week, that's his affair. But that particular young man's spoken for and I'm not having any of you forgetting it.'

'You think that's what's happening?'

'I know it is. This whole business about the opera's no more than a smokescreen. I've been watching Mr Belter on the rare occasions he looks in on rehearsals and I'll tell you that man's got no more music in him than that table. And yet this must be costing him thousands of pounds for the one performance. We were all of us wondering why—until the reason for it came wriggling in this afternoon. It's all to keep her happy.'

I said nothing, amused and impressed at how much she'd guessed. After all, Jack Belter's reputation was his own problem, not mine. The only question was whether this was likely to make my job more difficult.

'You think Jack Belter's in love with Oriana Paphos?'

'Besotted, more like.'

'He didn't seem to like her company very much this afternoon.'

'A pose because there were other people there, or perhaps it's some game they're playing with each other.'

'In that case, wouldn't you expect him to be more annoyed about the competition?'

'The Henson fellow, you mean, then her going for poor John? No, that's all part of it. He's feeding them to her like skinned rabbits.' She leaned forward until her knee was touching mine. 'I don't know how much experience of the world you've had, but I don't suppose you're straight out of Sunday school any more than I am. Men get to a certain age, can't do it any more or maybe not as often as they'd like, so they get their satisfaction out of thinking of other people doing it, even watching through little holes in the bedroom wall. You notice, it's young men he's hired that he feeds to her—not real competition.'

'It's an interesting theory.'

And I had to admit to myself that she was surprisingly close to the target, identifying Jack Belter's greed for Oriana. I knew that it was for the information she carried, but Elsie, not knowing, had noticed a lot.

She must have seen the change in my face, because she smiled. 'Believe me, Miss Bray, you don't sing opera for twenty years without picking up a few things about the way people go on. Now, I don't go round criticising people if they don't do me or mine any harm, but I'm giving you all a fair warning. I'm not walking out because I've never broken an engagement in my life. And I'm not taking young John out because this is his first big chance outside of oratorio and if he gets a reputation for being temperamental, he won't get another. But you can let Jack Belter and his pet python know from me that if she lays a finger on that young man, there'll be trouble. I'm not having happen to him what happened to the other one.'

'To Henry Henson, you mean?'

I thought of Jack Belter's comparison to the opened oyster. Elsie shook her head and leaned even more closely towards me so that our foreheads as well as our knees were almost touching.

'No. I mean the one who died.'

I must have given some accidental sign, because she drew back a little and laughed. 'Aha, so you knew about that one, did you? Did he kill himself over her?'

'I honestly don't know. I wasn't there at the time. As a matter of interest, how did you know about it?'

'I've got a lot of friends in London, and singers like gossip as much as anybody. More, probably, because of all the waiting. Anyway, I wasn't acquainted with that poor young man and I don't know the rights and wrongs of it. Just let Mr Belter know I'm not a fool and I'm not blind.' She stood up. 'When you see the housekeeper, tell her we'll have our suppers in our rooms and John must have plenty of red meat for his voice, but no more than half a bottle of Beaujolais because he's not used to it.' She took a step towards the door. 'And while we're on the subject of rooms, you can tell her I've exchanged with John. She'd put him too close to the python.'

She made her exit with a spring in her step that set the parquet floor vibrating. Not Salome exactly, but formidable all the same.

Chapter Twelve

I found Bridget in the smaller of the two kitchens, in conference with the cook, and passed on the word about trays. She seemed as unruffled by it as everything else.

'That makes it the lot of them apart from yourself. We won't be having to lay the dining table.'

'Is Miss Paphos having dinner in her room as well?'

'She is.' Bridget fished up the little notebook that hung from a string at her belt and flipped over pages. 'Clear soup, turbot, cold chicken with truffle sauce and a bottle of champagne. She said she never eats much when she's working on a new dance. And they must be white truffles not black, because today she's thinking white like the full moon.'

The cook, grating something, with her back turned to us, made a derisive noise. Evidently not everybody was taking the invasion as calmly as Bridget.

'What about Mr Sylvan?'

Bridget gave me a look, her sidelong eye implying a lot. 'Not much pale about that one. Steak tartare with two raw eggs and plenty of onion, two bottles of soda and a bottle of Armagnac. And he's having it served in her room.'

I passed on Elsie's news about exchanging rooms and she made another note on her pad.

'It's a funny thing about working here. People never seem to stay in the rooms we put them in, though they don't always have the kindness to let us know.'

Another derisive sound from the cook, and her knife went chopping away like a demented guillotine. The smell of raw onion, violently assaulted, rose round us.

Bridget caught my eye and smiled. 'Are you going to eat in your room too? Unless you'd like to join the butler and me.'

A kind invitation. I accepted it, always supposing that Jack Belter had no need of my society.

'Oh, you don't need to worry about Mr Belter. He's gone off to a dinner in London and won't be back until late, or he might not be back at all. He's got a little suite at his office and sometimes he stays there.'

The butler came in, slim and young for a butler but with a pate as bald as a fish's belly. He was carrying a tray loaded with various bottles. 'Here we are, Mrs B. The foreign gentleman's going to have to make do with the ordinary Armagnac because I'm not letting him slop soda water into Mr Belter's best.'

He put his tray down on a long side table against the wall. There were two more trays on it, already equipped with plates, glasses and cutlery and a list in Bridget's neat handwriting of the food requirements. A bell started ringing, one of a line of a dozen on coiled springs high up on the wall, each one labelled with the name of a room. This was guest room one. Bridget looked up.

'Mother of God, isn't somebody impatient? That'll be the dancing lady wanting her supper and I suppose Mr Sylvan's had better go up at the same time. Is that steak ready for him yet?'

Refusing to be hurried, with the three of us watching her, the cook chivvied the chopped onion into a little mound with the knife blade, then slid it accurately into the middle of a rampart of chopped raw steak. She fetched two large eggs from the pantry, broke them carefully and settled each in its half shell on either side of the onion.

'You watch the girl doesn't let them slip over when she carries it up.'

'Don't fret, I'll take it up myself.'

Bridget refused to be riled by the cook's bad temper, although the bell of room number one clanged into action again

211

while everything was being assembled on the two trays, and this time it didn't stop.

'Oh dear, it must be hungry work, this dancing with no shoes to your feet. Are we ready now?'

They weren't quite because there was no room on Oriana's tray for the champagne in its ice bucket, what with the broth, turbot and chicken under their silver domes, and the butler had his hands full with the steak tray.

'Don't worry, I'll take it for you,' I offered.

The whole point of being there was to get into conversation with Oriana, and taking her champagne up was at least a start. We went up the service stairs to the first floor corridor in a procession of three. Once through the servants' door, this corridor was as expensive as everything else about the house, with a runner of thick pale green carpet along the polished floor, electric light holders on the walls made to look like fat candles, and small tables outside each door. The effect was more of a high class hotel than a home, but as thoroughly done as everything connected with Jack Belter. Led by the butler, we padded up to the door of room one and stopped. There were raised voices coming from inside, hers first.

'... not my fault. You could see the way he was looking at me. Anyway, what is it to do with you?'

Then a lower rumble, the words inaudible, in what must have been her manager's voice. Perhaps it was advice to be quiet because we couldn't make out her reply. The butler coughed stagily, put his tray down and knocked on the door. It was opened in a few seconds by Leon Sylvan, looking more than ever like Jupiter in a bad temper.

'Well, what is it?'

'Your dinner, sir, and the lady's.'

He stood back and let us into the room. Oriana was sitting on a green plush sofa with her back to us, a coil of her heavy dark hair wound round her wrist, head bent forward showing a sweep of white, muscular neck. While Bridget and the butler were arranging the dinner things on a table, Sylvan watching them with hostility, I gripped the ice bucket and studied that neck. It didn't look a happy neck, weighed down with either weariness or depression, and the tension on her hair seemed enough to drag it out by its roots. I moved round the sofa to face her.

'Would you like your champagne over there?'

She looked up at me. I wondered if she'd been crying, but her great dark eyes were dry and angry. She'd changed into a long white robe, like a nightdress, and her feet were bare—long, high-arched feet that somehow looked more thoroughbred than the rest of her. She nodded and I drew up a low table beside her and put the ice bucket down.

'Is everything all right?' A query that, deliberately, could have meant anything.

'I'm hungry.'

She said it like a sulky child. The attempt at a French accent was there, though I hadn't noticed it when she was shouting at her manager a minute ago.

'Your dinner's over here, madam.'

The butler joined us, eased the cork out of the champagne bottle and poured her a glass. Her hand closed round it immediately. A squarish, almost plump hand when you saw it without its glove, though very white. The odd thing was that, whatever part of her body you looked at, you saw a different Oriana, like a doll that had been put together from scattered parts after some nursery catastrophe. She seemed, too, almost as lifeless as a doll, quite different from the vibrant woman who'd walked into rehearsal. Whatever had happened to her since must have come from Leon Sylvan.

'Is that the best Armagnac you have?'

Sylvan had a balloon of it in his hand.

'Yes, sir.' The butler's lie throbbed with controlled dislike. 'Will that be all for now, sir?'

Not condescending to answer, Sylvan put down the brandy glass and began to push raw steak into his mouth with a soup spoon. He grinned as he chewed, sensing the other man's disgust and his inability to do anything about it. He puddled the raw egg and meat together into a carnivore's porridge and repeated the process. Little gobbets of meat and a trail of egg yolk spilled over on to his beard. The contrast between the elegance of his clothes, manicuring and barbering and this method of eating was clearly a deliberate piece of showmanship. He might be a guest in Jack Belter's house, but he was making it clear that he accepted no obligation to behave well.

Oriana curled her bare feet on to the sofa, drank champagne and ignored him.

When it became obvious that he wasn't going to get an answer to his question, the butler left, followed by Bridget. Before I followed them, I bent down to adjust the position of the ice bucket on the table and got Oriaria's eyes to meet mine.

'If there's anything you want, Miss Paphos, or anything I can help with, please let me know at any time. My room's the next floor up, opposite the staircase.' Intense, perhaps, for a cultural attaché, and I thought I saw a spark of surprise in her eyes.

As I straightened up, Sylvan was looking at me and I knew that even if she'd missed the significance of it, he hadn't. 'Miss Paphos won't be requiring anything else tonight. If *I* want anything, I'll ring for it.' He chewed another spoonful at me.

I caught up with Bridget and the butler on their way downstairs as she was trying to talk him out of his professional disgust.

'They're foreign, after all, and artistic.'

'If that's being artistic, Mrs B, then I'm glad I'm not. I'll be pleased when it's Sunday and all over.'

The discussion was resumed later as the three of us sat at supper in the housekeeper's room—a comfortable little place with a pot of hyacinths on the table, a fire in the grate and painting of Galway Bay on the wall. By then it was after ten o'clock. Supper trays had been sent up to Elsie Wetherby and John Bartholomew; Jack Belter hadn't returned, and no more had been heard from room number one. The butler calmed down under the influence of some quite good claret, and he and Bridget started reminiscing about some of Mr Belter's other guests. A music hall comedian had knocked himself out one evening sliding down the bannisters in a race with a jockey. Half the Gaiety chorus performed on the terrace during a summer party. Young Mr Churchill had put away the best part of two bottles of brandy then accidentally set fire to his bed clothes with a cigar. Bridget seemed entirely tolerant of it all, even proud.

'The things this house has seen—if it could talk it would have to hold its tongue.'

At that point the screaming started. It came from upstairs, and, because the housekeeper's room was some distance from the staircase, it sounded quite faint to me. But Bridget and the butler had ears professionally tuned to anything wrong in the house and they were both on their feet and looking at each other. When the butler pulled the door open there was no doubt about it. The screams came spiking through the whole house, so loud and nearly continuous that it seemed impossible for one human being to go on making such a noise.

The three of us collided in the doorway and dashed out into the corridor. The cook was there, white-faced and glaring, with a maid hiding behind her. We pushed past them and pounded up the service staircase, through the door into the first floor corridor.

The screams were coming from guest room number one—Oriana's. Leon Sylvan was standing outside it in a purple dressing gown with a bored expression on his face.

'Oriana, don't be so silly.' He might have been talking to a dog.

Standing a little way off and watching him were Elsie Wetherby and John Bartholomew, still fully dressed, alarmed and white-faced. The butler asked, 'Has she locked the door?' All he got from Sylvan was a shrug. I tried the handle. Locked. Still the screams went on, so loud it was hard to think.

Bridget said, 'Is the bathroom door locked too?'

She elbowed aside John Bartholomew and tried the handle of a door a few yards to the left of the main one. It gave. She stood there for a moment surprised, then pushed it open a crack. The butler and I said simultaneously, 'Let me go in first,' and pushed in together. The light was on in the bathroom, and there was another doorway on the right, connecting with the bedroom.

Oriana was standing in the doorway between the two rooms, still in her white robe. Her mulberry mouth was wide open and the screams were pouring out of it like hot water from an Icelandic geyser.

Her hands were clutched together against her chest.

'It's all right. We're here. What's wrong?'

I heard an exclamation of disgust behind me and turned to look at the butler. He was staring at the bathtub. It was two thirds full of water. The water was red.

I got Oriana by the shoulders, and pushed her, still screaming, back into the bedroom and down on to the sofa.

'Will you stop, please. It isn't helping.' I sat down beside her, prised her clenched hands away from her chest and took them in mine. 'Stop it now. Breathe in, deeply.'

She took deep shuddering breaths at first, then calmer ones. There wasn't a speck of red on her hands or the white robe. Her eyes turned to the butler as he came in from the bathroom.

'There's nothing in the water. Just the ... the red.' He sounded shaken.

'Blood,' she said. 'It's blood.'

We looked at her.

'Whose blood?'

She just shook her head then dragged her hands away from me and curled up in the corner of the sofa, face hidden. Bridget came through the bathroom, walked over to the bedroom door and unbolted it. The other three came in, Sylvan first. He looked at Oriana but made no attempt to comfort her. Bridget took charge, sending John down to the dining room for brandy, Elsie to Oriaria's wardrobe to sort out something warm. It turned out to be the black sable coat which Bridget tucked round her with efficient gentleness. Oriana didn't move or speak.

The butler caught my eye and we went back into the bathroom together. The mirror on the wall was misted and the temperature in the small room was warmer than the bedroom. The water in the bath was a clear garnet-red, like stained glass with the sun shining through it. I knelt down beside it, dipped my finger in and smelt. Raw and rusty.

'I think it really is blood.'

'How did it get in there? Did she cut herself?'

'No sign of it.'

Time of the month? Miscarriage? Those possibilities occurred to me, if not to the butler, but there'd have been blood on her robe too.

'Somebody must have put it in there to frighten her, or as a nasty trick.'

A young man had killed himself in her bath. There would have been a lot of blood.

'Shall I pull the plug out?'

'We'd better, I suppose.'

No question of calling the police, and Oriana could hardly be expected to calm down with her bath awash with blood. But before he pulled the plug chain I had another good look. It was a big bath, two thirds full. It would have taken quite a lot of blood to colour it, perhaps a pint or more. I tried hot and cold taps. Both ran clear water.

'Nothing like this happened in the house before?'

'No.'

I left him to clear up and went back to the bedroom. Elsie and John had gone. Bridget was sitting beside Oriana on the sofa and had persuaded her to uncurl and sip brandy. Sylvan was in an armchair, watching closely but making no attempt to help.

'Would you feel like going to your bed now?'

Bridget's voice was kindly but brisk. Probably not the first hysterical guest she'd had to deal with. The counterpane on the big mahogany bed was turned back invitingly on snowy sheets. Oriana shook her head.

'I couldn't sleep.'

Her voice was husky, which wasn't surprising after all that screaming. Sylvan stood up, still looking bored.

'Miss Paphos will be all right. I shall

stay with her till she sleeps.'

'No.' Oriana sat bolt upright, slopping the brandy. Her eyes went first to Bridget then fixed on me. 'She'll stay with me.'

Sylvan shrugged and stood up. 'As you like.' But the look he gave me wasn't friendly. 'I shall require coffee in my room.'

As he walked out, Oriaria's eyes followed him.

Bridget said, 'Will you mind, Miss Bray?'

'Not in the least.'

She was conscientious, but obviously more than ready to have Oriana taken off her hands. She left and a few minutes later the butler put his head round the bathroom door.

'I've cleared up in there myself. No sense in frightening the maids with it. Ring if you need anything.'

I got up and switched off some of the lights, leaving only a small lamp on the table beside the bed, then went back to the sofa beside Oriana. She was calmer now, almost trance-like.

'What happened?'

A pause.

'I ... I went to have my bath. There was blood in it. Like the last time.' The fake French accent had gone and flat Midlands vowels were coming through.

'Last time? You mean when Laurence Gilbey died?'

A pause, then a little nod, as if it had taken her some time to recognise the name.

'Did you see him?'

A little movement of the head. She reached for the brandy glass on the table beside her, took a gulp.

'Do you think somebody put the blood in the bath deliberately to remind you of that?'

She bit her lip and gave the faintest of nods.

'Who?'

Not a word, but her eyes shifted upstairs, the way Sylvan had gone.

'Why would he do that?'

'To make me scared. He doesn't want me to leave him.'

It was said in an almost childlike way. When she wasn't putting out that electric energy, as she had on her entrance at the rehearsal, her mind and body went as passive as a sitting hen. It didn't seem to occur to her to wonder why I was asking questions.

'How will making you scared help?'

'Because if I leave him he'll tell the police Laurie killed himself because he loved me.'

'Is it true?'

Her huge eyes opened wide and she stared at me as if I'd questioned a law of nature. 'Of course.'

'Laurence Gilbey died because he loved you? You're sure of that?'

'He left a note in his own blood. "I love you." '

I sat up. The inquest had been told there was no note.

'You saw it?'

'On the chair by the bath. He'd written it with one of the little brushes from my dressing table.'

'What happened to this note?'

'He took it.'

'Mr Sylvan?'

'Yes. He said the police mustn't see it or they'd lock me up and ask me questions.'

'Why? It isn't a legal offence to have somebody kill himself over you.'

'I can't be locked up. I'm a free spirit. I can't have ugly men in uniforms asking me questions about people dying. It would get into my dance and poison it.'

Her eyes were blazing, her whole body suddenly electric with life. She'd been as calm as a hen when she'd talked about a man's death, but now she was urgently wanting me to believe her.

'Was that why you went away when you found the body?'

'Of course. Sylvan said I was to go away and he'd arrange everything. He knows I mustn't have ugly things round me.'

'And yet you think he's trying to scare you with blood in your bath. Isn't that ugly?'

She didn't answer, just curled up over her brandy glass.

'What happened that night? Did you come home and find him?'

'Yes. I'd been dancing at one of the big houses near the park. We came home after midnight, and he was there.'

'Did you love him?'

'I love everybody in the world. When I dance I am a priestess of the spirit of eternal love. Laurie Gilbey was going to write a book about me and my temple.'

'Temple?'

'I am going to build a temple of love and beauty by the sea in Greece where people can come to see me dance and find love.'

'What does Mr Sylvan think about that?'

'He keeps all my money. I've told him he must give it to me for my temple, but he won't.'

'So you talked to Laurence Gilbey about your dancing and your temple. Did you talk about anything else?'

'We talked about everything.'

'Did he talk to you about letters?'

225

Annoyance replaced the rapt look on her face. She wriggled round, half turning her back to me.

'Letters, letters, letters. I'm tired of people talking about those letters. They weren't even interesting.'

'So Laurie Gilbey talked to you about them?'

An angry twitch of the shoulder was all I got.

'You know about them anyway. Did you know Mr Sylvan had stolen them?'

'He steals from everybody. He steals from me.' This was muttered, still looking away from me.

'And you've seen them?'

'They're not interesting.'

'But you have seen them?'

'I asked Sylvan to show them to me. I thought they were love letters but they were all about silly things, the books he'd read, meetings, bridge games. What kind of man writes to a woman about bridge?'

'Did Laurie Gilbey read them as well?'

'He wanted to see them but he agreed with me. They weren't interesting.'

Impossible. Belter had regarded Laurie Gilbey as one of his brightest journalists. Even a journalist less than bright could hardly read a description of cabinet discussions in a private letter without realising he was dealing with something

226

unusually interesting. Either Oriana was lying or the late Laurence Gilbey had been playing a deep game.

'Did he take any of the letters away with him?'

'Sylvan wouldn't let him. But he must have taken one all the same.'

'How do you know that?'

She wriggled round to look at me. 'Because he'd written on the back of it—that he loved me.'

It took me a while to work out what she was saying.

'You're talking about that note that was written in blood by his body?'

She nodded.

'And you mean it was written on the back of one of those letters?'

Another nod.

'Where are the rest of them?'

'I suppose Sylvan has got them. He took them back.'

She stood up, shrugging the sables into place round her shoulders as casually as a dressing gown.

'I need to go to the bathroom.'

She took a few steps towards the bathroom door then stopped.

'I ... I can't.'

She was trembling, terrified, no affectation now.

'The blood's all gone. Look.'

I opened the door wide so that she could see the clean and empty bath. She took a step, shivered under the fur.

'Wait. Wait outside for me. Talk to me.'

So I did. She left the door open a crack and I kept on talking to her about channel ferries and music and nothing until water swooshed and she came out trembling and put out her hand to me. It was cold and grasped mine desperately as I led her over to the bed.

'His wrists ... and the water ... redder than that, but the same smell.'

I persuaded her to get into bed, spread the fur over the counterpane to try to stop her shivering, then drew a chair up and sat beside her. Her hand closed round my wrist, a surprisingly strong hand.

'I'm scared of him.'

'Do you want to leave Mr Sylvan?'

She thought about that for longer than my other questions.

'I think so.'

'But you're scared of what will happen if you do?'

'I'd have no money. He looks after all my money.'

'If it's yours you could take him to court and make him give it back to you.'

'No. No courts. No policemen. No

228

lawyers. They're all so ugly.' She shuddered.

I knew it was no good trying to explain to her the difference between a civil and criminal case or even to point out that I'd met one or two perfectly presentable barristers.

'You can always make more money from your dancing. You're the one with the talent, after all.'

'Genius.' She corrected me gravely. 'Talent is what little pink girls at dancing school have. Genius is like a god possessing you, making love to you.'

Her fingernails dug into my wrist.

'Whatever you call it, you could break away from him if you really wanted to.'

She gave me a long look, then sighed and released my hand as if I'd disappointed her.

'I'm waiting for a hero.'

'Hero?'

'A man brave and strong enough to take me away from him.'

I couldn't help laughing. She glared.

'What's funny?'

'Was that by any chance what you were doing with Henry Henson—auditioning him as a hero, poor man?'

From the time I'd seen them together, I couldn't see how anybody as ordinary as Belter's assistant had kept her attention for several days. Perhaps, spending his employer's money on sables, he'd looked to her like young Siegfried wrestling bears. Then he'd declined to lambkin.

She said, quite seriously, 'I wanted him to go away with me, yes.'

'And he wouldn't. You may just have to face the fact that there's a world shortage of heroes these days. Probably something to do with supply and demand.'

'Why are you laughing at me?'

'And if you're wondering about John the Baptist, you should save your energy. His aunt-in-law elect won't let him be a hero.'

She lay back against the pillow and closed her eyes, her face pale in its dark pod of hair. I sat beside her and did some thinking. I could have lectured her from then till morning on fighting her own battles instead of looking for a man to do it, but it would have been like trying to build a sea wall from meringue.

'There's somebody who might be able to help you.'

Her eyelashes fluttered, but apart from that she didn't move. 'Who?'

'The man who invited you here to dance, Jack Belter.'

A little moan of protest.

'No, listen. He's got quite indecent amounts of money. Only he wants something in return.'

'I don't like him.'

'Nobody's asking you to.'

I thought it best not to add that he thought she was at least an accomplice in murder.

'What does he want?'

'Those letters.'

Another moan. She curled up with her back to me.

'Not for himself. He wants to give them back to the person who owns them. If you could persuade Mr Sylvan to sell them to him there'd be plenty of money for both. Mr Belter would give you your share into your hand, so you'd have money to get away if you wanted to. He might even build you your temple.'

Judging by the architecture of his office and this house, it might be interesting to see what Jack Belter would do in the way of a temple of love and beauty. She didn't answer but I was sure she was still listening to me.

'They are stolen property after all. You wouldn't be doing anything wrong in getting them back to the man who wrote them.'

'To the Prime Minister?'

'What!'

I rocked back in my chair. I knew from what Lloyd George had told me that this incautious letter-writer must be somebody close to the Cabinet, but I hadn't reckoned on this.

Oriana turned to face me, clearly puzzled at my surprise. 'Isn't Mr Asquith still the Prime Minister? Laurie said he was.'

'Yes. Those letters were from him?'

'Why are you surprised? I thought you knew, with all this fuss about them.'

'So Laurie knew those letters were written by the Prime Minister himself?'

'Of course he did. I'm tired. I want to sleep now.'

She turned on her back and closed her eyes. I sat there trying to get my balance back, realising the stakes were even higher than I'd been told. No wonder Lloyd George and Belter were prepared to take risks—or have other people take risks for them.

After ten minutes or so she was breathing regularly. I got up and started to tiptoe to the door.

'No. Don't leave me. What will I do if I have to use the bathroom and the blood's come back?'

I suggested that I should go upstairs to fetch my nightdress and toothbrush, but she wouldn't even hear of that. She had dozens of nightdresses, toothbrushes, everything. I must take what I wanted. She watched, giving increasingly sleepy instructions, while I rummaged in drawers

overflowing with silk scarves and underwear, stockings, gloves, lace. Eventually,
wrapped in ivory lace and one of her older
mink coats, I took a cushion from the sofa,
put the light out and settled down on the
floor beside her bed.

She snored gently through most of the
night and I stayed awake and wondered.

Chapter Thirteen

At eight o'clock, the maid tapped on the
door to deliver Oriana's breakfast tray:
warm milk, grapes, soft white rolls and
honey. She seemed mildly surprised to
find me opening the door and Oriana
still in bed but, in the best traditions of
Jack Belter's house, made no comment. I
went over to the window, the lace and silk
of Oriana's nightgown sliding against my
skin like a wheedling cat. It was odd too
to get up to warmth all round me instead
of feet on a cold floor and the hurry to get
a fire going. The heating pipes made the
air in the room almost tropical, but when
I looked out of the window it was still a
winter morning, with the bare trees on the
island opposite black against a grey sky.

Oriana stirred sleepily and asked what

the time was but showed no inclination to get up. With maids around in the corridor it seemed safe enough to leave her and she was too drowsy to protest, so I went up to my own room to dress. On the way back downstairs I heard a soprano voice running up and down scales, presumably Elsie Wetherby greeting the morning. I knew that if I were to meet her over breakfast I'd be faced with a lot of questions, so I made for the back of the house and the kitchen area. As I'd hoped, Bridget was there, superintending breakfast trays. She broke off work and took me through to her own room, requesting coffee to be sent through to us.

'How's the dancing lady this morning?'

'Better, I think, but she was badly shocked. Tell me, have you thought at all about how that blood got into the bath?'

'That terrible man, I suppose, Mr Sylvan.'

'But where would he get the blood? Even assuming it was animal blood, not human, he'd have had to get it somewhere.'

'Raw steak. He had it for dinner.'

'Is there that much blood in even a large portion of steak tartare? Besides, he was eating it. Did anybody ask the cook for animal blood yesterday evening?'

'I'm sure not. I'd have heard about it straightaway.'

'Would you mind asking her?'

She was away about a minute.

'Cook says no, and she wouldn't have let them have it in any case.'

'So whoever put it in the bath must have brought it from outside. What sort of person turns up as a house guest with a pint of blood in his luggage? Or hers.'

I was wondering about Elsie Wetherby. She was determined to keep Oriana away from her protégé and might have been capable of this gesture as a warning. She struck me as a resourceful woman, but she hadn't known until the last minute that she'd be spending the night at Jack Belter's house. No chance to slip off to an abattoir.

'Did Mr Belter come home last night?'

Bridget gave me a surprised look. She thought I was changing the subject.

'No. He must have decided to stay in town.'

'What about Henry Henson?'

'He has his own flat in London. He only stays here overnight if Mr Belter needs him for foreign telegrams or so on.'

So Henry Henson would know the house well, certainly well enough to come up the back stairs. I was starting to ask her about the routine of pouring baths, whether the maids did it and so on, when there was a knock on Bridget's door and the butler's voice from outside.

'Mrs B, do you know where Miss Bray is? Mr Belter wants her on the telephone.'

The butler led me to a small lounge near the dining room where there was a telephone set on a table. As soon as he handed me the earpiece, Jack Belter's impatient voice leapt out of it.

'Well, have you talked to her?'

'Yes, quite a lot.'

'You don't need to shout. It's a good line. Any progress?'

'I think so, possibly.'

'All right, I'll be down in two hours. Don't do anything else until you've discussed it with me.'

That was it. The line went dead and I was left holding the apparatus and reflecting on the inherent discourtesy of the telephone as a means of communication.

I went back to Bridget's room for coffee and toast and to warn her that Mr Belter was on his way, then went back upstairs with the idea of returning Oriana's nightdress and mink coat.

The door of Oriana's room was open and a maid was inside, tidying stockings, underwear, spilt face powder. The lady had gone out, she said.

On the staircase on the way down, I passed Leon Sylvan coming up. Green brocade waistcoat this morning, pale green stock with a gold pin topped with malachite. He bowed in a sarcastic way and I asked him where Miss Paphos was. 'Practising in the small music room. She will need a pianist.'

I walked along the downstairs corridors, past more maids cleaning, and asked one of them the way to the small music room.

There was no sound coming from inside. I tapped on the door and opened it and there was Oriana sitting in the middle of the polished wood floor, one leg extended out to the side, the heel of it cupped in her hand. Her legs and feet were bare and she was wearing a loose tunic in what looked like white cashmere, her dark hair done up in a chignon. She glanced over her shoulder when the door opened, first alarmed then relieved.

'I am ready for my music. You will send somebody?'

I said yes. 'And about what we were discussing last night ...'

She stretched out an imperious white arm. As she was still holding her heel in the other hand, that in itself struck me as an athletic achievement.

'I am making a dance. I do not think about other things when I am making a dance.'

237

The French accent was back—perhaps she'd borrowed it from some dancing teacher in the distant past—but she meant what she said. Up to that point I'd assumed that her dancing was no more than a convenient cover for her real interests, men and money, but in her dance clothes there was an unmistakeable seriousness about her.

I closed the door and went along to the ballroom to find the orchestra had just arrived. Luckily Madoc was more than happy to let Oriana have the rehearsal pianist all day as long as it kept her out of his way. He said she disturbed the concentration of his orchestra. From his sidelong glance at Elsie Wetherby, I guessed that it wasn't only the orchestra's reaction that worried him.

Once I'd seen the pianist on his way, I looked for Bernard. He was on his own, carefully unwrapping his viola, so preoccupied that he jumped when I came up to him.

'Hello, Nell. I've brought the mail from home. The cats are well.'

I wondered why I should be so grateful for this touch of normality, grateful enough to want to hug him as he handed over my routine mail. I didn't, of course.

We talked about Madoc and the singers

and how rehearsals were going. Well, it seemed, with remarkably little panic about the dress rehearsal the next day. He asked how Miss Paphos was in a tone of voice that suggested that he at any rate was immune to her. 'There are some odd rumours going round the orchestra about that one. Did you know a man killed himself over her?'

It was obvious that Elsie Wetherby had been spreading the word. I replied noncommittally that I'd heard something about it, and asked if he'd had a chance to make any more inquiries about the player who thought he'd remembered Sylvan from a long way in the past.

'Yes, I have. In fact, when the Paphos woman came in yesterday, he remembered her too. It's quite a sordid little story in its way.'

'He remembered Oriana Paphos?'

'Yes, only she wasn't called Oriana Paphos then. This was ten years ago and they were Princess Lotus and the Priest of the Nile.'

'Where?'

'Music halls. It was around the Birmingham and Wolverhampton area, only minor halls. I gather the act wasn't quite respectable, not the sort of thing you'd take your wife to. This man in the second violins was no more than a boy then,

239

hardly out of school and taking any work he could get to pay for music lessons. He had a friend in the band a few years older who fell heavily for Princess Lotus and his ardour was apparently, um, requited, so to speak.'

'You mean they became lovers?'

'Yes. For a while all goes as well as it could in the circumstances, then one night this Sylvan character, or Priest of the Nile, makes it clear that the pair of them expect some financial contribution from him. In other words, the lady wanted paying. Well, naturally the young man had no money or he wouldn't have been playing in flea pits. So Sylvan informs him that in that case he'll just have to let the young man's father know about it. As luck would have it, the father was a vicar. You can probably guess what happened next.'

'Tell me.'

'The young man steals the takings from the place where they're all working, gets found out and does six months in prison while the Princess of the Nile takes up with a rich businessman. More or less wrecked this young man's life. According to the man I was talking to, the last he saw of him he was still scraping a living in the lower sort of music hall and killing himself with drink.'

'While Oriana and Sylvan are swanning

round Europe in luxury. I wonder what took her from being Princess Lotus in Wolverhampton to being the height of fashion.'

'That's not difficult to guess, is it?'

'Yes. Plenty of women have started out like her and ended in the gutter.'

'Sylvan, then. He looks like a shrewd man as well as a nasty one.'

There too, though I couldn't say it to Bernard, it was a big step from blackmailing vicar's sons to stealing Cabinet secrets.

'Thanks for what you've done. I wonder if you could find out where this man they ruined was living or working last. It might be interesting to talk to him.'

He said he'd try, but there was clearly something else on his mind.

'Bobbie came round again late last night.'

He said it in an embarrassed way, plucking a string of his viola, turning a peg.

'Oh yes.'

'She was looking for you.'

I almost said 'oh yes' again but it would have been in a different tone of voice. I held it back.

'I think she might be coming down to see you later.'

'Bobbie, down here! Why?'

'I think she wants to talk to you about something.'

My pleasure at seeing him disappeared. I was sore at the way they were treating me, like some awkward rock that needed careful navigation to get round, and it was a relief when Madoc called the musicians to their places.

In the middle of the morning's rehearsal, an anxious face wearing spectacles looked round the door and Henry Henson beckoned to me.

'Mr Belter wants to speak to you.'

I followed him across the terrace towards the main part of the house. I presumed that he'd just arrived in the motor car from London with his employer but it struck me that he didn't look quite as sleek as when I'd seen him in the office. The heels of his shoes were muddy; there was a light scattering of dandruff on the shoulders of his jacket; and his shirt collar looked wilted. In cold weather like this, that must mean yesterday's shirt, and yet I was prepared to bet that such an orderly man would keep a drawerful of clean shirts at home. Therefore, Henry Henson hadn't been home since the day before.

As he stood aside for me to go into the house, I said, 'You've been up all night, haven't you?'

He looked at me. There was a foggy desperation in his eyes and even from several steps away I could feel a sick heat radiating from him. Perhaps there hadn't been a woman in his life before Oriana so she'd got into his unvaccinated blood like a fever. He didn't reply but held the door open for me like the polite man he was, even in this state.

There was a long smear of blood on his white cuff. He might have cut himself shaving but he didn't look as if he'd shaved that morning. Anyway, Henson would shave in his dressing gown and then put his shirt on. I followed him into the house and up three flights of carpeted stairs to the top floor where I hadn't been before.

He knocked on a door and opened it on to a room that reminded me of a university don's—bookcases everywhere, leather armchairs, a feeling of male comfort. Jack Belter was standing beside a big window looking out on the river, flowers and a telegraph machine on the table beside him.

As soon as Henson had closed the door and we were left alone he said, 'It seems I must congratulate you, Miss Bray. There's one thing that puzzles me. Where did you get all that blood?'

He was smiling and yet there was a

concentrated, almost fierce look under the smile.

'You think I put the blood in her bath?'

'I've just been hearing about it from Bridget. You scare the woman into hysterics then spend the night with her to protect her. I'm supposed to be a ruthless man but I really couldn't have done better myself.'

'I didn't do it.'

He raised his eyebrows. 'You're refusing to take the credit?'

I decided to say nothing about the smear of blood on Henry Henson's cuff.

'Oriana herself is convinced it was Sylvan trying to scare her.'

I gave him a full account of what she'd said, leaving out only the fact that I now knew who'd written the letters. When I got to the part about the note written in blood he practically jumped out of the chair.

'She told you that Laurie left a note saying he loved her?'

'That he loved somebody, presumably meaning her.'

'It's a lie. Or if there was a note, one of those two wrote it.'

'That wouldn't make sense. After all, the whole point of that would be to make it look like suicide. Why go to that trouble and take the note away before the police could find it?'

'It never existed then.'

'According to Oriana, it was written on the back of a page from those letters. She says Laurie Gilbey knew about them and discussed them with her. At least she's not denying they exist or that Sylvan stole them.'

'Where are they now?'

'She thinks Sylvan's still got them, but she doesn't seem very concerned. At any rate, I've tried to open the bidding on your behalf.'

He seemed less pleased than I'd expected. I guessed that there was enough vanity in him to resent the possibility that Lloyd George's tactics were working.

'She's just stringing you along. If I were to hand over money, we'd find that what I've bought is a pup.'

'Suppose you were to offer her a lot of money for the sight of just one of those letters. That would at least test whether they've still got them.' While he was thinking about that I said, 'Incidentally, you might have told me that those letters were written by the Prime Minister himself.'

His eyebrows went up and he grinned. 'I told our friend we wouldn't be able to keep it from you.'

I hadn't expected him to be so amused about it, but then I remembered that he was a journalist and not a politician.

'So do we make her an offer? You've nothing to lose. If she can't produce at least one of the letters, you don't pay her anything.'

'Yes.'

'It might help if you could offer to protect her in some way from Sylvan. She seems to be genuinely scared of him.'

'There isn't a genuine bone in her body. You realise that you're proposing we offer our protection to a murderess?'

'I'm not convinced she had anything to do with killing Laurie Gilbey.'

His eyebrows shot up again. 'Don't tell me you're falling in love with the woman as well.'

'Hardly. But it would be possible to check her dancing engagement for that evening. Her story is that she came home with Sylvan and saw Gilbey dead in the bath. She can't have been dancing at a house near Regent's Park and slitting his wrists in Mayfair at the same time.'

'She wouldn't need to. She gives poor Gilbey something to drug him, goes off and does her cavorting while Sylvan comes back, dumps him in the bath and slits his wrists.' He shook his head. 'In any case, that's not our job, is it? It's not a question

246

of whether she's a murderess, just whether she's a murderess we can do business with. You think she is.'

'I think it's the best chance we have.'

He sat staring at me, biting a knuckle. His uncertainty lasted seconds then: 'All right, play it your way. Tell her that for the sight of one of those letters she can have a thousand pounds in cash in her hand. If she needs to go up to London or back to Paris to get it, go with her. Take Henson too. I'll leave him with you.'

'What about her dance?'

'Oh, to hell with her dance. I'll get a Gaiety Girl in.'

He seemed exhilarated from the speed of his own decision making, his power to move people and money around. There was a boyish quality about it that stopped me from resenting taking orders as much as I usually did. After all, I'd had my way. He was chuckling to himself as he got up to show me out.

'If you see young Henson, send him up to me. I might even forgive him for those sables—after I've made him sweat a bit.'

I didn't tell him that Henson had been sweating enough already, for a different reason.

Speaking to Oriana turned out to be more difficult than I expected. Salome's dance

247

was being played on the piano as I walked along the corridor to the music room and when I opened the door she was standing in the middle of the floor, moving her body like seaweed in a slow current. She gave no sign of knowing that I was there so I tiptoed to a sofa by the wall and sat down. When the piece ended she nodded to the pianist and he started it all over again. By the end of it her arms were beginning to move, apparently in spontaneous response to the music. Another nod and it started yet again. The pianist had loosened his collar and tie and was already looking wilted, but it was clear that Oriana wasn't stopping for anybody.

I looked in at various points through the day, between sitting in on the other rehearsal in the ballroom and the situation was much the same every time, except that Oriana's movements were becoming more spacious and the pianist closer to exhaustion.

It was six o'clock and dark outside when I tried for the final time. In the ballroom they'd finished off the John the Baptist and got to the most testing scene for Elsie Wetherby, the long passage where she's gloating over his severed head. At dress rehearsal and in performance, Oriana would mime while Elsie sang, but at this stage, singer and conductor had serious work to do and didn't need her. As I slipped out of the side door and walked across the terrace, Elsie's voice came after me, singing the same phrase time after time.

'In the whole world there was nothing so red as thy mouth.'

Inside the house I listened for the sound of the piano playing Salome's dance, but it was quiet at last. In spite of that, I decided to check the music room. There was no answer when I knocked, but I thought I heard a movement inside. When I pushed the door open there was just one light on at the piano, the rest of the room in shadow with the curtains undrawn. There was a warm smell of sweat in the air. Then I saw them, all three of them at once.

On the sofa against the wall two people were twined together. The third wasn't in the room at all. He was standing there, just outside the window to one side of the sofa. His feet must have been on a path or a flowerbed. His dark suit merged in with the night sky so that all you could see of him was a face. It was a round, pale face with a dark circle for a mouth and two staring eyes in spectacles. The expression on it was shock and a kind of struggle, as if trying to register something for which the face hadn't been designed.

Before the two people on the sofa were

aware of me, the staring eyes refocused. The head gave me one horrified glance then ducked away from the window and into the darkness. I must have made some sound because there was shuffling on the sofa then one of the figures on it jumped up, cannoned into me, swerved sideways and made for the door as if running for his life, sliding on the polished wood in stockinged feet. The door banged shut behind him. I staggered and almost fell, but when hit by somebody of John Bartholomew's height and weight, that was hardly surprising. When I got my balance, I found the electric switch by the door and put on the main light.

'Did you want something?' asked Oriana.

She was still lying along the sofa in her Greek tunic, making no attempt to move. Her chignon was coming down but she looked drowsily happy, as if she'd just got up from a sound sleep instead of dancing all day. Or most of the day. John Bartholomew's discarded jacket was draped over an arm of the sofa, like the skin of a trophy, and his tie writhing in loops on the floor.

'Did you know somebody was watching you through the window?'

That scared her. 'Now?'

'Yes.'

'Who? Sylvan?'

'No. Henry Henson.'

'Who?' She seemed genuinely puzzled.

'Oh, for goodness' sake, Jack Belter's secretary, the one who came to collect you in Paris.'

'Oh, *him.*'

The drowsy smile came back to her face, not worried now. I was almost as staggered mentally by her lack of embarrassment as physically by young John Bartholomew's excess of it. Trying to get my balance, I asked if her dance had gone well.

'I think it is growing.'

Time to get to the subject, though I'd seldom been in less likely circumstances for talking business.

'Remember what we were talking about last night?' A guarded look came over her face. 'The person I mentioned is prepared to pay a thousand pounds to you personally if you can let him see one of those letters. That would just be the start of negotiations.'

'I have my dance to think about. It is like a baby growing inside you. You must be full of love and think of nothing else.'

She stared at me with great soft eyes, turned passive as a sitting hen again, and just as hard to shift.

'When can you think of anything else?'

'After my dance tomorrow, if it goes well.'

She stood up, paced over to the piano, heavy-limbed with tiredness and satisfaction, and wrapped herself in a long velvet cloak. 'I want a bath now. You will come and see it's all right?'

No blood, she meant. I went up with her, waited in her bedroom while she ran the bath then, at her urgent request, waited some more until she came out draped in purple velvet, smelling of lily of the valley, and settled on the couch. She was more than half asleep by then and didn't protest when I said I was going. I'd remembered that John Bartholomew's jacket, shoes and tie were still in the music room and doubted whether he'd have the presence of mind to retrieve them.

I was on my way there when I met Bridget walking along the corridor with both garments folded over her arm, the shoes in her hand and a quizzical look in her eyes. 'Would these happen to belong to any of your musical people, Miss Bray?'

'Yes, thank you.'

I took them from her just as Elsie Wetherby came round the corner in a hurry. Her face was flushed and she'd probably just come in from rehearsal.

'Has anybody seen John?'

I managed to tuck shoes, tie and jacket behind my back before she saw what they were. 'I think he may be in his room,' I said. 'I'm on my way up. Shall I tell him you want him?'

'What's he doing up there? Would you tell him Mr Madoc wants to see him about tomorrow?'

She went striding off and I breathed a sigh of relief. Bridget hadn't missed anything.

'Was your John the Baptist doing some barefoot dancing too? I didn't know the prophets went in for it.'

John Bartholomew's room was next door to mine. I tapped on the door, delivered Elsie's message and heard a scared and miserable acknowledgement from inside. 'I'm putting your shoes down here.'

I put the jacket and tie beside them and went hurriedly back downstairs to spare his blushes.

The grandfather clock in the hall struck seven. Bridget put her head round the door.

'Are your men doing the scenery going to want feeding?'

I'd forgotten that a gang of men would be working in the ballroom late into the night, putting up scenery for the next day's dress rehearsal, and that they were nominally my responsibility. Bridget took over as usual.

'Would tea and sandwiches every two

hours be about right?'

'Just right, I should think. I'll go and see how they're doing.' It was a dark night, not quite raining but the air full of damp and the smell of the Thames over everything. A noise of sawing and hammering came from the ballroom with slabs of electric light falling on the lawn from the uncurtained windows.

'Nell, is that you?'

A voice from the darkness, Bernard's voice. He came towards me into the patch of light, wearing his trilby hat and dark overcoat.

'I thought you'd have gone home by now.'

'I waited. I wanted to talk to you when the others weren't here. You look cold. You should be wearing your hat and coat.'

I started telling him not to worry about that but he unbuttoned his coat and draped it round my shoulders.

'I don't need it.'

We walked up and down the lawn with the sound of the river swollen with rain quite close to us, in and out of the rectangles of light. Though I'd said I didn't need it, his coat felt heavy and comforting round my shoulders. After the complications of the day, I wished we could go on walking like that in silence for a while, but of course he wanted to talk.

'Bobbie's worried. I know I shouldn't ask, but it's something to do with the Movement, isn't it? She's pretty deeply into what's going on.'

'We both are.'

'That night when you and she came in late and she was soaked through—I didn't ask then, but I asked her when she came this morning. She told me.'

That was a shock. If Bobbie had told him, a supporter on the fringes, something that belonged to the inner councils of the WSPU, she must be much deeper in than I'd expected. I'd thought that poor Bernard's case with Bobbie must be hopeless, but it seemed I was wrong, as I tended to be with affairs of the heart. Perhaps it wasn't poor Bernard after all. Poor who then? Bobbie? Did there have to be a victim? Shouldn't I just be feeling pleased for the pair of them?

'What exactly did Bobbie tell you?'

'That she's afraid there's a spy in the Movement and you were helping to find her. That was what you were doing the night she went in the pond.'

So she really had told him, and in some detail.

'And then, you see, you went away and got involved with this. She can't understand what you're doing, Nell.'

'She doesn't have to.'

'I don't expect you to tell me everything, or anything if you don't want to, but I don't like to see you or Bobbie getting into danger. Is there anything at all I can do?'

'Nothing.'

We were in one of the light patches. He looked at me.

'I owe so much to you, giving me a roof over my head, introducing me to Madoc and so on.'

'You don't have to be grateful, you know.'

All that apology in his voice. Why couldn't he say it out straight: Nell, I'm in love with your friend. You don't mind, do you?

'But I am grateful, you know that.'

'Right, you're grateful and I'm grateful to you for telling me. Now, you'd better take your coat back. Are you walking to the station?'

I took it off and pushed it at him. I felt cold now, in a way that I hadn't before he put it on me. Instead of wearing it, he folded it over his arm. No sense. Now we were both cold.

'As a matter of fact, I don't think I'll go back to London tonight. I'll get a room at a pub in the town. Madoc wants us here early tomorrow.'

And Bobbie was coming here tonight.

'Just as you like. See you tomorrow, then.'

I left him standing there and walked towards the lights and the noise of hammering.

Chapter Fourteen

Inside the ballroom, scene shifters were hoisting the backcloth. Even Jack Belter's money didn't run to three-dimensional scenery for only one performance but the painter had done a fine job with the columns of Herod's palace, date palms, white peacocks and a pale full moon. To the left of it was a screen painted with blocks of stone for John Bartholomew to sing behind as the Baptist. I found the foreman, reassured him about refreshments and lingered for a while, watching the team work.

'Up a bit to the left.'

'Hold on, it's tangled round the hook. Give me some slack. Is that better?'

The question was addressed to a man standing with his back to me, trim in shirtsleeves and waistcoat. He stepped back to judge, caught his foot on a stray offcut of wood and stumbled, half turning as he tried to get his balance.

'All right now.'

As he turned, I got a glimpse of his face; surprisingly authoritative for a scene-shifter and no youngster either. His brow was creased into more lines than seemed likely for such unambitious work. I took a few steps so that I could see him full face. His eyes caught mine, registered, looked away.

'Bit of a wrinkle bottom right. Yes, that's got it.'

I waited, seething, until I could get him on his own while the rest of the men were occupied with something on the platform. He didn't try to avoid me but looked a little apprehensive as I walked up to him.

'Well, Inspector Merit, what brings you here?'

The sad protruding eyes looked into mine. 'The course of duty, as ever, Miss Bray.'

'And I suppose the course of duty is checking on what I'm doing.'

Didn't anybody trust me? I'd not the slightest doubt that he'd been sent there by Lloyd George as a reminder that I must keep to the bargain. It was very unlikely that he'd know what it was really about. Levers must have been pulled very high up in the Home Office and a long way down Scotland Yard. I could imagine the briefing he'd been given. That Miss Bray of yours, getting mixed up in some rum opera production. No telling what she's doing. Just get down there, keep an eye on her and report back. But, of course, there was no need for him to report back. Lloyd George would know through his friend Jack Belter all that was going on, far above the head of a mere Scotland Yard inspector. Merit might not know it, but he was there for no other purpose than to keep me worried.

'I'm not about to blow up Mr Belter's house, you know.'

'I'm sure you're not.'

His air of melancholy was always his strongest weapon, as if burdened with problems that I could solve for him if I chose. I didn't choose.

'Inspector, I have, on this occasion at least, committed no crime. I am here by invitation as a free citizen and I've done nothing whatsoever to earn the attention of Scotland Yard. I'd be very much obliged if you and whoever sent you would simply leave me alone to get on with my work.'

A call from the men on the platform. 'Anything wrong, Charlie?'

They thought one of their team was getting a dressing down from me and were protective. Was Charlie his real name?

'Nothing wrong. Just coming.' He hesitated for a moment then, speaking with great emphasis, 'Miss Bray, I shall be here all night and every day until Saturday. I'd like you to think that if you needed any help you could come and ask me.'

He turned and walked over to join the rest of the men while I was still reeling from the cheek of it. They landed me in this situation and set a police spy on me who talked about helping.

Fuming, I went back into the house intending to have it out with Jack Belter but was thwarted in that because he was still in London.

As I was sitting down to dinner with Bridget and the butler the next annoyance arrived. There was a long and imperious ring at the front door. The butler went to attend to it and came back smartly.

'A Miss Fieldfare asking for Miss Bray.'

Any other person might have felt some hesitation about intruding uninvited into somebody else's home. Not Bobbie Fieldfare. The butler had put her in the small front lounge and when I came in she was standing glaring at one of Jack Belter's bright new Constables, still with her coat and hat on.

'What a ghastly vulgar place. You'd think with all his money he could at least afford some good pictures.'

260

'There are worse things than vulgarity. At least he pays for what he wants and doesn't waste time being apologetic about it.'

Bobbie stared at me. 'Is anything wrong, Nell? You are acting in a most peculiar way these days.'

'Isn't everybody?'

I felt tired, but Bobbie looked even worse. Her coat was mud-splattered; her hat looked as if something heavy had trodden on it; and there were dark rings round her eyes.

'I suppose you've come about the spy hunt. Are there any developments?'

'I'm not sure. Yes, I have come to ask you something.'

'Sit down at least.'

She sat reluctantly then, untypically for Bobbie, seemed to be struggling for words.

'It's not easy to ask this.'

'Go on. Ask away.'

She took a deep breath. 'You know that night at Walton Heath—you guessed we were going and went there.'

'Yes, and I told you how I knew.'

'Did you mention it to anybody else, after you left the office?'

I stared at her, while the significance of it sank in.

'Are you by any chance asking me if I informed the police?'

'I know you wouldn't do it directly. But you do know some police officers and you do disapprove of the arson campaign. If you'd mentioned it to one of them you thought you could trust and he'd—'

I'd never seen her look so ill at ease and I suppose I should have pitied her, but for the black anger that was rising up inside me. 'So you've come all the way down here at night to ask me if I'm a police informer, is that it?'

'No, Nell. Really no. But this could destroy us if I don't settle it. I've got to ask everybody, however much I hate it. You'd do the same.'

And had done, with June. She hadn't resented it and I shouldn't, but then I'd been in the Movement since June was at school and Bobble riding hunters over her aunt's estate.

'All right. It's a fair question and here's the answer. I went to see Max Blume; I went home; I went to Walton Heath. I didn't tell anybody. And before you ask, I didn't tell anybody about the Albert Memorial business either.'

She took a deep breath. 'Thank you. It's what I thought. At least it eliminates one other thing.'

'Leaving?'

'Leaving something I'd rather not talk about at the moment, until I'm sure.'

'I see.'

She believed me, and yet I wasn't trusted, not one of the inner circle any more. Now I'd suppressed my anger enough to start thinking again an idea had come to me and I at least owed it to her to discuss it.

'June's friend Gwen talked about a gentleman who bought some of her bookmarks and so on. If you haven't asked her for a description of him yet, you might do it and let me know.'

Before all this started, the possibility of Inspector Merit posing as a suffragette sympathiser wouldn't have occurred to me, but then I hadn't expected him to go in for scene-shifting either. Bobbie gave me an odd look.

'Who?'

'No sense in putting a name to it. He wouldn't have used his own, would he?'

I asked if she'd like me to get her some coffee before she went and she said no thank you, but made no move to go.

'Nell, how long are you going to stay here?'

'Not much longer, I hope. No later than Saturday, at any rate. That's when the performance is.'

'I don't suppose you're going to tell me what you're really doing here?'

When it all started I'd been tempted,

very tempted, to tell Bobbie in spite of my promise to Lloyd George. Not now. She didn't trust me. I shook my head.

'I see.' She started buttoning her coat, turned towards the door then, impulsively, turned round again. 'Nell, I wish you were back with us properly. Terrible things are going to happen. You know the word's round London that the Government are planning something worse to use against us.'

'Worse than Holloway and forcible feeding?'

'Yes. We don't know what it is, but there's going to be some new law. And if Mrs Pankhurst goes to prison again and dies there—I don't know what will happen.'

'I haven't gone away. Not really.'

'Oh!' A groan of anger and frustration. 'Why aren't things simple any more?'

I couldn't answer that. I asked instead if she'd seen Bernard on her way up from the station. She looked away.

'Why should I?'

'He said he was staying here tonight. I thought you might have arranged to meet him.'

'Oh.' Quite a different tone this time then, still turned away, 'You like him, don't you, Nell?'

'I like a lot of people.' (What was I

supposed to say? 'Bless you, my children'?)

'I suppose I'd better go.'

Now that she knew he was somewhere in town she was suddenly anxious to get away. I took her to the front door, opened it and closed it behind her. There were no lights on the road back to the bridge and the rain had started but she'd find her way. Bobbie always did.

I didn't fancy finishing dinner so I went up to the first floor and knocked on Oriana's door. It was opened by Leon Sylvan, brandy glass in hand. In the room behind him, Oriana was sitting on a sofa in her purple velvet gown with her feet tucked up and her hair down. In spite of that I had the impression that I'd interrupted a business conference.

'What do you want?'

I told him I'd come to see if Oriana needed anything.

'She wants nothing.'

I looked at her to see if she wanted rescuing from him, but she gave no sign. He stood back to let me come a little way into the room and closed the door.

'Miss Paphos has been telling me about Mr Belter's kind offer. You should know you're wasting your time. We haven't got those letters. Except for one.'

The voice was mocking but the eyes

staring into mine from a few inches away were like marbles.

'Which one is that?'

He slid a hand into the pocket of his smoking jacket and produced a small leather folder. I took it, aware of his strange eyes on me, and found a folded sheet of white paper inside. On one side it was an ordinary-looking letter in firm, forward-sloping handwriting that I had no chance to read because I was distracted by the other side. The firm handwriting covered only a few lines of it and the rest had been blank. Over the blank three-quarters of the page, three words were scrawled in another style, big broad strokes: I LOVE YOU. They were rusty brown in colour and a little raised and crusty at the edges.

Before I could see any more he twitched it back from me and the leather folder fell to the floor.

'Is that the letter you found by Gilbey's body?'

'It is.'

'Why didn't you leave it for the police to see?'

He glanced over his shoulder towards Oriana. 'Because she didn't want me to.'

'Where are the rest of the letters?'

A shrug. 'Who knows?'

'Did Laurence Gilbey have them?'

'All I know is that they're not in my hands. Now, if you'll excuse us, Miss Paphos is tired.'

She was still tucked up on the sofa, staring at us. There was a long silence until, as I turned to go, he said, 'And if you were thinking of searching my room, please take care not to crease my cravats.'

I slept badly. My thoughts kept trampling round the same dreary circuit, like the exercise yard in Holloway—Emmeline, Lloyd George, Bobbie, Bernard—and why I was so annoyed with the four of them. Occasionally the wrinkled and worried face of Inspector Merit added itself to the circuit.

I got up when I heard the maids moving about in the corridor, washed and dressed. Outside the bathroom window the sky was still dark grey but my watch told me it was half past six. I put on my hat and coat, went downstairs and out of the back door, needing to clear my head from the bad-tempered fuzziness of the night. There was just enough light outside to find my way across the lawn to the little bridge over the creek. I stood on it watching a pair of swans paddling against the rushing water, getting nowhere. Faint sounds of hammering were still coming from the ballroom and the lights were on. I supposed Merit, along with the rest of them, had been working all night.

Back at the house, the breakfast room was deserted but there were already pots of tea and coffee on the table and silver-covered dishes on warming stands. As I was pouring coffee Bridget came in looking worried.

'Miss Bray, have you seen Mr Henson?'

'Not since yesterday.'

And then only as an open-mouthed face at a window, although I didn't say that.

'Mr Belter's back and looking for him. He's not in his room and his bed hasn't been slept in.'

I asked if she wanted me to help look for him, but she said to get on with my breakfast, he'd probably turn up. By the time I'd finished my toast, Elsie Wetherby and John Bartholomew came in together. Luckily, like a good professional, she had her mind on the night's dress rehearsal and only wanted to talk about that. Had Mr Belter invited any critics down from London? Would I make sure the costumier let out her bodice? If she had to sing in it as tight as it was it would split open the first time she took a deep breath—'...

and I leave that kind of thing to Miss Paphos.'

John looked pitifully nervous, like a schoolboy caught scrumping apples. He jumped and gave me a look when Elsie's back was turned that asked whether I'd told her. I tried to signal back that I hadn't and didn't intend to, while Elsie piled up her plate.

'These devilled kidneys are very good, John, and you should have some of the sausages. On dress-rehearsal days you must always make sure to eat a really good breakfast.'

He slithered a fried egg on to his plate and sat there staring at it miserably, as if he expected it to rise up and denounce him. Since my presence might have been making things worse for him, I gulped down my coffee and went out, to be intercepted by Jack Belter in the hall.

'Miss Bray, a word.' He drew me into the small lounge. 'We can't find Henson. Apparently nobody's seen him since yesterday.'

'Perhaps he's gone home.'

'No, I told him he was to stay here last night in case you needed him. In any case, he has a telephone in his flat and he's not answering. When did you last see him?'

'Early yesterday evening.'

Belter took a deep breath. 'Did you say anything to him?'

'No.'

A dilemma. In the ordinary course of events, what had happened to Henson was too humiliating to pass on to his employer, but Belter had lost one man already and had reason to be worried.

'You hadn't told him to do anything stupid, like searching Sylvan's room for instance?'

'No.'

'Damn, damn, damn.' He looked out of the window. It was light now, but the sky was grey. One of his motors was parked on the gravel sweep by the front steps with chauffeur in attendance.

'Perhaps he's simply gone off to lick his wounds. It would be natural enough.'

'Wounds? What are you talking about?'

'To his self-esteem. He meets a woman of very powerful sexual attraction, buys her furs and flowers ...'

'On my money.'

'... and, incredibly, finds that she is attracted to him. Which she probably was for a couple of days when there was nobody else available.'

'You know, when it comes to sheer cold-bloodedness, I think you women beat men every time.'

I wasn't sure whether he meant Oriana

or me, so I let that pass.

'He escorts her back here, only to find that she simply blots him out of her mind.'

He said nothing for a while, looking at me, then, 'There's something you're not telling me. What is it?'

'Yes, I'm afraid there is. Yesterday evening he saw Oriana Paphos in what you might call intimate circumstances with another man.'

'Well, I'll be damned. That singer fellow?'

'It doesn't matter who it was. The fact is any man would find that humiliating, especially a man like Mr Henson.'

'The silly fool.'

'Well, it was you who sent him to Paris to bring her back.'

'What do you mean? I didn't tell him to fall for the woman.' He barked it at me, really angry.

'You might have guessed it would happen. Putting him into contact with her was like giving brandy to a teetotaller.'

'Did I ask him to fall for her? After what happened to poor Laurie, it was the last thing in the world I wanted. Surely you can see that.' Distress as well as anger in his voice.

'But it's not the same, is it? Laurie was much more immediately involved than Henry Henson, unless there's something

271

you're not telling me.'

He shook his head. 'No. I wasn't risking having that happen again. That's one of the reasons we brought you in.'

'I think you may be worrying unnecessarily about Henry Henson. If I'm right, he's realised that it's all over with Oriana, that he's made a bit of a fool of himself, but he can't stand being around while she's here. By Monday he'll probably be reporting for work as usual, quite his old self.' Having in the meantime gone through hells of jealousy, fury, self-reproach—but that was Henson's business and nobody else's. 'Then in six months' time or so he'll find some nice sensible young woman to marry and you can send a cheque to their wedding.' Signed, probably by then, Sir John Belter or Lord Whatsit. Perhaps that occurred to him too, because he cheered up a little.

'I hope you're right, Miss Bray. Anyway, to our business. I'll be back for the dress rehearsal tonight, starting at six o'clock sharp. Dinner will be at nine, so you'd better tell the conductor fellow not to hang about.'

A message I decided not to pass on. Ten minutes later he left for the office, with a spattering of gravel and a toot on the horn. He was driving himself, the chauffeur sitting stiff-faced beside him.

Chapter Fifteen

By six o'clock on Wednesday evening, when the tenor sang the opening line, *How beautiful is the Princess Salome tonight*, there was still no sign of Henry Henson. As a dress-rehearsal audience, there were just five of us to appreciate the efforts of a dozen singers and an orchestra of forty or more.

Jack Belter had returned from town a few minutes before, in a tetchy mood. I was puzzled that he was attending the dress rehearsal, as he'd made clear that even one performance was too many for his tastes, then saw the way he looked at Sylvan and understood. Having to tolerate Sylvan's presence in his house and being outfaced by him in front of the orchestra was an almost unendurable irritation to someone so used to having his own way. It hurt Belter not to be able to follow his instincts and throw him down the steps. The idea of Sylvan holding court unchecked at the rehearsal, possibly even giving orders, was too much for Belter to swallow. Rather a double helping of Strauss than that. So there they were, sitting only one chair away from each other, Leon Sylvan on one end of the short row, a friend of the conductor next to him, then Jack Belter. I sat next to Belter on the other side, along with Bridget who'd been co-opted as Oriana's dresser. The situation reminded me of the stories of mad King Ludwig of Bavaria, who'd commissioned his own private performances of Wagner opera. The difference was that Ludwig presumably enjoyed his Wagner, while Jack Belter took Strauss like a patient at a spa downing foul-tasting water on medical orders. By nature, he wasn't a man accustomed to sitting still and listening to other people. We'd got no further than the quarrel at King Herod's banquet before he was hissing at me from the side of his mouth, 'Is there much more of this?'

'Quite a lot.'

His 'Oh God!' brought glances from the singers and players not immediately engaged. Luckily, the sheer power of young John Bartholomew's voice, singing the Baptist, impressed him enough to keep him quiet for a while, then he started again.

'Why is he singing behind a screen?'

'He's supposed to be imprisoned in an underground cistern.'

'When do we get to the dance?'

'Not for an hour yet.'

'Oh God!'

I've sat next to children at pantomimes who've been less trouble. Leon Sylvan kept glancing at Belter and giving silent exasperated sighs, a man fallen among barbarians, which made Belter even worse. At one point he even asked me if we couldn't skip some of the singing and get on to the dance. Only my hissed assurance that if he tried anything of the kind Madoc would immediately walk out and there'd be no dance at all brought him to order. The infuriating thing was that it had the makings of a superb performance and I'd have given a lot just to be able to listen and enjoy. The reputation of Madoc and the novelty of being able to perform the opera nearly as the composer intended had brought together musicians who deserved better than this. When Elsie Wetherby, magisterial in blue velvet robes, sang, *I will dance for you, Tetrarch,*' Belter's sigh of relief was audible above the orchestra.

In a stage performance the action sweeps on with no interval, but that was impractical here. The platform was large enough to accommodate only the singers, with the orchestra at floor level in front. To make space for Salome to dance, the orchestra's seating would have to be reorganised. Madoc put his baton down; Bridget went to tell the maid to bring in the tea urns and to give Oriana any last minute help that was needed; and a group of workmen came in to shift chairs and music stands. Among them, with irritation, I recognised Inspector Merit. I was even more annoyed when he came up to me as I was drinking tea and talking to Bernard.

'Excuse me, miss, do you know which side the double basses are supposed to go?'

There was nothing in his manner to show that he'd seen me before, but Bernard gave me a startled look. He obviously recognised Merit from the time he came to collect me at the house and knew very well that this chair-shifter was a policeman. It was only as I crossed the floor with Merit that I realised the significance of this. Bernard had seen me talking with a police officer in disguise. Naturally, the next time he saw Bobbie, he'd mention that to her as a curiosity, nurturing that grain of suspicion in Bobbie's mind that Nell, of all people, might be the police informer. I stopped.

'Anything wrong, Miss Bray?'

'Yes. No. Oh damnation.'

I couldn't do what I wanted to do—go back to Bernard, explain. I couldn't explain without untying the whole cat's cradle. Anyway, I owed neither of them an explanation. I followed Merit over to a cluster of music stands, knowing it wasn't double basses he wanted to talk about. I was surprised, though, by his question.

'Did you know that foreign fellow, Sylvan, has been following you?'

'How do you know?'

'I've been watching all day. You've been dashing all over the house, but he's never far from where you are. Hadn't you noticed?'

'No, but I can't say I'm surprised. He thinks I'm a bad influence on Miss Paphos.'

'I think you should be careful, Miss Bray.' Now that we were out of hearing of the others he'd dropped the deferential tone.

'Careful of what, in particular?'

I was still annoyed with him for being there, even if it wasn't his fault. I was in a mood to be annoyed with everybody. He hesitated before replying.

'I wouldn't say this if I weren't concerned about you. I know we've been on opposite sides in the past and you probably think—'

'Oh for goodness' sake, if you've got anything to say to me, come out and say it.'

'Very well, then.' I'd annoyed him now. 'What I intended to say to you was you shouldn't trust people too easily. You're mixing with an odd lot and I don't like to think of you getting into trouble.'

He took my breath away. 'Trust people too easily? What do you mean?' As far as I could see, the problem of my present position was that I could hardly trust anyone at all. I wondered if he might be having an attack of prudery about the uncensored *Salome*. If so, the last thing I needed was a literary chaperon. From his face, he wished he'd never opened the subject and when one of the other men shouted to come over and help move the music stands he went without another word.

Before I could spend any more time wondering what he meant, Sylvan appeared at my elbow. 'Have you seen about the head?'

This question of the head of John the Baptist was one of the things that had me running about all day. We'd intended to use a plaster head of Goethe that had been standing in Jack Belter's library, probably wished on him by an interior decorator. As it would be covered with a red velvet cloth throughout the action, the identity didn't matter. But Oriana had objected. She'd tried at her private rehearsal in the music room and decided that Goethe simply wouldn't do. He was far too heavy. He'd tire her arms and cramp her movements. After some frenzied searching, Bridget and

I had discovered a wooden hat block in a wardrobe, presented it to her and heard with relief that it was acceptable. I explained this to Sylvan, who gave an Olympian nod.

'You will please make arrangements for Miss Paphos and me to return to the Savoy in Mr Belter's car after the performance on Saturday night.'

'I'm sure Mr Belter expects you to stay here for the night.'

'It's no matter what Mr Belter expects. Miss Paphos's contract ends as soon as the performance is over. And you will kindly keep away from her. You are unsettling her.'

'I thought you were the one doing the unsettling. If Miss Paphos herself asks me to keep away, of course I shall.'

Over his shoulder I could see Inspector Merit watching us in his sad way, a chair in each hand. Bridget came in. I heard her say to Madoc, 'She's ready.'

'Right, gentlemen, the dance, from the top. Can we have those teacups out of the way, please?'

Whatever I'd heard of Oriana Paphos before—or have heard since—there's one unarguable thing about her: she could dance. The day before, I'd seen, to my surprise, that she was completely serious about her art, but plenty of people are serious and still perform abysmally. As she came in with a dark cloak round her, then dropped it to reveal draperies that suggested a vestal virgin having second thoughts about her vocation, legs and feet bare, it was still in my mind that the experience was going to be embarrassing. She came to the space cleared for her like a sleepwalker. Madoc brought down his baton and the music began. For the first few bars she simply stood, eyes closed, so that it looked as if she'd been seized by stage fright. Then gradually her body began to sway as if the music itself were moving it. Her toes moved and arched and it was as if instead of sliding against the polished wood floor they were exploring cool sand. The toes seemed to like what they felt and so the arms began to rise in that seaweed movement I'd seen in the music room. It was like watching a body create itself. Unexpectedly, she made no attempt at a dance of seven veils. Not a veil in sight, only a more subtle series of revelations. Her feet, though finely arched, were much like any other feet, her knees like any other knees, and yet somehow she managed to make it seem as if nobody had looked at a foot arching or a knee bending before. My cynical friend had been right about her thighs. As the dance got wilder and her draperies flew you could see that they were on the brawny side and her raised arms were frankly plump, and yet that didn't matter. This is my arm. Look at it. Isn't this arm an amazing thing?

Surprised, I glanced round to see the effect on the others. Jack Belter was on the edge of his chair. The singers on their platform were fascinated. John Bartholomew's jaw had dropped open and stayed that way. Elsie Wetherby looked furious but couldn't take her eyes off Oriana. The audience had increased because the men who'd come in to move the chairs had stayed and were standing by the wall, Inspector Merit among them. It would be unfair to say that his eyes were protruding because they always were, but he was watching her with more than his usual sad intensity. Only Leon Sylvan, sitting beside Jack Belter, watched coldly and critically, hands folded on the silver knob of his walking cane.

The music came to its climax, ended. I'd always imagined Salome kneeling in front of Herod to claim her reward, but Oriana stayed on her feet, staring not at the singer playing Herod but at Jack Belter. I've given you what you wanted, now give me what I want. That was what her look said. Deliberately, in the silence, Jack Belter started clapping. It was echoed by one of the workmen then, gaining force, by some of the players in the orchestra. There shouldn't have been applause. In the opera, the action goes straight on, and Madoc looked disconcerted for once. He tapped his baton and the orchestra hurriedly stopped clapping and shuffled with music and instruments. Bridget came forward with Oriana's cloak, draped it round her and led her to a chair. Once the dance was over, the arrangement was that Oriana would sit beside the platform, until the time came for the climactic mime with the head of John the Baptist.

Now it was the turn of the singing Salome again, and Elsie Wetherby sang as if determined to eclipse the memory of Oriana's body. Salome demands her reward, *the head of Jokanaan*. In that charged atmosphere, the brutality of the request hit home. I heard Bridget gasp, although she must have known the story. Herod, appalled, offers her anything else she can name: the biggest emerald in the world, his white peacocks, the veil of the temple. *'Give me the head of Jokanaan.'* Herod gives in. Muted drum rolls, nervy little notes from the strings. An arm from behind the screen offers the head on a silver charger, covered on this occasion in a red velvet cloth. The oddity of the whole thing was increased because John

Bartholomew, his singing role over, was standing there at the side of the room in his rough Baptist robe, watching his own supposed head emerging. Oriana stood on cue, discarded her cloak again and walked forward to receive the head. *'Thou wouldst not suffer me to kiss thy mouth, Jokanaan. Well, I will kiss it now. I will bite it as one bites a ripe fruit.'*

Elsie's voice sang the words but most eyes were on Oriana's mulberry mouth and her bare white arms. John looked both fascinated and revolted, as if he'd have liked to turn away and couldn't. In the earlier rehearsals, work on the music had taken away the shock of it, but now the full charge of words and music was there, plus Oriana. *'In the whole world, there was nothing so red as thy mouth.'* She bent her arms, bringing the head closer, leaned her upper body towards it until lips and velvet were only inches apart. Either the wooden hat block was heavier than we'd thought or Oriana was tired because she was finding it a real burden, her arms sinking under the weight, her eyes glancing round for somebody to blame. Because of that, Bridget and I were both looking at the head closely. Bridget gasped. A heavy drop had fallen from under the red velvet cloth and splattered on the floor, then another. Bridget's eyes, horrified, probably mirrored mine. Nobody else seemed to have noticed it. Only a few bars to go now to Elsie's exultant *'I have kissed thy mouth, Jokanaan'* and Herod's *'Kill that woman'*.

We never got there. As Oriana's arms bent, the salver tilted and the red velvet cloth began to slide. Bridget gripped my arm, probably fearing the anticlimax of the hat block. Once it started, the thing went on sliding into Oriana's startled face and slithered between her arms. Then a loud exclamation from her, anger or disgust, and salver and head fell to the floor together in a tremendous clatter of metal. No thump of wood, though. The head landed with a wet, heavy sound. Flup. There were gasps from the singers. Madoc glanced over his shoulder, still conducting, and with perfect discipline the orchestra went on playing but nobody was taking any notice of them. All the attention was on the thing on the floor.

It lay there, round eyes staring, lips drawn back from yellowed teeth, surrounded by the sticky red drops that had been shaken out as it fell. A fleecy head. A sheep's head. It had landed upright so that it looked as if the rest of the animal should still be attached to it under the floor. Some of the red stickiness had got on to Oriana's white draperies and she started ripping and tearing at the material.

Jack Belter, Bridget and I were on our feet. Bridget grabbed Oriana's cloak, and she and I bundled her into it. Her body was stiff with disgust or anger. Jack Belter's voice, loud above the music, demanded to know what was going on. Then, even louder, the sound of male laughter. It came from John Bartholomew. His face was red, his eyes screwed up and he stood there howling with laughter as loudly as he'd sung the Baptist's denunciations a little while before. I thought it was mostly nerves. Oriana and the excitement of his own performance, then the impact of Wilde and Strauss combined, had totally unsettled a young singer without much experience of the world. All the same, the effect of it was horrible. The orchestra faltered and murmuring and laughter broke out. Madoc tapped his baton.

'Gentlemen.'

Oriana's alarm had become fury and for some reason Madoc was the target of it. She pulled away from Bridget and me, caught up the sheep's head by its wool and threw it, with all the force of her magnificent arms, full at the conductor. It hit him in the midriff and he staggered. His music stand fell over with a crash and most of a shocked orchestra put down their instruments and rose in a body to pick him up.

Elsie, the train of her blue velvet dress swishing behind her, went striding across to John. 'Stop that. It isn't funny. Stop that.'

Sylvan, meanwhile, was on his feet and shouting at Jack Belter. 'Miss Paphos has been insulted. The contract is terminated. You will have the car ready and we shall go immediately.'

For the next few minutes everything was pandemonium. I think I was the only one who noticed what happened to the head, and that was because I was watching Inspector Merit. He walked quietly across and picked it up from under the feet of the orchestra, replaced it on the salver and took it away to a chair by the wall, carrying it carefully in both hands. I had no chance to discuss it with him because the whole quarrelling party of Belter, Sylvan, Oriana and Elsie Wetherby swept out and carried on several arguments at the top of their considerable voices all over the house. Sylvan blamed Belter, Oriana blamed everybody, Elsie blamed Oriana, Belter seemed inclined to blame Bridget and me. Outside we were dimly aware of the noise and bustle of the orchestra going home, Madoc having decided that there was no point in trying to do any more work that night. In the end Elsie decided on a tactical withdrawal. She must have hated conceding any ground to Oriana, but John was clearly in a state of shock and had scarcely said a word after his hysterical laughter. She announced that they would spend the night at a hotel back in London (at Jack Belter's expense, of course) and demanded a motor car immediately. The chauffeur was summoned from his supper while Bridget delegated a maid to help Elsie with the packing and found the boot boy to carry cases downstairs.

While this was going on, Belter took my arm and steered me into the empty dining room.

'If that was your idea, I don't like it.'

'It certainly wasn't. What would have been the point of it?'

'To scare her.'

'It seems to have infuriated her.'

'What was the point then?'

'I don't know. I have to admit I wouldn't put it past Elsie Wetherby.'

'Why a sheep's head?'

'Goodness knows, and where did it come from? Do you keep whole dead sheep in your kitchen?'

'I should hope not. This isn't a Bedouin encampment.'

'So somebody took a lot of trouble.'

'Where is the thing now?'

'Back in the ballroom, I suppose. I saw one of the scene-shifters pick it up. And

I don't know if you know it, but that scene-shifter is—'

I was interrupted by an imperious knocking on the door and Elsie Wetherby stalked in, wrapped in a fur-trimmed travelling cape. John hovered in the hall behind her, looking so helpless that I wondered if Elsie had needed to button him into his overcoat like a child.

'Goodnight, Mr Belter. We shall need the motor to collect us for rehearsal tomorrow. Nobody can say we walk out on an engagement.'

I took the opportunity to escape out of the back door. The ballroom curtains were drawn but lights were on behind them. When I opened the door the huge room looked empty at first. Chairs and music stands were tidy in their places and the sticky patch on the floor had been mopped. The painted moon and Herod's white peacocks glimmered from the backcloth in the dim light.

'Hello, Miss Bray. I was waiting for you.'

Inspector Merit stood up from his seat beside the wall. On a chair beside him was the head on its salver.

'Well, what do you make of it? Why a sheep's head?'

I'd been thinking since I left Jack Belter

and I didn't like what had occurred to me. 'I think it might have been meant to be a lamb's head, but they'd be hard to come by at this time of the year.'

'Why lamb?'

'You've probably heard about Oriana Paphos arriving with Henry Henson in tow.' He nodded. 'She called him lambkin. Everybody heard it.'

'And nobody's seen him since last night.'

'No.'

'Is it a message?'

'Who from?'

'Henson himself? He's telling her she's had his head on a charger—metaphorically speaking.'

'Did Mr Henson strike you as the kind of man to go in for metaphor?'

'Not when I first saw him, but he hadn't met Oriana Paphos then.'

I told him what had happened the evening before and described Henson's shocked face at the window of the music room. A few minutes before I'd been too angry with Inspector Merit to think of sharing information with him but now a sense of crisis was growing. He listened and looked worried.

'And you haven't seen Mr Henson since then?'

'As far as I know, nobody has.'

We stared at each other.

'Of course, there's nothing to prevent a man going away for as long as he pleases.'

'Jack Belter's worried though.'

He nodded. 'Well, I don't think either of us can do anything for the moment. If Mr Henson does turn up tonight, perhaps you'd be kind enough to let me know.'

'You're staying here?'

'I think so.' He seemed to take it as a matter of course. The bedrock patience of the man was formidable. 'You know, a police officer can't pick and choose the jobs he's given. If I had my choice I wouldn't have taken this one. The fact is, I don't like it when I'm not being told the full story, and I'm sure I'm not being told the full story here.'

He waited.

'No, that's quite likely.'

'I thought it was.'

His voice was flat and his face had that creased, sad look. He was inviting me to tell him what I knew, which was no surprise in the circumstances. What was surprising was the urge I felt to do exactly that.

'You know, I wish I could tell you more, I really do. Only, I've given a promise.'

'I see.'

I said I'd come and tell him if anything happened and made for the door. He fell into step beside me.

'I'll see you to the back door.'

'I don't need an escort.'

But he wouldn't be shaken off. It was past eleven o'clock by then, pitch dark outside and the kind of damp cold that strikes straight to the bone. We went across the terrace and were twenty yards or so away from the back door when it opened quietly and somebody came out. For a few seconds, before the door closed again, we saw him in silhouette against the light inside, a tall man in a cloak with a dark cap on his head. Inspector Merit took my arm and dragged me back into a rose bed so that the man walked past us in the darkness. He was smoking a cigar and there was enough glow from it to make out a stiff beard and sharp profile. Besides, he had an arrogant way of walking even in the dark that was unmistakeable. We watched as the cigar glow crossed the terrace then disappeared down the steps and on to the lawn. Inspector Merit let go of my arm and spoke in a low voice, close to my ear.

'Sylvan. I told you he was following you.'

'He's not making a very good job of it then. Perhaps he's just come out to smoke his cigar.'

'By the river on a night like this? I'll see

you in, then I'll go and have a look what he's up to.'

'I'll come with you.'

He didn't argue. We untangled ourselves from the rose bushes and went to the top step of the terrace. There was no sign of him but half of our view of the lawn was cut off by the ballroom sticking out at a right angle. We walked down the steps and round it then we picked him up again. The red glow was right down on the river bank, travelling slowly now.

'He's just pacing up and down beside the river.'

'There's nothing there except the landing stage and the boat house. Perhaps he is just out for a walk.'

'Or waiting for somebody.'

We were both in our indoor clothes and I felt freezing cold. Once Sylvan's cigar must have gone out because two matches flared. Inspector Merit hardly moved. He'd probably learned the art of waiting as a young constable on the beat. A match flared again.

'Having trouble with that cigar.'

Then no glow at all, so he'd probably turned away from us.

'Where's he gone now?'

Then, out of the silence, a noise of cracking wood and a scream. We went running across the lawn, stumbling against each other on the damp grass. As we ran there was a shout for help, then silence.

Chapter Sixteen

The noise had come from the far end of the lawn, near the boathouse. We stumbled down the steps and ran, but as we got near the river, Inspector Merit caught my arm.

'Steady. Don't want you in there as well.'

Then a voice, from somewhere below us, above the rushing water. 'I'm here. Can you throw a rope?'

The voice of Leon Sylvan, terribly calm. Most people would have been simply bellowing for help.

'Hold on,' Merit called. 'We're coming to you.'

There was a smell of sulphur and the flare of a match, illuminating Merit's hand and beyond it the grassy edge of the bank. It was the point where the creek ran down to the river and even a glance by matchlight was enough to show something missing from the view. The wooden bridge had gone, with only a rail slanting down to

293

the water that was already dragging at it, pulling it away. The match went out and Merit pushed something square and brittle into my hand.

'Keep striking them.'

I fumbled handfuls of matches out of the box, kept striking as instructed. What we saw, illuminated by the burst and dying of match after match, was the creek rushing down into the river and, just at the point where they joined, Sylvan clinging to one of the surviving bridge posts, both arms wrapped round it. He was chest deep in the water, his pale face and dark beard upturned to us, cloak still round his shoulders, dragging along in the current. He was staring towards the light of the matches but after that shout to us made no sound, saving his energy. There was a shocking intensity about his calm. Panic would somehow have been easier to cope with. I sat down on the grass, put down the matches and started sliding down the bank into the creek, hoping the water directly underneath might be shallow enough for a foothold. Merit grabbed my shoulder.

'No, you'll be swept away. Have you got a belt?' Then, to Sylvan, 'Hold on. We're coming to get you.'

I tore the waist belt away from my jacket and started striking matches again. Merit took it and knotted it to his, then threw off coat, jacket and braces. I thought he was getting stripped to dive in and started to protest, but he knotted the braces round his ribs, hitched the end of the belts through them and gave the other end to me.

'I think there's a post beside you. That's it. Does it feel firm? Right, sit down and get your arms round it and keep hold of this. I'll try not to put a lot of weight on it, but I can't guarantee.'

No spare hand for matches now. I improved on his instructions by dragging my skirt up and getting my knees on either side of the post—probably put there for hitching boats—like riding a thin mule. I twisted the end of the belt round both hands as the dark shape of Merit moved down the bank and into the water. A little gasp from the cold, then splashing.

'All right, coming for you now.'

The belt in my hands went tight.

'Nearly there.'

Tighter. I wondered about the tensile strength of braces—considerable probably, but not built for this.

'Right, let's get rid of this for a start.' A snap of metal, audible above the noise of the river. I imagined the lion clasps parting and the cloak floating away in the current. Merit went on talking to Sylvan, voice breathless but calm.

'Now, can you stretch out a hand and see if you can touch me? That's it. When I say now, I want you to reach out and grab for me, anywhere you like. Understood?'

'I understand you.'

Sylvan's voice sounded more tired now, but there was amazingly still that tone of arrogance in it, as if to a servant.

'Right. Miss Bray, are you ready?'

'Yes.'

It still seemed to me all too likely that the arrangement of belt and braces would snap and they'd both be swept away. If I had to dive in and try to save one of them, I hoped it would be Merit I got.

'NOW.'

Splashing and wallowing, like seals at feeding time, heavy breathing, then Merit's breathless voice from just below my feet.

'That's got it. I'm standing up now. Keep holding. Reel in, Miss Bray.'

The belt went slack in my hand as a black shape came up the bank. I let it fall, untangled myself from the post and went to kneel down beside Merit as he helped Sylvan. Then we were all three of us on the grass, the two men wet and dripping, myself covered in river mud.

'The young man will be drowned, I'm afraid.'

'What?'

Merit and I asked the question together.

Sylvan had said it so matter-of-factly, sitting beside us on the ground, that it was hard to take in what he was saying.

'What young man?'

'The secretary.'

'You mean Henry Henson?'

'Yes. Young Henson.'

'He was in the water?'

'He was waiting for me on the bridge. He'd sent a message that I was to meet him there. Unfortunately, when I set foot on it, the whole thing collapsed.'

'Let's get this clear, sir, you're telling us that Mr Henson was waiting for you on that bridge?' Merit, from his voice, was more shaken than Leon Sylvan.

'Yes.'

'You actually saw him?'

'It was too dark to see who it was. When it broke, I heard his voice as he fell.'

'What happened?'

'I imagine he was swept away. I was lucky enough to take hold of a post, as you saw. That was probably not the way it was intended to happen.'

Merit drew in his breath then, neutrally, 'I think we'd better get up to the house as soon as possible, sir.'

'As you like.'

We all stood up. Merit shouted Henson's name a few times but the sound went out hopelessly over the river, with no response.

It was obvious that there was no point in trying to find him in the dark and—if Sylvan had spoken the truth—the only hope was that he might manage to swim along with the current and land somewhere downstream. I said I'd run up to the house and raise the alarm, being less waterlogged than the other two.

I ran back across the lawn, across the terrace and into the house. There was a light on in the corridor leading to the hall.

'Bridget!'

I shouted for her, not wanting to face Jack Belter at once. She appeared in a blue woollen dressing gown, hair in a plait down her back.

'What in the world—'

'Could you telephone the police? Somebody's fallen in the river. And I'm afraid we're going to have to wake up Mr Belter. He's—'

'What's going on?'

Belter himself appeared from above, looking over the rail on the top landing. He was wearing a blue velvet smoking jacket over trousers and might have come from his study.

'We've just pulled Leon Sylvan out of the river.'

'Dead?'

'No, but he says Henry Henson was

there too and he's been swept away.'

At once Belter disappeared from the rail and came running downstairs. By the time he was back in sight, on the last flight, he was firing out questions. When did it happen? Where was Sylvan? Before I could answer, Merit and Sylvan appeared along the corridor from the back of the house, leaving a wide smear of wet like a snail trail behind them. Belter jumped the last two stairs and landed practically touching Sylvan. The man was a head taller, but took a step back and—for the first time since I'd met him—looked off balance.

'So that's another man of mine you've killed. What had he done to you?'

He looked and sounded ready to hit Sylvan, but Merit intervened.

'We'll go into the circumstances later, Mr Belter. Meanwhile I need a telephone.'

Belter stared. I don't think he'd even registered Merit until then and certainly wouldn't have recognised him as the former shifter of music stands. Merit had put jacket and overcoat over his soaked clothes but was hatless, gloveless and looked generally like a retriever left out in a rainstorm.

'Who the hell are you?'

'Inspector Ernest Merit of the Metropolitan Police.' Calmly, Merit produced a wallet from his jacket, took out a card and handed it to Belter.

'When did you get here?'

'I've been here for some time, sir. We'll discuss it later, but if you'd please ...'

Bridget came back. I hadn't noticed that she'd gone, but typically she was the only one who'd done anything useful. 'I've got the police station holding on the telephone. They want to know exactly where it happened.'

Merit said, 'Excuse me,' and he and Bridget rushed into the lounge.

Belter switched his attention back to Sylvan. 'How did you do it this time? I suppose she decoyed him down there and you pushed him in. Well, this time the pair of you are going to hang for it and I don't care what happens. That young man was no more danger to you than a day-old puppy.'

Sylvan had regained his composure by now. His jacket clung to him in wet creases; he'd lost his shoes; and his trousers were rucked up, showing his sock suspenders. And yet he was still an impressive figure, with his wet hair moulded to his head like a helmet and his classical beard.

'No danger to me? Was that why he tried to drown me? I went to that place because he'd sent me a note telling me to meet him there after the performance.'

'Henry Henson sent *you* a note asking

you to meet him by the river in the dark? You expect me to believe—'

'On the bridge to the boathouse. He was quite clear about it. He was waiting when I got there.'

'That much I will believe. He was waiting because you or that woman had told him to be there. Where is this note he's supposed to have sent you?'

Sylvan shrugged. 'Probably in the river too.'

'Of course. There never was a note. If he was down on the river bank it was because you or that woman had told him to be there.'

Inspector Merit came back and spoke to Belter. 'They're organising a search down river, but there's probably not a lot they can do before daylight.'

'I want every man they've got on it. Every man.'

'I'm sure you can trust them for that, sir. Meanwhile, it might save time if you could give me the name and address of the missing man's next of kin. I understand you are his employer.'

'Certainly, officer, as soon as you've arrested this man on suspicion of his murder. His accomplice is probably upstairs. She goes by the name of Oriana Paphos.'

Sylvan made a contemptuous noise.

Merit was unmoved.

'All in good time, sir. When my colleagues arrive I shall be taking statements from anybody who can tell us anything. Meanwhile I'd be grateful if all your guests and staff would remain in the house.'

Sylvan said, speaking to Merit, 'If he thinks I killed his secretary, ask him why.'

I expected an outburst from Belter, but there was a moment's silence. At some point, if a murder charge were to be brought against Leon Sylvan, the matter of the letters would have to come into the open. If that happened, then the huge investment of Belter's time and money, and the sacrifice of a life or two lives, would have been wasted. Not to speak of the baronetcy. Not to speak of the political consequences. It was a difficult calculation to have to make and I could hardly blame Belter for putting it off—which was what he did.

'As to his next of kin, they'll have it in the office. I keep somebody on duty there at all times. I suggest we go up to my study and we'll telephone from there.' Then, to Bridget, 'Wake up two of the men and put them on guard by the back and front doors. Nobody's to leave. When the other police officers arrive, let them in and tell me. Send coffee and brandy up to my study—and some dry clothes and towels for the inspector.'

He turned away without another glance at Sylvan and went upstairs. Merit, leaving damp splodges on the stair carpet, followed him.

Sylvan said to Bridget, 'I also require a bottle of Armagnac in my room. I shall be taking a bath.' He went upstairs with some dignity. I listened to hear if he stopped at Oriana's door, but he didn't.

Bridget, still in her dressing gown, said she didn't care what, she was going to get herself decent before she did anything else, and disappeared towards her room, leaving me alone in the hall. My nerves were tight with the need to do something, although I knew the police would make a more efficient job of looking for Henson than any of us. In the end I went up and knocked on Oriana's door.

It took me some time to get an answer and longer to persuade her to let me in. She was bleary eyed, her satin nightgown creased and she moved as slowly as a lizard in winter as she went back to her bed. I thought probably she'd taken a sleeping draught. Back in her rumpled nest of sheets and pillows she looked at me and wrinkled her nose.

'You smell of cold water.'

I sat on the end of the bed. 'I've

been down by the river. Leon Sylvan was in it.'

'In the river? Leon?' She frowned as if trying to get her mind round it, then, 'Is he drowned?'

A flat, simple question. Impossible to guess from her face or the tone of her voice what she felt about it.

'No, he was pulled out. But it looks as if somebody else may be drowned.'

'Who?'

'Henry Henson.' Then, since from the blankness of her face it might have slipped her mind again, I added, 'The secretary.'

'Oh. Were they fighting?'

'Did you expect them to be?'

Silence. There was more life in her eyes now, but her mind still seemed to be moving slowly.

'Had you told Henry Henson to meet you anywhere tonight?'

'Why should I do that?'

'I don't know. Did you?'

'No.'

'Did Leon Sylvan ask you to write a note to Henson?'

'Why would he do that?'

'Look, just answer the question. Yes or no?'

'No.'

'Have you ever met Henry Henson by the river?'

'No. I didn't even know there was a river.'

Which, I supposed, was just possible, given her self-absorption.

'Did Leon say anything to you about going to meet Henson tonight?'

'No.'

'You thought they might have been fighting. Why was that?'

Silence.

'Had he made any threats against Henson?'

'No, no, no. Why are you asking me all these silly things? I'm tired. I want to sleep.'

'I think you'll find the police will be asking them too.'

'Police?' She was alarmed now, as far as her bleariness allowed. 'Why police?'

'Because if Henry Henson is dead, they'll have to find out why he died.'

'It's not my fault. Why are you looking as if it's my fault?'

'Am I?'

'Yes. Yes, you are. Is it my fault if men love me?'

'You think that's why he might be dead—because he loved you?'

'I don't know.' Her voice was almost a wall. 'I don't know anything. Go away and leave me.'

I went. There was a bathroom a few

305

doors along from my room. The towels were soft and thick, the water scalding hot. I threw off my damp muddy clothes and lay back, trying not to think of Henson in the river. Before I'd finished soaking I heard motor car wheels on the drive, voices and the front door opening. Inspector Merit's colleagues had arrived. By that time, I'm sure, the news had reached Downing Street and long before the cold daylight when police were going along the river bank looking for Henson, he had become tangled in politics as inextricably as in water weed.

Chapter Seventeen

They found Henry Henson's body soon after it got light. I was in my room, looking from the window at a grey, drizzly morning when a car drew up. Two uniformed policemen in rain capes knocked on the door and were let in by the butler. I went out to the landing and saw them being shown into the lounge. They came out again almost immediately, Jack Belter with them, shouting to the butler to bring his hat and coat. Then they drove away together. When I went down, Bridget was carrying a coffee pot into the breakfast room, looking weary to the bone.

'They've found a body down towards Windsor. They're taking Mr Belter to identify it.'

We found out later that it was a place where some pleasure boats were moored, notorious to the police as a point to which the current delivered bodies on this stretch of river. They'd looked there at first light and found him in the water alongside a steam launch. Half an hour later Belter came back, face grim, and went straight up to his study. Although nothing was said, the whole house knew and it felt as if the cold drizzle had found its way inside.

Neither Oriana nor Sylvan came down, and I was sitting on my own in the breakfast room over a cup of coffee when Inspector Merit came in. He was wearing grey flannels and a jacket too long in the sleeves for him, possibly the butler's clothes, but his air was as official as if he were at Scotland Yard and back in uniform.

'Miss Bray, I'm sorry to tell you that Mr Henson has been found dead. I'm not the officer in charge of this investigation, but I have been asked to speak to some of the people who were in this house yesterday.'

'Are you taking official statements?'

'Not yet.'

'I've no objection.'

He sat down opposite me. His face was grey, drained of everything except determination. 'I don't need to ask you why you were in the garden last night, but describe what happened as if I hadn't been there.'

'Leon Sylvan came out of the house on his own and walked down to the river. He was walking along the bank for some time.'

'Was anybody else there?'

'No sign of anybody. He lit a match, then there was the sound of wood breaking, a scream and a shout for help.'

'Was it Sylvan himself who shouted for help?'

'Yes, I think so, though it's hard to tell with a shout.'

'Who screamed?'

'Henson, I suppose.'

'And the wood breaking sound came first?'

'I think so, but when you hear things close together and unexpectedly, you can't be certain.'

Good question though. He was asking whether Sylvan might simply have pushed Henson in, then somehow broken down the bridge and plunged in himself to make it look like an accident.

'Sylvan didn't know we were there, so who was he calling to?'

'Anybody. If somebody had gone in the water by accident he would shout out, wouldn't he, just in case anybody heard?'

'Then?'

'By the time we got there, Sylvan had managed to grab hold of a post.'

'A lucky man, wouldn't you say? Unless he knew the post would still be standing.'

I understood now why Merit had decided to see me on his own. He was taking risks, surprisingly for such an orderly man.

'You think Sylvan arranged to meet him there and planned it?'

'Do you?'

'There's one argument against it. When you went to help him, the first thing you had to do was to get rid of his cloak. It was dragging him away. If he knew he was going in the water, wouldn't he have taken the cloak off first?'

'Perhaps he forgot in the heat of the moment.'

'He doesn't strike me as a man who does anything in the heat of the moment.'

'Did you see that bridge by daylight?'

'Yes, but I didn't take much notice of it.'

'Did it look rickety, likely to break?'

'I don't think so. It was a flimsy little thing and it wouldn't have taken much to saw through some of the struts, but I don't think Mr Belter would tolerate rickety things on his property.'

He didn't rise to the bait about sawing through struts and changed tack. 'Did you notice what Sylvan said to me when he and Mr Belter were quarrelling last night? "If he thinks I killed his secretary, ask him why." You know Mr Belter better than I do, Miss Bray. What did you make of that?'

I hesitated. Pull too hard on that end and the whole skein would come apart.

'Was it something to do with Miss Paphos?'

'I doubt it. Not directly anyway.'

'I take it we may assume that Miss Paphos and Mr Henson rapidly became intimate when he went to Paris to collect her?'

I was amused that he seemed to consider me an expert and said as demurely as possible that I thought we might assume it.

'Mr Sylvan is her manager but we may also assume a closer relationship there?'

'You know, I'm not sure about that. I suppose they might have been lovers in the past, but now he probably even encourages her to have love affairs with other men.'

The python keeper and the python. Or, more than that, the quickest way

310

into the social circles that interested him. That aspect was something Inspector Merit probably didn't know about, and I couldn't tell him. I noticed he'd looked away when I talked about love affairs and supposed he was remembering Bernard blundering downstairs with his pyjamas showing. Still, if he was determined to treat me as his expert witness on affairs of the heart, I'd do my best for him.

'If you're asking me if Sylvan might have murdered Henson because he was jealous of him, I'd say no. There'd be a trail of corpses across Europe if he killed everyone who was intimate with Miss Paphos.'

'Some people would say there've been two in this country alone.'

'Laurence Gilbey, you mean?'

'Yes.' His eyes stayed on me, still hoping for an answer.

I tried a question of my own. 'I suppose Henson did die from drowning.'

'We're not sure of anything until they do a post mortem, but it looks likely. There were no obvious signs of injury.'

He was looking at me again, waiting. I waited too. There was the noise of wheels on the gravel outside.

'That other young man, the Baptist ...'

'John Bartholomew.'

'He reacted very oddly to that head business. Hysterical.'

'He'd been going through a nervous time. His opera debut, Miss Paphos and so on.'

'You think she ...? Him too?'

'Trying, certainly.'

'Is there anybody in this house the damned woman hasn't ...? I'm sorry.'

'Anyway, that would hardly be a reason for John Bartholomew killing Henson. If it had been the other way round I might have wondered.'

'Have you thought any more about that head business? Who'd do a thing like that?'

Silence again. I had the impression that he was trying to make a decision. It came reluctantly.

'Mr Henson was still wearing his jacket when they found him and some of his things were in the pockets. Most of them were what you'd expect: wallet, keys and so on. Then there was this.' He put his hand into his jacket pocket and brought out a small paper parcel. 'It will have to go to the coroner's officer, but I wondered if you'd ever seen it in Mr Henson's possession.'

He unwrapped the brown paper and showed me a silver-plated cigarette case. It looked unremarkable, quite new, not particularly expensive, no initials on the outside.

'No, I don't remember seeing him with

it. In fact, I don't think I ever saw him smoking a cigarette, but then he was on duty I suppose.'

Merit pressed the fastener and opened it. 'It's well made. The contents were still dry, after all night in the river.'

No cigarettes, just a piece of white notepaper folded into four. He unfolded it carefully and handed it to me. I read.

... can't agree with you about George Meredith. There's the worst kind of dandyism about his style, like a man who looks at himself in drawing-room mirrors. Dim people at bridge last night, three rubbers and I, though guiltless, lost a shilling. Today we had a largely satisfactory Cabinet. It occurred to me, when Winston was going on and on about the naval estimates, repeating points made twenty times already, that ...

The same firm, forward-sloping handwriting as on the other letter, though this was certainly a different one with no empty spaces and no message in blood. I turned it over. The address at the top of the page was 10 Downing Street.

'Oh ye gods.'

'You recognise it?'

I gave him back the piece of paper,

trying to collect my wits, and chose my words carefully. 'I've never seen it before this moment.'

'But you know what it is?'

'I think I can guess what it is, but I'm simply not at liberty to tell you.'

He went stiff, as if I'd tried to hit him. 'Miss Bray, this is not just a friendly chat. I'm a police officer and this is an inquiry into a fatality.'

'Did you show this to Mr Belter?'

'Yes. He said he didn't know what it was and he didn't know why Mr Henson should be carrying it.'

I thought that he must have known as soon as he set eyes on it. In the balance between the interests of the Empire and the deaths of his young men, the Empire was still weighing more heavily. Was that his final decision or was he playing for time? Even somebody as decisive as Belter must have been knocked sideways, as I'd been, by this development.

'You've told me you can guess what it is but you won't tell me.'

'I'm sorry, I've made a promise.'

Consciously or not, he moved his chair a little away from me. 'I see. Well, I should warn you that, although I can't insist on an answer now, either I or one of my colleagues will be asking you again later.'

'Yes.'

Ridiculous to mind about going down in his estimation. He was a policeman after all. And yet I did mind.

'There's ... there's one thing I think I can tell you. The fact that it was found in Henson's possession makes it likely that there was a secret meeting between him and Leon Sylvan.'

Sylvan had been in possession of the letters. Belter had sent, through me, a message that he'd pay a thousand pounds for the sight of one of them. But when it came to delivery and payment, Henson had been the messenger. I couldn't say anything of that to Inspector Merit.

'You say that because of this bit of letter?'

'Yes.'

He stared at me, eyes as bleak as the sky outside. I'm sure he'd have asked more questions, but there was a knock on the door and a uniformed constable looked in.

'Inspector Merit? You're wanted on the telephone from London, sir.'

He stood up, put the letter back in the cigarette case, wrapped up the case and returned it to his pocket.

'Excuse me, Miss Bray. Would you mind waiting here for me?'

He went, leaving me alone and not pleased with myself. The worst thing was that in trying to make a deal on the letters I might have contributed to Henson's death. It seemed all too likely that he'd gone to give Sylvan the thousand pounds and taken delivery of part of one of the Prime Minister's letters. Belter had said Henson didn't know about the letters. If that were true, then he'd simply used his secretary as a messenger. But why not use me instead? It was supposed to be my job. And if Henson had just handed over a wad of Belter's money, with the prospect of much more to come, why should Sylvan want to kill him? I wondered if Henson might have died by accident after all, but decided not. One suicide and one fatal accident in a matter of months was stretching coincidence too far.

Inspector Merit came back sooner than I'd expected. He'd been angry enough when he went out but now there was a cold fury in his face and the way he walked that I'd never have expected in such a conventional man.

'I'm sorry to have kept you waiting, Miss Bray. I don't think I need to ask you any more questions.'

'What?'

That was the last thing I'd expected.

'You've given me your account of what you heard of the accident. Sometime over the next few days I'm sure the coroner's

316

officer will take a statement from you. So I don't need to take up your valuable time any further.'

'Accident? I thought you ...'

He remained standing, hands behind his back.

'As I've just been informed over the telephone, it doesn't matter whether I'm convinced or not. It has been decided at levels far above my head that the death of Mr Henson is a regrettable accident and is to be investigated entirely on that basis.'

'But that's ridiculous.'

'It may seem ridiculous to me, Miss Bray. It may even seem ridiculous to you, though I strongly suspect that you've been allowed to know more about it than I do. But somewhere in the Home Office or, for all I know, at the house where you took breakfast the other day, the decision has been taken and a mere inspector of police can't expect to be told the reason.'

'I'm sorry.'

That was putting it mildly. I was almost as shocked as he was.

'Are you? I'm sorry too. Sorry that I've wasted more than twenty years of my life in the police force. I'm sure you've got your own ideas about police officers. We're brutal, stupid, agents of oppression and all the rest.'

'No. Some of you—'

But he was unstoppable. Usually the most civil of men, even when we were on opposite sides, this time he wouldn't let me speak.

'But strange though it may seem to you, I chose this work because I believed in certain standards in society. Standards of public life and honesty and all men being equal before the law. But I was being naïve, wasn't I? The intellectuals like you know better, and the Chancellor knows better and the newspaper owners know better. It's only poor stupid police officers like me who think it matters whether a man's murdered or not ...'

'That isn't true.'

'... if it happens to interfere with what they want. And God knows what they want. You know too, apparently. You who've thrown bricks through windows and done time in prison, you're allowed to know what's going on and I'm not.'

'I don't know half of—'

'And when it all falls apart, and believe me it is going to fall apart in ways you can't even guess at, with all your cleverness and all your connections in high places ...'

'I haven't got—'

'... then it's going to be the likes of me it falls on, when the politicians and the newspaper owners sit up there out of it telling each other what a pity it was that it all went wrong. If that sounds like disloyalty to you, then I'm sorry, but after this I don't know what loyalty is any more.'

He stopped at last. His face that had been alive with anger turned back to sad grey frog, but the protuberant eyes that hoped for answers from me in the past didn't expect them any more. He turned away, his hand on the doorknob.

'Goodbye, Miss Bray.'

I'd had time to think while he was talking and a decision had made itself.

'I think you should stay,' I said. 'I'm going to break a promise.'

Chapter Eighteen

It was nearly ten o'clock before I finished talking to Inspector Merit. At the end of it I said, 'Well, you know now, and if you do anything about it, it will probably wreck your career.'

'Yes.'

From the expression on his face, he'd thought of that.

'Are you a family man?'

'Yes. A girl of twelve and a boy of ten.'

319

He'd thought of that as well, but I hadn't. It was like being caught in a sticky cobweb. Whichever way I turned made things worse.

'It could have been an accident after all,' I said.

'No.'

Since there was nothing else to say, I stood up. He stayed sitting down, a little breach of manners that he'd committed only once before to my knowledge and that time I'd been a prisoner in Holloway. As my hand was on the door he asked me what I was going to do now. I said I wasn't sure. In fact there was one thing I needed to do urgently, but it wouldn't help him to know about it.

Jack Belter's red motor car was still parked outside the house, so he hadn't left for his office yet. I went up three flights of stairs and knocked on the door of his study.

'Come in.'

He was on the telephone and signalled to me to sit down and wait. He looked less affected by a sleepless night than anybody else in his household, dark business suit, hair sleeked back. But the events of the night had reduced him from his usual, almost indecent, level of energy to something more like most people's normality. He'd already put on a black

320

tie. When he hooked the telephone receiver back on its stand I said, 'I resign.'

His eyebrows went up.

'I thought I could do it. I can't.'

'I can understand you're anxious about your safety ...'

'You think I'm worried that I'll be the next.'

'It would be an understandable fear.'

'I could deal with that. What I can't stand is the underhandedness. Two men have died to save a Government that doesn't deserve it. Also, you lied to me, by implication at least.'

The eyebrows again.

'Yes, you did. You implied that Henry Henson wasn't involved in this, and yet you must have sent him to meet Leon Sylvan and collect that letter. You pretended not to recognise it when the inspector showed it to you this morning, but I assume it's one of the stolen ones.'

He nodded.

'Why didn't you tell him so?'

'Never show your hand too soon.'

'Are you going to show it at all?'

He got up, walked to the window and stared out. It was still drizzling.

'Another thing—Laurence Gilbey wasn't as loyal to you as you thought. Did you know he was trying to make his own deal over those letters?'

His back twitched. Either he hadn't known, or he had known and the knowledge still hurt him.

'So what are you going to do?'

He turned round. 'You came in here to resign. Did it occur to you that I might just have done the same thing?'

That gashed melon of a smile, but no humour in it.

'As I see it, you could only do that by telling Lloyd George that as far as you're concerned he can wait till doomsday for those letters.'

'That's exactly what I've done, by telephone half an hour ago, and in rather stronger language.' Then, seeing the look on my face, 'For goodness' sake, you can't be surprised at that. It was bad enough losing Laurie Gilbey and having to invite the couple who killed him to live under my roof. Do you really think I'd let them do it again and walk off scot-free?'

'Can you prevent it?'

'I'm going to see the pair of them in dock on a charge of both killings if I have to overturn the Government to do it. I've had enough of being the man who picks up the bill.'

'And yet it's been decided from on high that Henry Henson's death is an accident.'

'What!'

He'd been half turned away, looking out of the window, but when I said that he turned to face me. His face went quite blank for a moment, like a turnip lantern with the candle snuffed out.

'The police have been ordered to investigate it as a fatal accident, not a murder.'

'How do you know that?'

'You have better sources at the Home Office than I have. Check with them and see if it's true.'

I wasn't going to land Inspector Merit in even more trouble. He stared at me for a second, still with that blank look on his face, then reached for the telephone.

'Would you wait outside for a few minutes, if you don't mind.'

I waited on the landing, looking down over the bannisters at a shaken household trying to go about its normal business—a maid sweeping the stairs, Bridget bustling in and out of rooms off the hall. Two floors below me Oriana's door was still closed. One floor below, Leon Sylvan's door was open and a maid was throwing used bed-linen out on to the landing. It was five minutes or more before Jack Belter opened his door and asked me to come in.

'God knows how you knew, but you're right. That callous, scheming, cold-blooded little Welsh bastard.'

I didn't need to ask who he meant.

'Anyway, he's chosen the wrong man for once. I'll crucify them. If they think they can use me and my men like so much cannon fodder ...'

He sat down at his desk, hands clenched, as if he couldn't trust himself to say any more.

'Do I take it that you're not accepting that his death was accidental?'

'You do. I'm going to prove it and you're going to help me.'

'I've had enough of this.'

'You can't walk away from it and you know it. It might have been you drowned instead of poor Henson, if I hadn't sent him there in your place.' It was unfair and we both knew it, but he had me caught.

'What do you propose doing?'

'We have to set some sort of trap for them. Use her against him.'

'I'm still not convinced she's involved.'

'She's in it up to her neck, and I'm going to prove it.' He was silent for a while. 'I need time to think about this. Can you come to my office in Fleet Street this evening? Make it late, eleven o'clock, and come in by the side entrance to the composing room. I wouldn't put it past our friend to set spies on both of us now.'

A knock on the door. Bridget's voice.

'Mr Belter, the musicians have arrived. What do you want done about them?'

'Damn. I'd forgotten them.' He raised his voice. 'Thank you, Bridget. Miss Bray will be down to see them in a few minutes.'

I'd forgotten about them too. I said I supposed the one public performance of *Salome*, due the day after next, would be cancelled.

'Yes. The only advantage in this business is that I won't have to sit through that again. Only we're not telling them that until the last minute. I'm keeping the pair of them tied down here. You'd better go and break the sad news to the band, if they don't know it already, but give out that we're going ahead with the performance because it's what Mr Henson would have wished.' He added, under his breath, 'Though I don't suppose he cared for that rubbish any more than I did.'

The band knew about it already. That is to say, they knew that an assistant to the patron, the young man so smitten by Oriana, had died in mysterious circumstances. It unsettled them enough to delay the start of the day's rehearsal and when I got to the ballroom Madoc was making notes on the score while orchestra and singers milled around and drank coffee.

Elsie Wetherby came up to me at once, sleek from her night at a hotel.

'Well, did he drown himself over that woman?'

'The police think it was an accident.'

She made a disbelieving face. 'After what happened with that head last night? Well, I hope at least somebody has the grace to apologise to poor John.'

'Apologise?'

'Blaming him for that head business. In the light of what's happened, it's obvious who was responsible.'

'Who?'

'Oriana Paphos. She knew he'd killed himself over her and she was flaunting it, making a mock of him.'

'He was still alive when that happened.'

She was pressing me for more details when rescue arrived in the shape of Bernard bringing me coffee, face full of concern. He led the way to a couple of chairs against the wall at some distance from the rest of the orchestra.

'Were you involved in this business?'

'Yes, I'm afraid I was.'

'Nell, I'm sorry. Do you want to talk about it?'

'There's not a lot to say.' Or far too much. If I started I might tell him everything, which would be unfair on him.

'Elsie says he ...' He stopped himself, then started again. 'It's ironic. Here was I, pleased you were getting involved in something that would take you away from trouble for a while, then this happens.'

'Getting involved in ...? Oh, you mean the *Salome.*'

'Of course. Do you know what will happen about that now? Madoc's behaving as if it's still going ahead but ...'

'Officially it is, but between the two of us I shouldn't rely on it.'

He looked unhappy. 'Will you be coming home, after Saturday?'

'I suppose so.'

I couldn't think more than a few hours ahead. It would have been good to be back in the living room at Hampstead with nothing to worry about but politics and other people's arson, he writing *Joan of Arc* at one end of the table, I writing reports and speeches at the other.

'I wish there was something I could do.'

'Did you manage to find out where that musician who had the love affair with Princess Lotus is living?'

'His friend gave me the address of a place in Holborn where he was lodging a few months ago.'

'Could you try and find him? Find out if he knows what happened to Princess

Lotus after she left him. You said she took up with a rich businessman, but I don't suppose she stayed with him. Does he know if she went abroad or what happened?'

'When do you want me to do it?'

'Today. Now. I don't suppose Madoc will miss one viola after all that's happened.'

'You don't know him. He'd miss a jangle off a tambourine.'

'Well, he'll just have to put up with it. Can you meet me somewhere in London this evening? Meet me ... let's see, that café near Victoria Station that does anchovy toast. Can we make it quite late, nine o'clock, say.'

He nodded in a bemused way and walked over to confer with one of the violinists. I felt guilty about him, but if he intended to be a partner for Bobbie he'd have to get used to an unpredictable life.

I went back into the house and up to Oriana's room. After a long wait she opened it herself, just wide enough to see who was there.

'May I come in?'

'If you must.'

Her hair was down, reaching below her waist, and she was wearing a silk robe, embroidered all colours of the rainbow.

The room looked like a flower show tent after a whirlwind, with dresses and scarves flung haphazardly over the bed and the chairs. An empty wicker basket gaped open on the rug.

I said, 'The police have found Henry Henson's body.'

I think she must have heard that already. In any case it didn't surprise her. She made no attempt to sit down, just standing there in the middle of the disorder. One foot, in a purple Turkish slipper, arched and fretted like a small animal wishing to be elsewhere, but apart from that she hardly moved.

'Do you remember I warned you last night that if he were dead the police would be asking everybody questions? That's what will happen now.'

No need to tell her that police inquiries would be of a not very searching kind.

'They can't blame me. It's not my fault.'

'Then whose fault is it?'

The foot made a bid for escape, was drawn back.

'There was part of a letter found on his body. It was still dry because it was inside a cigarette case. It came from that batch of letters that was stolen. Do you know how it came into his possession?'

'Why should I?'

'Did you give it to him?'

'No.'

'Did Mr Sylvan?'

The foot came out of its slipper, described a half circle on the floor, was drawn back in again. The outside of the little toe was hard and calloused.

'I don't know.'

She turned away, scooped up a haphazard armful of silks, and stuffed them into the wicker basket.

'What are you doing?'

'Packing. Sylvan says we're leaving.'

'Where to?'

'Greece. He says he'll give me the money for my temple if I come with him now.'

'But you haven't performed your dance yet.'

'I danced for them yesterday. They mocked me, laughed at me.'

The door opened and Sylvan came in without knocking. He said to Oriana, 'Haven't you finished packing?' Then, to me. 'It seems your colleagues in the police can't arrest me. They'd like to, of course, but there's some little problem of lack of evidence.'

'Although there was something in his pocket that you gave him.'

'Oh?'

'A cigarette case, quite plain, with the

page of a letter in it. One of the letters you stole.'

I could have sworn that the news surprised him. He blinked and hesitated before replying, the second time I'd seen him less than totally in command.

'If that's true, it didn't come from me.'

'Didn't the police ask you about it?'

'No.'

'I suppose they asked you about the note you claim to have had, asking you to meet him.'

'I don't claim to have had it. I had it.'

'Then lost it.'

'Unhappily, yes.'

'Why did you think he wanted to meet you?'

'He was a confused young man. Perhaps he blamed me for what had happened.'

'And yet you went to meet him by the river in the dark.'

'To give him some good advice.'

'What was that good advice?'

'That he'd had three days with Oriana, which after all is three more than a very ordinary man is entitled to expect. He should thank the gods for three days and walk away.'

'But before you could deliver this fatherly advice, you were both in the river?'

'Sadly, yes.'

'What happened?'

'As I've told the police, that bridge collapsed as soon as I set foot on it. Henson was standing there, waiting for me.'

He crossed the room and settled himself into a chair. It was piled with her clothes but he made no attempt to move them.

I said, 'A coincidence, isn't it? A few months ago another man died with a page from those letters beside him.'

'A man sent to spy on us.'

'A man sent to get those letters back. Henson was trying to do the same.'

'Was he? In that case, he was wasting his time and his life. I told you I haven't got those letters.'

'Who has?'

'When the police find out who killed Mr Gilbey, perhaps they should ask him.'

'You think Laurence Gilbey was killed then? That he didn't kill himself?'

A nod, so slight that the angle of his beard altered by no more than a degree or two.

'And Henry Henson?'

'Ah, in that case we were both of us meant to die, only I was unobliging enough to survive.'

No acknowledgement of Inspector Merit's help in that process, or mine.

'Nor am I obliging enough to wait until it happens again. Miss Paphos's contract has been broken by the insolent and brutal way she was treated last night.' He looked at her, kneeling on the floor, listening to him as if this was all new to her.

I said, 'Why did you come back to England after what happened last time?'

'She wanted to. Perhaps she hoped I'd be arrested and hanged.'

'No. No, I didn't.'

'She can't do without me. She'd like to, but she can't.' He stood and said to her, not unkindly but without any emotion, 'I'm leaving in ten minutes. What you haven't packed will have to stay here.'

As soon as the door shut behind him Oriana was on her feet, shoving armfuls of clothes into the wicker basket.

'Oh, help me. Help me pack.'

I stayed where I was.

'Tell me something. You thought Laurie Gilbey was writing some pieces for the newspapers about you?'

'A book. He was writing a book.'

She was darting around in a frenzy, hardly noticing what she was saying.

'Did he ask you things about your early life?'

'Of course. My father was an English

lord and my mother was a Gypsy from—'

'Not quite that far back. I was thinking about Princess Lotus. Did he know about that?'

She stopped, hands full of perfume bottles, eyes hurt. 'Yes, he knew about that but it is not important.' Then she dropped a bottle and the smell of jasmine spread around us. 'Oh, oh, help me. He'll go without me.'

I left her but she must have managed to pack after a fashion because only a little over ten minutes later I watched from a window as the two of them were driven away by Belter's chauffeur in the red motor, every cubic inch of it stuffed with luggage. Soon afterwards there was an almighty row when it turned out that they'd commandeered the motor without permission. Jack Belter damned the chauffeur, the police and his entire household and refused to believe that there was nothing legally they could be charged with, not even motor theft since his chauffeur was at the wheel. He raged around shouting for someone to bring him his Sunbeam, which was apparently the name of his green two-seater motor, and set off for London in hot pursuit. I kept my distance. I was going too, but in my own time.

Chapter Nineteen

I went up to my room without meeting anybody and hurriedly put the few things I'd brought with me into my suitcase. On my way out, I put my head round the staff door to say goodbye to Bridget.

'Are you leaving us? Where will you be if Mr Belter comes back and asks for you?'

'Here and there. I'll let you know.'

She clearly didn't know about my appointment with Jack Belter later. I let myself out of the front door, passing the room where, for all I knew, the police constable might still be waiting to take a formal statement from me about the regrettable accident of the night before. At least I was sparing him and myself a scene of that farce. For once there were no motor cars parked on the wet gravel. I walked to the station, just missed a train. By the time I got back to London it was past four o'clock. No time to go out to Hampstead. I made my way to the WSPU office, dumped my case and commandeered a corner of a desk and a stack of paper.

Of course there was no chance of being undisturbed. People who hadn't seen me for weeks kept coming by with pieces of news, much of it gloomy. Emmeline was still out on bail, trial in three weeks' time. Probable sentence three or four years. Various wild schemes like people chaining themselves to the prison van outside if she were found guilty, mass attacks on government offices. And yet—was it my imagination?—some of the people who stopped to talk to me seemed odd and awkward in their manner, as if not sure how I'd react. Bobbie, I knew, would have tried hard not to be suspicious of me, even harder not to let it show to anybody else, and yet the slightest hint of treason in a movement is like a damp smell that spreads to everything, and I felt as tainted with it as a wet woollen sock. I tried not to think about that and got on with writing. Nobody asked me what. Luckily, nobody was around when I put the pages into a large envelope and addressed it: 'Inspector E. Merit. Scotland Yard.' Nobody was around either when I wrote a much shorter letter, only one page, and gave it an address almost equally unpopular: 'Rt. Hon. David Lloyd George M.P. 11, Downing Street.'

It was past seven o'clock by then. I was

in a hurry to deliver them before keeping my appointment with Bernard and was rushing out of the door when I cannoned into somebody coming in. Bobbie Fieldfare of all people.

'Nell, I've been looking for you. I want to—'

'Later, tomorrow.'

'We've got to talk. I've been putting it off until—'

'I know. Tomorrow. Come up to the house.' I went on through the door and out. She followed me on to the pavement, caught my arm.

'What do you mean, you know? You can't know.'

'For goodness' sake, it was obvious enough from the start.' I pulled my arm away. 'Now, if you don't mind, I've got something important to get on with.'

'Nell ...'

The stricken look on her face in the lamplight almost halted me in my tracks, but not quite. 'I'm sorry, I know this is important to you too, only it will keep. Tomorrow.'

I left her standing there, still with that look on her face, and went off almost at a run. At Downing Street there was a different police constable on duty under the lamp outside Number Ten, and the sight of a woman in a hurry made him jump like a nervy horse. Not surprising, I suppose. Asquith and Lloyd George both lived in fear of the next suffragette attack. I knocked on the door of Number Eleven and it was opened by the disapproving housekeeper.

'Is Mr Lloyd George in?'

'He's over at Parliament.'

'Will you see he gets this as soon as possible? It's urgent.'

She accepted the note, but with no sign of urgency. It was much the same round the corner at Scotland Yard. The duty officer took the plumper envelope and said he'd make sure it would get to the inspector, but in a tone of voice that said tomorrow would do. I got to the café to keep my appointment with Bernard ten minutes or so late.

It was the time of the evening when London is comparatively quiet, between the going in and coming out times of the theatres. There were just two couples at tables, a tired waitress and Bernard over in a corner, reading an evening paper. An empty coffee cup was in front of him and a plate with crusts of anchovy toast. A waitress came over at once and I ordered the same again, for two this time. I was suddenly ravenously hungry. The waitress went away.

'Well?'

'I saw him. It ... it was pretty awful. The man's living at this place in Holborn, not much more than a doss house. Empty bottles all over the place. He doesn't play any more. Sold his instruments to buy drink. Anyway, his hands shake so much he couldn't ...'

He took a deep breath and rubbed the back of his hand across his forehead. I guessed that a wrecked musician would be a kind of phantom from the future for him, a sign of what might happen if his own luck or talent ran out.

'Anyway, there was no trouble getting him to talk. I think for the price of a bottle he'd talk to anyone. But it wasn't much use for what you wanted, Nell. He lost track of her. Didn't know she'd turned into Oriana Paphos and didn't seem all that interested when I told him.'

'Well, thank you for trying. You did all you could.'

Irrelevant now anyway. Unless Jack Belter had pulled some very powerful strings, Oriana Paphos and Leon Sylvan could be round the corner at Victoria this moment, ready to catch the next boat train.

'As far as he's concerned, the story finished when she went off with that businessman ten years ago. That *is* a

339

coincidence by the way, or did you know?'

'Know what?'

'His name.'

'Go on.'

'Prepare to be surprised, Nell.'

He told me the name. I wasn't.

'You knew?'

'Not for sure. Thank you, Bernard.'

I looked at him across the table and my heart did a painful extra beat.

'Is it to do with the man who died?'

'Two men.'

'Nell, I don't know how you got into this, but leave it now. Let the police handle it, whatever it is.'

'The police can't.'

'Why not? Is it to do with Bobbie and the arson campaign?'

I made a face at him to be quiet. The waitress was coming with our coffee and anchovy toast. When she'd put it on the table and moved away he said, more quietly, 'Are you or Bobbie being blackmailed, Nell?'

'Not quite that, no. And Bobbie's not concerned in this.'

He couldn't keep the look of relief from his face at that.

'You then. You're in trouble of some kind. I wish you'd let me help. You know I do care about you?'

He did, which was one of the worst

parts of it. Then it struck me that the sanest thing to do, the most helpful for both of us, was to take him at his word.

'You can. I'm keeping an appointment later tonight. You can't be part of it, but I'd like to know you're somewhere at hand.'

'Yes, of course I will be. Wherever it is.'

'Not far. And one thing before I tell you about it. I bumped into Bobbie this evening as I was coming out of the office. She said there was something she had to tell me. I said it would have to wait until tomorrow, and it will.'

His eyes had been on me up to that point. Now he picked up a finger of anchovy toast and stared at it as if he'd never seen anything like it before. I picked up another piece from my own plate and bit into it. My appetite had gone but no need to let him know that. 'It's good, isn't it?'

He looked up and smiled, rather shakily I thought. 'Oh, Nell. I wish—'

'Come on, eat up. We've got a long evening ahead.'

Chapter Twenty

At eleven o'clock at night, Fleet Street is near its busiest. Windows are lit up in all the great cliffs of building, motor vans dash westwards to the main railway stations, headlamps blazing and horns blaring, and the pavement vibrates with the thump of printing presses. On good nights the walk from the Temple Bar to Ludgate Hill, with all that life and urgency in the air, is as exhilarating as a ride on a fast horse or a windy day by the sea.

That night, with Bernard walking beside me and the lights from the ground floor windows reflected on the damp pavement, I felt as if I were walking through mud. I didn't want to talk any more and I suppose he sensed that and didn't try, except to say thank you when he stepped off the kerb and I had to snatch him out of the way of a speeding newspaper van.

Jack Belter's office was as busy as the rest. We walked past the front entrance and I led the way into an alleyway to the right of the building, just about wide enough for two people to walk side by side. Some distance along it was a side doorway with no nameplate, only a lamp over a green door with thick glass panels in the top of it. I pushed the door and it opened at once, letting out a flood of light and a battery of machine sounds into the alleyway.

'Are we allowed in here?'

'Nobody knows who's coming and going in a newspaper office.'

Bernard looked like a man with misgivings but he followed me inside. Ahead of us a passageway led to another green door. Nearer at hand on the right were the grille round a lift shaft and a stone staircase with a metal rail and bronze bannister that needed polishing, leading austerely upwards or down to the basement where the presses thumped and thundered.

'We go up. Do you mind if we use the stairs instead of the lift?'

If we were challenged, which was unlikely with everybody busy, I could say that I was there at Belter's invitation but there might be questions asked about Bernard. I wanted him with me. The large presence of him, anxious but unfluttering, was reassuring. I was only borrowing him for the night. Bobbie could have him back tomorrow. We walked up the staircase with the lift shaft on our left. As we climbed, we could look down on the first floor through its ironwork at long rows of linotype machines, their distributor arms rising and dipping like black swans' necks. There was the whiff of hot metal and printer's ink in the air and a constant whirring of machinery and clicking of lines of type falling into galleys.

Bernard said, 'I wonder if I could score them—percussion piece for printing machines.'

'Why not? Wagner did anvils.'

The next floor was probably the territory of the writers and sub-editors, but all we saw of it were some lights behind glass panels. As we climbed, feet echoing on the stone stairs, the noise of machinery died away into the background and the lights were few and far between. One more floor then the staircase stopped against a maroon-painted door.

'This is it.'

'Do I come in with you or wait here?'

'Let's see.'

I pushed the door open and saw green carpeted corridor, clean white paint and a series of doors on the right and nothing on the left but a wall with a brass rail on top that ended at waist height. Bernard came through the door behind me, looked over the rail and took a hasty step back.

'You need a head for heights. I haven't got one.'

I went to where he'd been standing and looked down the whole height of the building to the front hall. The lights were on down there, illuminating the great mosaic map of the world on the floor, with its sprawling red patches of empire. An angel that didn't know the world was round might have seen it like that in its flight. I glanced away and there was the glass dome between our heads and the night sky.

'Architecturally audacious,' Bernard whispered, sounding a little shaky, 'but not homely—'

Then a voice, not from one of the doors to our right but from somewhere unseen, round a corner. 'Who's there?'

Jack Belter's voice.

I mouthed at Bernard, 'Stay here. Wait.'

He looked as if he was going to protest, but I put my finger to my lips and he nodded reluctantly.

'Nell Bray,' I called.

I went quickly round the corner, in case he came to look for me and saw Bernard. Once round the corner I was in familiar territory, recognising the desk where the secretary sat by day. Now there was only Jack Belter, dressed comfortably in a dark lounge suit, small cigar in his hand. He came towards me with his melon slice of a smile, holding out his hand.

'Were you talking to somebody back there?'

345

'I was admiring the view.'

'Let's go in.'

It was his sanctum, the room where we'd had our first meeting. The big table was still scattered with proof pages, but not penguins this time. There was a full-page colour picture of a suffragette, idealised, golden hair blowing in the wind, sash of green, white and purple, lilies round her knees, holding a scroll: 'Our Vote—the Time is Now'.

He looked at me. 'You like it?'

'I certainly like the slogan. What are you proposing to do with it?'

'Run it as our front cover next week, with an editorial inside committing us firmly to the cause of women's suffrage.'

'Your friend Lloyd George won't like it.'

'Lloyd George might have to put up with several things he won't like.' He seemed reluctant to leave the subject of the picture, picked it up and gave it to me.

'Have they got the details right? I sent to your office for a sash and so on.'

There it was, a flare of green, white and purple draped over a chair. On the table beside it were some of our hat rosettes in the same colours and various badges and leaflets.

'You've certainly been very thorough.'

'I could be very useful to your movement, you know that. None of the popular press backs you wholeheartedly.'

Not smiling now, he moved over to his desk and settled down behind it, lodging his cigar in a marble ashtray. I put the picture back on the table and sat down on a chair in front of his desk.

'You said this morning that you were going to prove that Henry Henson's death wasn't an accident. Do you still feel that way?'

'I do, and you're going to help me. Did you make any progress today?'

'I don't know if you'd call it progress. Sylvan denies giving Henry Henson the page from that letter.'

'A waste of time talking to him. She's the one we needed to break down.'

'Do you know where they are now?'

'Still in London, I think. I spent the day trying to get them arrested on some holding charge.'

'Like attempted blackmail?'

'What do you mean?'

'I think that was why Sylvan let Oriana come back to England. He'd been thinking it over and thought he could take another bite at the apple.'

'Trying to push up the bidding for those letters, you mean?'

'No. He claims he's already sold them. I

think he may be telling the truth about that. After he sold them he worked out that the person who'd bought them wanted to keep the transaction secret. Properly handled, that might have been worth another few thousand pounds, and they're both of them very greedy for money.'

He picked up his cigar and drew on it but it had gone out and he crushed it back in the ashtray.

'After all,' I said, 'they've been making money from blackmall for a long time. They were doing it back in the Princess Lotus days.'

Nothing visible changed, and yet there was a difference like a hardening in the air between us. 'Princess Lotus?'

'That was what she called herself when they were doing a music hall act ten years ago.'

'It's the last few months we're concerned with.'

'Not entirely. You know, there's one question that's been worrying me from the start of this—why they stole those letters.'

'We know that. Merchandise. The only question was—who was the customer?'

'Yes, but the customer didn't just come out of the blue. If it was Germany, you'd look for a German link somewhere. Have we found one?'

'She's probably had as many lovers as there are countries in the world.'

'I don't know about the number, but her background's not quite as cosmopolitan as she likes to pretend.'

'That wouldn't stop them being traitors.'

'Of course not, but if they were in the pay of Germany, there'd be more direct ways of going about things. After all, the Prime Minister's hardly going to be putting battleship plans in letters to a woman friend, is he? And they couldn't have known in advance that he'd be writing to her about disagreements in the Cabinet.'

'Then why steal them?'

'Yes. Why steal them? We have to assume that Sylvan was using the entrée to society that Oriana's dancing gave them and stealing them to order. Somebody knew that the Prime Minister was writing regularly to a woman. That person couldn't know what was said in the letters. Only two people knew that. Wouldn't he have jumped to the obvious conclusion?'

'Which was?'

'That the Prime Minister was writing love letters to a woman who was not his wife.'

'According to our Welsh friend, they're nothing of the kind.'

'I think I believe him. About that at any rate. Oriana found them disappointing.'

349

'So would the person who wanted them, according to your theory.'

'No. A sophisticated political mind would see the potential for blackmailing the Government with that information about Cabinet meetings.'

'Sylvan is as clever as a cageful of monkeys.'

'Possibly. But then, he had to know the letters were there to steal in the first place. You'd have to be pretty deeply into English society to know who the Prime Minister was writing to. You don't get that sort of knowledge from organising exotic dancing events for country house parties.'

'You might be surprised.'

'So we come back to the starting point of all this. Oriana and Sylvan stole those letters, but they stole them to order for somebody who was enough of an insider on the British social and political scene to know they existed. Lloyd George must have guessed that from the start. This business of German spies was just his way of trying to drape a patriotic flag round an operation to save the Government's blushes.'

'I admit he'd be quite capable of that.'

'So the letters are stolen. General panic once the Prime Minister's admitted there might be Cabinet secrets in them. Lloyd George is the one who keeps his head as usual, calls in his loyal friend who might pull their chestnuts out of the fire for them. He tells you most of the story—though perhaps not quite all of it.'

'I'm sure he never does that to anyone.'

'You promise to do all you can to get them back—and two people die.'

'Which is all that we're talking about now.' He stood up from behind his desk and started walking up and down the room, hands behind him. He spoke slowly and deliberately, two words to each stride.

'Miss Bray, I don't know how I can impress on you that it's the only question that matters to me now, the deaths of two of my young men in the Government's service. I don't care about the letters any more. As far as I'm concerned they can publish them in full in the *News of the World*. I don't care about the survival of the Prime Minister, Lloyd George, or the Government. All I want is to see the people responsible for their murders in the condemned cell, and if you can help me do that you and the suffragette movement may depend on me for anything my magazines can do for them.'

'Which is why I've been looking into Oriana's past.'

He groaned. 'You keep coming back to that. It's irrelevant.'

'I don't think so. She and Sylvan had

351

the chance to steal those letters because they were mixing in high society. They could do that because of the reputation of Oriana's dancing—risqué, undoubtedly sexual, but Art with a capital A. The perfect entertainment for guests at country house parties if you wanted something titillating and respectable at the same time. She certainly wouldn't have been invited to those big houses if she were still Princess Lotus from the music halls.'

'Well?'

I stood up, tired of sitting still while he paced.

'How did she make the transition from low-bill act on the halls to society entertainer? I found the answer today. She did it because she found a patron who recognised her talent and her usefulness. He was a rich man but like her in some ways, a talented outsider who wanted a wider world than the one he was born into. He gave her what she needed—financial support, publicity, an audience.'

He moved over to the table and stood toying with the edge of the green, white and purple sash.

'Perhaps he did it because he was her lover, for a while. But he was a far-sighted and ambitious man too. He might have had an idea even then of how useful she might be to him. When he heard about

352

those letters it was time for her and Sylvan to repay the debt—with interest. Only Sylvan was ambitious too and saw a chance of his own for blackmail. Making the second time somebody had tried it over those letters, first Laurence Gilbey then Sylvan.'

'Did you get this from the Paphos woman?'

'Not directly. You know, in some ways Oriana is very innocent. As long as she can dance and have admiration and nice things round her, she doesn't worry her head about anything else.'

'Innocent! They've killed two men between them and you call her innocent.'

I shook my head. 'Oriana didn't kill either of them, nor did Sylvan. The man who employed them to steal the letters did that.'

He turned away from me, screwing the sash up in his fists.

'You'd better go. I don't think we can do anything for each other after all.'

'No.'

I looked at his tense back, hunched over the table and started my walk across the soft carpet to the door. When I got there he still hadn't moved. As I stepped into the corridor the only sound was the distant thump of his printing machines in the basement.

'Miss Bray. Wait.'

I'd almost closed the door. The call came from just inside it. As I hesitated he came out at a run. I thought he was asking me to go back into the room, then felt his hand on my arm and instinctively pulled away into the corridor. Instead of trying to pull me back as I expected, he threw his whole weight against me, catching me off balance. I felt something broad and soft going round my neck, tightening against it as I lost balance and pitched forward. I might have gasped or tried to say something, but didn't even have a chance to scream. Then there was something pressing against my stomach. The rail on the top of the low wall. Beyond that rail, the angel's view of world and empire, five floors down to a brightly lit marble floor. I glimpsed it, closed my eyes, tried to push back against the gasping, thrusting weight that was forcing me over the rail. My hands had gone to my neck, trying to tear at the thing round my windpipe. Then they were away from it, flailing for a hold on the rail, but the thing round my neck was jerked tighter. I trampled the floor, trying for an instep then, when I didn't find one, simply trying to keep my footing.

A yell. Not my yell. Not Belter's either. From the side. Then something cannoned into me, knocking me to the floor. Not the floor of the world spread out down there. No seas and continents and red patches. What I saw when I opened my eyes, more than half expecting to find myself winging downwards, was the green wool pile of the corridor carpet. Then somebody trod heavily on me, a door slammed and I heard Bernard's voice.

'Nell. Are you all right?'

I got to my knees and he helped me up the rest of the way. I could feel him trembling, or perhaps it was my trembling.

'I was nearly ... round the corner waiting, then I thought I heard something ... for heaven's sake, why didn't you shout out for me?'

No obvious damage except a tender spot where my head had banged against the wall on the way down and what felt like the hoof print of a dray horse on my back. 'Where did he go?'

Bernard pointed to the door to Jack Belter's sanctum. I tried it, shakily. Locked, no sound from inside.

'Was that ... was he ...?'

I nodded.

'Then for God's sake let's get out of here.'

Round the corner, through the doors to the echoing staircase. On the first landing

Bernard said, 'I'm sorry,' put his hands against the wall and was sick. 'Oh, I'm so sorry.'

'Don't worry about that. Natural. Come on.'

As we went down we could see the swan-necked printing machines still dipping and rising. Another flight, another door and we were out in the alleyway and the damp night air. It felt as if it were the first breath I'd taken since I stepped out of Belter's door and for a moment I went shivery and had to lean against the brick wall opposite. Bernard stood there, a twisted look on his face, and his arm went round me.

'It's all right. You're all right here.' Then a figure appeared in the alleyway from the Fleet Street end, silhouetted against the light, and started walking towards us. Bernard's arm tensed and I tried to stand upright. It was coming at a run now. A woman.

'Nell. Bernard. Get away from her, you traitor.'

Bobbie's voice. Bobbie coming like an avenging fury, not slowing down, cannoning straight into us. It took my breath away, as much the situation as the impact of her, though that was considerable. I knew about jealousy, but not like this—and from Bobbie of all people. Bernard removed his arm from my waist. I waited for him to explain to her but he didn't. For a moment he just stood there in between us, looking at Bobbie's face under the light. Then, without a word, he pushed past her and was running full pelt up the alleyway towards Fleet Street.

'Bernard. Wait. There's no need to ...'

I took a few steps after him, but Bobbie caught my hand. 'Let him go, Nell.'

'But it's not what it looks like. He's just saved my life.'

'Saved it, for goodness' sake? It looked as if—'

'No, in there. I'd have been down there on Africa or Asia or somewhere with every bone of my body broken if he hadn't been there.'

'Asia? Africa? Nell, what are you talking about? You haven't been drinking, have you?'

'I wish I had.'

'Nell. We've got to go somewhere and talk.'

She still had hold of my hand. No cafés open past midnight, not even in Fleet Street. In the end we went across the road and into the little churchyard of St Bride's, with Wren's extravagant wedding cake of a steeple soaring overhead. We sat on a bench and I told her everything that

357

had happened since that night in Walton Heath.

'So you see, I've no claim at all on Bernard. But if it weren't for him I'd be dead and if he hadn't happened to put his arm round me in the alleyway I'd probably have fallen over. He's done nothing whatsoever to be ashamed of—quite the reverse—and I really don't know why he bolted like that.'

'Nell, why are you saying this?'

There was just enough light from Fleet Street to make out Bobbie's face in the dark. It was angry and puzzled.

'Because it's true.'

'The man's got everything to be ashamed of. And what do you mean about having no claim on him?'

'That I'm perfectly aware that he doesn't love me, he loves you. That's grand. I wish you every happiness. Bless you, my children.'

'Nell Bray, have you finally and completely gone stark, staring mad? You think I love *Bernard?* That I *love* him?'

'Don't you?'

'Listen. I mean this. God knows what's got into your brain, but there isn't a creature, male or female, in this whole wide world that I hate and despise more than him. When I saw you together in that alleyway I thought he was trying to kill you

358

and it wouldn't even have surprised me. I've been following the pair of you round all evening expecting something to happen. That's how much I *love* Bernard.'

'But why?'

'Because he's a spy and a traitor. Don't look at me like that. I tried to tell you earlier this evening when you were coming out of the office. You told me you knew. You said it had been obvious from the start. Then you go and spend the whole evening with him.'

'He was helping me, really helping me. I'd never have worked it out without him.'

'For his own purposes. Nell, don't you understand? He's a spy. The police informer. The one we've been looking for.'

'No.'

'Yes, Nell. Look, we'd narrowed it down, hadn't we? You told me yourself about June's friend Gwen, the one she lives with. You found out she had a man friend in the Movement who'd come and talk to her and buy the things she made. I went back to Gwen and asked her. That friend was Bernard.'

I said nothing. A truck clattered along Fleet Street. A starling above our heads woke up and clicked its beak.

'He seemed to know a lot anyway, so

Gwen assumed he was part of the inner ring and there was no harm in talking about what June was doing.'

'But we worked out ...' My mind was moving slowly, reluctantly. For once Bobbie waited without interrupting. 'We worked out that it couldn't all have come from June and Gwen. The police spy could have found out about the bombs from them, but they didn't know what night it was going to be.'

'No. He had to find out that from you.'

'From me?'

'Yes, look, that night when you came out to Walton Heath, did you go back home first?'

'Yes.'

'Was Bernard there?'

'Yes. But I didn't tell him where I was going.'

'He knew you were going out in a hurry. And did you look up trains?'

'Oh God, yes I did.'

I could see it, Bradshaw lying face down on the cluttered table beside his music manuscript paper. In your own home, you don't worry about things like that.

'As for that business in Kensington Gardens, he could have steamed open the note I left for you. And he knew you were going out in a hurry that night.'

'Yes. Not where, I thought, but he knew I was going out all of a sudden.'

After our fish and chip supper, to celebrate the work I'd got for him with Madoc.

'Then when I walked in later that night, he thought he had me as well. Two for the price of one.'

'But you came to see him. You even sang songs with him.'

'I wasn't sure. I wondered, yes. I wanted to find out more about him. It was only after I talked to Gwen that I knew for sure.

No argument left. I felt bruised to the marrow of my bones, wondered if I'd ever move again or just stay on this bench in the churchyard until I calcified.

'It was for the money, I suppose. He wanted it for his opera. Do you know, even Inspector Merit tried to warn me. He must have recognised him as a police informer. He told me not to trust people but I didn't understand what he meant. Oh, I'm a fool, a fool, a fool.'

I must have said it, I suppose. My voice did anyway.

'Nell, don't think that. Anyone would have been taken in. You'd have seen through him before I did, if it hadn't been for this other business.'

'This other business, yes.'

There was something round my neck, working its way under my collar. In the way you concentrate on irrelevant things while your mind tries to deal with the big ones I took it off, spread it out in my hands like a skein of wool. In the dim light you could only see the stripes, not the colours.

'What's that, Nell?'

'Our colours. Belter said he'd got it to do a magazine cover. Only I think it was for another reason. He put it round my neck just before he tried to push me over. He'd got some badges and leaflets and things too.' Dead on his map of the Empire, sash round my neck, leaflets scattered round me. Fleet Street Protest Suicide of Fanatic Suffragette.

'Do you suppose Lloyd George would have sent a wreath?'

I started laughing. Bobbie put an arm round me.

'Come on. Home.'

The fire was out. His things were still scattered over the table. Bobbie got the fire burning, poured brandy, made tea. To make room for the cups and glasses I picked up a handful of his manuscript pages. Act Two, I think, the battle scene. I stood with them in my hands, staring at the fire. A sparkle came back into Bobbie's eyes.

362

'Are we going to burn it? Like Hedda Gabler.'

I took the top sheet with just a few bars on it and shoved it between the bars of the grate. It writhed slowly, charred and then burst grudgingly into flame. Sickened, I put the rest back on the table.

'Aren't you going to?'

'It might be good, after all.'

'How could it be?'

But we left them anyway. Later I went upstairs and Bobbie settled down to sleep on the sofa. The lodger's room was free of course, but she didn't fancy that.

Chapter Twenty-One

The weekend doesn't matter. I took a train somewhere, walked in the rain till my boots fell apart, came home. On Sunday night I delivered a note to Inspector Merit, personal, at Scotland Yard suggesting that we should meet at a certain teashop in Victoria Street at midday on Monday, plain clothes. He was there waiting, bowler hat on the table, umbrella hooked over the back of the chair. He stood up as I came in.

'I got your letter.'

We both sat down. He'd chosen a table away from the window and there were no other customers within hearing distance.

'Something else has happened since then. On Thursday night he tried to kill me as well.'

I told him about it.

'Was there a witness to this?'

'As it happens, there was. A man known to Scotland Yard—although I didn't know that until afterwards.'

I thought at first he was going to pretend not to understand. Then, 'The viola player?'

'I don't blame you for him. In fact, you tried to warn me but I didn't understand. Thank you for that anyway.'

'He saw Jack Belter trying to push you over?'

'More than that, he stopped him. Then he ran off, but I'm sure Scotland Yard could always find him. If it wanted to.'

He'd had the chance of a few nights' sleep since I last saw him, but those bullfrog eyes still looked tired.

'Do I understand you want to make a formal complaint that Jack Belter attacked you?'

'And what would happen if I did?'

'The police would naturally investigate.'

'The way they're investigating the murder of Henry Henson?'

He looked hurt.

'I'm not blaming you. But it was murder on that bridge. Belter fixed it up to make it collapse when there was two men's weight on it, and Sylvan is a big man. Neither of them was meant to survive.'

'But Mr Sylvan did.'

'Because he's stronger than Belter allowed for and because we happened to be there. But Belter had a plan in case he didn't drown. If Sylvan survived, it would be as a suspect for another murder. Belter was confident that in the circumstances Sylvan would vanish overseas as soon as possible. He pretended to be trying to stop him. It was a good act.'

'Why did Sylvan come back here? He'd got away without trouble after Gilbey's death and picked up a lot of money selling those letters he'd stolen to Belter. Why not leave it at that?'

'Greed and arrogance. He'd thought about it and realised that Belter was sitting on the letters until he could blackmail the Government with them in his own good time. And he probably guessed that Belter had killed Laurence Gilbey. Sylvan thought there was a lot more money to be made out of Belter if he kept his nerve—and he's got plenty of that.'

'What is Belter playing at? If you're right, and he'd had those letters for months he could have named his price from the Government. Any title he wanted would be his for the taking.'

'We all underestimated him. His friends in the Government thought he was angling for a title like the rest, but he's more ambitious than that. He wants to be part of history. He plans to sit on those letters till there's a really serious crisis, probably something involving the Empire, then use them to dictate policy. Laurence Gilbey got in the way of that, so Laurence had to go. Belter killed him and tried to make it look more like suicide by scrawling the note in his blood, only Sylvan spoiled that part of the plan by taking it before the police got there. But it was still in everybody's interest to go for a suicide verdict.'

Except for a barmaid, crying into her pillow for a man who never would have bought her a ring. No need to mention her.

'Because Gilbey was trying to blackmail Belter?'

'Either that or get in ahead of him. He certainly guessed what Belter was doing.'

'Was Henry Henson trying his hand at blackmail as well?'

'No, poor man. Can you imagine him as a blackmailer? But you can see why Belter was worried. When he knew that

Henson had spent several days alone with Oriana he naturally thought he had another Gilbey on his hands and that Oriana had told Henson everything. Poor Henson was so besotted I don't suppose he'd have taken any notice. But devious men like Belter and Sylvan don't understand simple ones.'

'And the simple ones die of it. Do you think Henson really had sent Sylvan a note telling him to come to the bridge?'

'Yes, on Belter's orders. Henson was never really missing that day when Belter pretended to be worried about him. He'd seen Henson and told him to keep out of the way. Remember, Henson would be in an even more humble mood than usual because of the sables. He wouldn't question anything he was told. I'm sure Belter told Henson to fix up the meeting and gave him that cigarette case with the letter in, ostensibly to hand over to Sylvan. But it worked just as Belter had intended. The letter was still on Henson's body when it was found. We leapt to the conclusion that it had come from Sylvan.'

'Why did Belter encourage Miss Paphos and Sylvan to come back to this country? As far as he was concerned, surely the further they stayed away the better.'

'Can't you guess?'

He stared at me, twisting a coffee spoon round and round in his fingers. 'Would it be something concerning the man you went to breakfast with?'

'It certainly would. The letters are missing, the Government's in a panic and—as usual—the man I went to breakfast with assures them he'll get them out of trouble. He goes to his good friend, Jack Belter. Imagine the position Belter is in. He's offered title, influence, the eternal gratitude of the Prime Minister for getting his hands on something he has already. But he can't claim his reward without admitting he was getting ready to blackmail his good friend as soon as the stakes were high enough.'

'And they weren't high enough then?'

'He's a gambler. I suppose all business-men are. It must have amused him to sit down with Lloyd George and hatch this elaborate plot to get hold of letters that are probably sitting in Belter's safe in his study. I'm sure Belter hoped that Sylvan would simply refuse the bait. Then he'd have the credit of having tried without any of the danger. But Sylvan accepted. Among other things, that meant Belter had to spend a lot of money on financing an opera he hated. But he kept his head and did his best. The first night they were under his roof he tried the blood in the bath trick, hoping it would scare Oriana away.'

'Did he put the blood in himself?'

'No, I'm sure he told Henson to do it. There was blood on his cuff.'

'The sheep's head?'

'He probably did that himself. If you were investigating, you might try asking his chauffeur if he had to wait outside a butcher's shop. If.'

He sighed and looked away from me. Over by the window a plump man was making a fuss about his bath bun not having enough currants in it and the waitress was trying to pacify him.

'But you're not investigating, are you? That man committed murder twice over and tried it again. Gilbey was suicide and Henson was a regrettable accident. If I were to make a complaint, would what happened on Thursday night turn into another of those regrettable accidents?'

I waited a long time for an answer. He stared at me, massaging his temples, looking sorrowful. 'Miss Bray, I've always done my best to tell the truth to you.'

'Well?'

'You wouldn't want me to spoil it now, would you?'

Silence.

'I see. Thank you.'

I finished my tea, stood up.

'What are you going to do now?'

'I think I need another invitation to breakfast.'

When I got home to Hampstead the gap in the living room struck me as soon as I opened the door. The piano had gone. I went upstairs and found that Bernard's room had been cleared down to the last sock, the bed stripped and the bed-linen folded in a tidy heap. He always had been neat, the perfect tenant. His key was on the mat inside the front door, posted through the letter box as he went. I pulled furniture round to fill the gap left by the piano, rearranged books, tried to concentrate on work. The attempt must have been more or less successful because I was still reading and making notes in the early evening, with the fire burning and the curtains drawn, when the knocks came at the front door. Tentative knocks, apologetic you might have said, but then he always scored well for percussion. When I opened the door he stood there on the step, head bent, hands hanging down.

'I moved my things.'

'So I saw.'

'Can I come in for a moment?'

I let him in just far enough for me to close the door. He took his hat off, moved automatically to hook it on its usual peg on the back of the door, saw my expression and held on to it.

'It ... it wasn't only the money.'

'No? How much does the Special Branch pay its spies?'

'Not as much as you might think.'

'Enough for music paper at any rate. Nearly enough for board and lodging with the people you're spying on.'

'I never intended, or rather I suppose I did intend but ... they have a way of pulling you further in, of making you feel important.'

'How clever of them.'

In other circumstances we might have compared notes. After all, I'd been pulled in too, but not like this.

'And I never meant you any harm, or did you any harm. I told them you were really against the arson campaign.'

'Am I supposed to feel grateful for that? You give me a certificate of good character at Scotland Yard while using me to spy on my friends.'

'Bobbie Fieldfare's dangerous company. She—'

I walked round him to the door and opened it. 'I choose my own company. Out.'

He hesitated. The fire flickered in the draught from the door.

'Out.'

He went.

It took me all of that week to get to Lloyd George. I delivered more letters to both Number Eleven and the Commons asking for an appointment. I even obtained his telephone number at the Treasury, mastered my dislike of the instrument, and rang it. I got the Balliol first, suave and totally unconvincing, sure that Mr Lloyd George had got my letters and I'd be hearing from him. I didn't. I even tried waiting for him in Downing Street one evening but got threatened with obstruction and moved on by a police constable before he came home. The policeman had recognised me and seemed certain that I was bent on kidnap or assassination. In the end, I had to track him to his native territory.

I'd found out from a newspaper that he was due to address a meeting in South Wales on Saturday on the place of the Sunday school in national life. I caught an early train wearing a respectable coat, a most unbecoming hat in floppy black felt and the nearest thing I could manage to a chapel-going aspect. His speech was in Welsh, a musical language and a pleasure to listen to, even if I didn't understand a word of it. On his way out, I caught him, jostling with all the others who wanted to shake him by the hand, walk next to him.

'A wonderful speech, Mr Lloyd George. Would you permit me to give you this hymn book?'

He looked, recognised me, and took a step back. A large man beside him who was probably his detective made a move towards me then halted, uncertain. Lloyd George made a little sign to him not to intervene and took the book I was holding out to him. Since I'd had no hymn book handy at home, it was in fact a Hungarian dictionary, but it was the note inside it that mattered: 'I must see you. I know where the letters are.'

'Mrs Williams, isn't it? Didn't you want to talk to me about your son? Is he any better? Come in here and tell me about it.'

The thinking was instantaneous and the warmth in his voice so genuine that I looked over my shoulder for this motherly Mrs Williams. Then the crowd parted with sympathetic murmurs and I found myself alone with him in a little side room, not much more than a cupboard, along with three chairs and a broken lectern.

As soon as the door closed the warmth faded from his voice and manner. 'What are you doing here?'

'I've been trying to get to you all week. I know where those letters are. Your friend

Jack Belter had them all the time. He had them already when you asked him for his help getting them back. He was just waiting for the right time to blackmail the Government with them. Just before the next election probably.'

Standing there in the cupboard of a room I told him everything, except Bernard being a traitor. He listened to the end. I never even saw him blink. Even when I'd finished, he took a long breath before speaking.

'You know, Miss Bray, if I were the ruthless, devious man my opponents believe me to be, I should say you were a madwoman. You come here in disguise, you spin me a story involving the Prime Minister himself and a highly respectable magazine proprietor. You have served several prison sentences. I know for a fact that you planted bombs in my own house ...'

'I did not.'

But he swept on. ' "Away with her," I'd say. "Insane, poor woman. Lock her up somewhere safe where she can't hurt herself and spread slanders about respectable men ..." '

'You might have to explain why you invited this madwoman to breakfast.'

'I said "if", didn't I? Perhaps I'm not so ruthless and devious as you all like to think me. Perhaps, Miss Bray, I even believe you.'

'What?'

It was as if he'd managed to talk himself back into a good humour. He was even smiling.

'You have friends in high places, Miss Bray.'

'*I* have?'

'Or perhaps you don't regard Scotland Yard as a high place. You evidently have a very warm admirer there.'

Bernard, I thought. I felt my face flaming, black anger welling up.

'Indeed. A certain Chief Inspector Merit.'

'Ye gods.'

'You're surprised? I wonder who you thought I meant? Have you so many warm admirers at Scotland Yard? The fact is that Chief Inspector Merit has been creating quite a rumpus within that excellent force, a rumpus which has even reached the office of the Home Secretary. The chief inspector seems entirely convinced that you're right. And do you know, I think you might be.'

'You said *chief* inspector.'

'So I did. You may congratulate your friend on a promotion.'

'To stop him creating the rumpus, as you put it.'

'Not at all. We're not the Czar's police.

An entirely fitting reward for his initiative and devotion to duty. However ...'

'I knew there'd be one of those.'

'However, his well-deserved promotion has brought a transfer to administrative duties within Scotland Yard.'

'In other words, you know he's right so you're putting him behind a desk to keep him quiet. Well, if Chief Inspector Merit's right and I'm right, why aren't you doing something about it? Get a warrant. Search Belter's home, his office. He must keep those letters somewhere close at hand, otherwise he couldn't have got at that page so quickly when he needed it.'

'Ah yes, those letters.' He ruffled the pages of the Hungarian dictionary, frowned at it in an abstracted way, put it aside.

'As it happens, they've come back.'

'They've what?'

'Come back. Or rather, they have been sent back. They were delivered by unknown messenger to Ten Downing Street in a large brown envelope.' I stared, off balance, expecting a trick. He smiled. 'It was some time before anybody opened the envelope, not expecting anything of the kind. But I can assure you, they're all there.'

'Except two pages.'

He nodded, reluctantly. 'Yes, except the two pages.'

'When did this happen?'

'The envelope was delivered some time last Friday week.'

'You see, it fits. Once he'd tried to kill me and failed he knew he was backed into the corner. That was late on Thursday night. On Friday he sends back the letters.' Another nod. 'Those letters would never have been returned if it hadn't been for what I did. I've earned my fee.'

'And you'll get it. I think I can give you my word that there's no intention now of prosecuting you for your part in blowing up my house.'

'I didn't blow up your house. Anyway, that's not the point. It's Mrs Pankhurst we're talking about. Are you going to drop the charge or aren't you?'

'The situation is not quite what it was when we had our little talk, is it?'

'No. You thought then that the letters might have got into the hands of a German spy. Now you know it was a man you play golf with, biding his time to blackmail the lot of you. You might not like the result, but I've done what you asked me and more. So do I get my fee?'

He smiled, opened the door before I could move to stop him and called up the corridor. 'Ready to go now. Will you send somebody to see Mrs Williams out?'

He turned to me, smiling warmly as if he'd done me a favour. 'Nobody will believe you, you know.'

'Your friend Jack Belter has killed two people. What are you going to do about it?'

There were steps down the corridor, stopping by the door. He dropped his voice to a murmur. 'Well, I think we can safely say he won't be getting his knighthood.' Then, aloud, 'Good morning Mrs Williams. So nice to meet you again.'

He was away in his motor car before I got out of the building.

Chapter Twenty-Two

Five days later, early on a Thursday morning, in his study at home in Maidenhead, Jack Belter shot himself. Bridget and the butler found him. There was no suicide note but within a few days the world knew that he'd done it because he was facing financial ruin. His empire, like many others, depended on credit. Unluckily for him, and inexplicably, several of his major creditors had decided to call in their debts at the same time. Just one of those things if you're over-extended.

Lloyd George sent a wreath to the funeral but did not attend in person.

Oriana Paphos and Leon Sylvan were among those absent. I heard later that she was already in Athens, negotiating for land to build her temple of love and beauty. Madoc managed to keep his orchestra together long enough to give a concert performance of *Salome* to great acclaim. He may have noticed the lack of one viola player, but I don't suppose it spoiled things.

And Mrs Pankhurst? At the beginning of April she went on trial at the Old Bailey charged with being an accessory before the fact of the bombing of Lloyd George's house and was sentenced to three years' penal servitude.

I wrote letters, waited outside the door of Number Eleven until the police moved me on as soon as they saw me. I even got Max to put a reference to part of it in one of his wild radical publications—the most he could manage without getting sued three times over, he said. The security around all the members of the Cabinet was tighter than ever. I couldn't get within talking distance of the man, although I tried as hard as I've ever tried at anything. One spring night when he was addressing a Liberal rally in London, I was there as usual. This time at least I managed to get in, standing room only near the aisle at the back. There he was, up on the platform, eyes glittering, hair swept back, playing on his sympathetic audience like a maestro with a Stradivarius. If I'd even tried to shout I'd have been bounced from the hall before he'd finished a sentence. But I had to do something or explode. All the resentment about what had happened, Bernard and the rest of it was concentrated on that distant, untouchable figure on the platform.

A young woman came and stood beside me, huddled into a grey coat with big pockets though it wasn't a cold night. She moved suddenly, jogging me with her elbow. She was taking something out of her pocket. A bag of big sweets it looked like. But who sucks sweets at a political rally? Then I saw her face and knew who it was.

'June. June Price.'

She was paler than ever. She looked up at me and put a finger to her lips. The bag was in her other hand and I saw what was inside it. Not sweets. Short glass tubes, sealed at the ends with a dark liquid inside, memorable from childhood. Simple schoolboy stink bombs. She plunged her hand in the bag, selected one and gauged the distance between us and the platform. I moved behind her and, catching her by surprise, took both bag and single stink bomb from her hands. She whirled round, hissing a protest.

'No. Don't stop me. He deserves it.'

'Indeed he does. But my necessity is yet greater than thine.'

Besides, I'd learned from a cricketing brother to throw accurately overarm for quite long distances and I'd back my throwing skills against June's any day. A fierce joy blazed through me. I weighted the little tube in my palm, ran up the aisle and let fly. It got him right on the shirt front, stopping that flow of eloquence in a gasp and a splutter of coughing. I landed another two on target area before anybody realised what was happening, then the whole crowd rose up in pandemonium and a weighty portion of it landed on me. Still, I felt another weight had lifted. It wasn't much—not nearly enough—but it was something. I hoped he guessed it came from me.

This Large Print Book for the Partially sighted, who cannot read normal print, is published under the auspices of

THE ULVERSCROFT FOUNDATION